D0802740

ISBN 1-56315-171-5

Trade Paperback
© Copyright 1999 M. Diane Vogt
All rights reserved
First Printing --1999
Library of Congress 98-87024

Request for information should be addressed to:

SterlingHouse Publisher, Inc.
The Sterling Building
440 Friday Road
Department T-101
Pittsburgh, PA 15209

Cover Art: Michelle Vennare - SterlingHouse Publisher
Minarét Photo: Robert A. Vogt
Typesetting: Pam Muzoleski

Printed in Canada

ACKNOWLEDGMENT

This book would not have been possible without the unflagging support of my husband, Robert. My great friend Lori-Ann Rickard was a constant source of encouragement. My book club read the early drafts and gave me invaluable insight and constructive criticism. Each of them has a special place in the development of this project: Michelle Bearden, Kate Caldwell, Betty Cohen, Linda Gibson, Laura Howard, Allison Jennewein, Deborah Jordan, Rochelle Reback, Robin Rosenberg, Wendy Cousins Savage, and Amy Sharrit. My parents, Austin and Evelyn George and my brothers, Stephen George and Stanley George, who have loved me and supported me, are a part of all things I do successfully. My assistant, Linda Lee, provided much more assistance than her job required, for which I am grateful.

I must acknowledge my editor, publisher and my agent, Dianna Collier, without whom this book would never have found it's way to print, and my gratitude to all my friends and neighbors who showed so much interest in my efforts.

Finally, this is a work of fiction: pure imagination. Any resemblance to real people, places and events are coincidence.

DEDICATION

For my Buddy, who is better than George, with all my love.

CHAPTER ONE

Carly's visit was probably urgent, at least to her; she'd never come to me with just a minor problem. It was a perfect late afternoon in January. Even with the early evening fast approaching, the day was warm and clear. We sat outdoors on the patio of the Sunset Bar and I played with the pink flamingo swizzle stick in my iced Bombay Sapphire and tonic, moving the lemon twist around the cubes, waiting. Gin, yellow lemon and white ice were vivid and mesmerizing. I raised my eyes from the swirling liquid and looked at my surrogate sibling.

My thoughts drifted to the first time we met. We were gathered around the bassinet, looking into the small face with the blue eyes and curly red hair. Mom cooed over the little feet and perfect hands. The boys murmured in hushed wonder as they examined the tiny fingernails and perfect eyelashes. Mark, not quite ten and very clever, wanted to call her Curly, but his mother insisted on Carly, and his brother Jason punched him in the arm whenever Mark refused to get it right. No one noticed me, standing off to the side, already over five feet six inches tall and still growing. Nothing about me was petite or cute, then or now. I was gawky, awkward. Even my earlobes were big. I'd been the only girl in what I considered my family, and now this baby had arrived. My feelings for Carly were born in that minute and hadn't changed. I'd always had conflicting feelings about Carly: awe, jealousy, irritation and protectiveness. I'd always taken care of her and she resented it. Her view was she could take care of herself. I knew better.

All grown up now at 110 pounds and 5'2", Carly's style was anything but cute. Brightly polished artificial nails and perfect makeup, a glamour hound. "It's better to look good than to be good" is her personal creed. I don't know if she can't be good, or just doesn't try. Although the late afternoon sun reflected off Hillsborough Bay in glistening orange light that flattered her copper coloring, today was not one of her better days. Her clothes were wrinkled and the dark circles under her eyes showed through her concealer. Her lipstick was smeared and the bright pink blush on her pale cheeks made her look more like

Bozo than Garbo. Even her curly red hair was dirty. I felt sorry for her and annoyed at the same time. She was fiercely independent, but perpetually getting into something that I had to get her out of. I like to think we've both matured in the past 29 years, but maybe not.

I came home early and found Carly waiting for me. I hadn't seen her in over a year. We'd been sitting at the Sunset Bar for twenty minutes and she still hadn't told me why she'd come. When I couldn't wait any longer, I stopped playing with my gin and pushed it aside. As much as it would have helped, I knew I'd need to keep all my wits about me to deal with Carly and I was running short on time. In a couple of hours, my husband George would have more than 500 guests arriving for an AIDS benefit.

I said, "OK, the suspense is killing me. I don't know what it is you have on your mind, but it can't be that bad. What's up?"

"It's worse than anything you can imagine," Carly said quietly, with none of her usual bravado.

My annoyance vanished when I saw how distressed she was. "Hey, come on. I have quite an imagination," I joked. "Just because you haven't talked to me in a while doesn't mean I don't care about you." She smiled a little, sheepishly, and it seemed to take the edge off. The young are so dramatic. She slumped back in her chair and looked out at the water. There were a couple of late afternoon sunfish sailors out, racing back and forth from Davis Island to a spot about 100 yards off the edge of our island, Plant Key.

About a year or two later, or at least it seemed that long, Carly finally started to talk. "Did you see NewsChannel 8 yesterday morning?"

"Sure, I always watch Frank Bendler."

More silence. She picked up her white wine, took a sip, put it down, picked up the blue paper cocktail napkin and concentrated while she folded it into a fan. She never looked directly at me.

"Did you see the story on the body they found out by the Skyway?" I nodded. Frank Bendler had the report. He'd said pieces of a body were pulled out of Tampa Bay in the morning hours just before dawn. Hands and feet were bound together by clothesline and tied to small slabs of cement. The largest portion of the body, the part the fish hadn't eaten, was found banging up against the pilings of the Sunshine Skyway bridge over in Pinellas County. It was completely unrecognizable.

"Let me ask you a hypothetical question." Oh, brother. Once a law student, always a law student.

"Hypothetically speaking, what if you thought you knew the identity of that body? Would you be obligated to go to the police and tell them who you think it is?" She asked.

By now, Carly had shredded the cocktail napkin into tiny blue pieces and dropped them all over the floor. She'd need collagen on those frown lines sooner than later if she didn't relax. She wasn't looking at me, and I took that to be a lack of frankness. Like most legal hypotheticals, this one was probably a thinly veiled version of what she believed to be the truth. She was sitting on the edge of her chair and looked like she was ready to spring up and run any minute.

I'm a Federal District Court Judge. I'm supposed to be the law and it's a role I'm well suited for. Just like she's been doing all her life, Carly was putting me in a hell of a spot, even if she was telling me the whole story, which I was very sure she wasn't. There had to be more to this. Just knowing who this "floater" was wouldn't be enough to scare her so badly. Carly had a habit of revealing only what she thinks you need to know. As a kid, she'd say, "If I tell you, I'll have to kill you," but that wouldn't be such a funny line today.

"Are you asking me as a lawyer, a judge, your friend or does it matter?" I visualized my dilemma: reporting Carly to the local police for withholding evidence or being an accessory to obstruction of justice and facing impeachment myself. Lately it seemed the judicial qualifications commission investigated judges at the drop of a gavel. Just great. My patience was evaporating and I eyed the now watery gin, tempted to drink it anyway.

"I don't know," Carly said quietly. "I mean, let's assume you don't know for sure who it is, but you have enough facts to suggest a realistic possibility."

"Why wouldn't you want to try to help the police if you could? I would think anyone would volunteer whatever information they might have about the identity of a murder victim. Unless you have some reason to keep it quiet, and hope your guess is wrong." She didn't notice that I'd slipped into personalizing her facts. As always, Carly was totally focused on Carly. Carly could lose her license if she handled this the wrong way. Neither one of us wanted that to happen.

My old annoyance with Carly was pushing its way into my concern. It was bad enough that she showed up here, unannounced, at a seriously inopportune time. If Carly had a real problem, she should tell me about it and stop acting like some kind of flaky child. How could I fix it if I didn't know what it was? I love Carly, if love is a way to describe the feelings for the only sister I'd ever had. And I'd do anything for her mother, Kate. But Carly doesn't make it easy. I could see her calculating how much to reveal: just enough to keep me interested, but not enough to overplay her hand. I may not have seen Carly in a while, but her methods of dealing with me sure hadn't changed.

"Well, hypothetically speaking, suppose you had been spending a lot of time with a guy and he missed an important meeting with you and for a month after that you were never able to get in touch with him," she said.

"That's it? I know a number of people I haven't seen in a month, but I don't believe any of them have been submerged in Tampa Bay all that time." What the hell. I reached for the gin and drank about half of it. Even with mostly melted ice water filling the glass, I felt it hit my stomach with a jolt. It relaxed me almost immediately. I should have had lunch.

"Yes, but then stories started appearing in the paper about his disappearance." Carly looked out at the water for several seconds. When she finally continued, her voice was so quiet I had to lean closer to hear her. "And the last time I saw him, he told me someone was going to kill him."

The effects of the gin evaporated. Years of listening to clients' stories, sitting stone-faced in court while your theory of the case gets flattened by opposing counsel, then on the bench listening to all manner of ridiculous tales, I'd learned to appear cool and calm no matter what happened, to trust my instincts. But appearing cool and being cool are two different things. My pounding heart and racing pulse gave me the real story. I could feel my hands starting to shake, so I put them on my thighs under the table. I didn't need what Kate calls my "inner wisdom" to tell me Carly believed, absolutely, she knew whose body was found in the Bay and she believed that he had been murdered. It wasn't just another of Carly's attention-getting maneuvers. I hadn't been sure. Knowing the dead man made Carly much closer to murder than I wanted either one of us to be.

Now, the legal hypothetical gave both of us a little bit of protection.

"Hypothetically speaking, who does this person believe the dead man is?" I barely recognized my own voice, and I wasn't sure Carly heard me.

"Carly?" I cleared my throat and said a little louder, more assured. Hearing the change, she turned her head and looked at me directly, unblinking.

"Doctor Michael Morgan. Here." She thrust a small piece of newspaper toward me. She'd been holding it crumpled up in her hand. It was wet, the ink smeared with her sweat. I flattened it out so I could read it. It was short, from the *Tribune*, dated about two weeks earlier. No pictures.

DOCTOR MISSING

Once prominent plastic surgeon Dr. Michael Morgan has been reported missing by his friends. Dr. Morgan lives alone and has become a recluse in recent years following his conviction on drug- related charges eight years ago. He was last seen at his weekly golf game.

I realized I'd been holding my breath. I sat back in my chair and tried to breathe normally. Carly continued looking at me, through me, steadily. I couldn't say anything. Dr. Morgan was a locally prominent plastic surgeon. A boy wonder. Some said a genius. I'd never met him, but I've seen his resume in my court files many times. It was 64 pages long. He had been published more than once in every major American medical journal, authored two textbooks and done plastic surgery on three-fourths of Tampa's affluent citizens, males and females alike. He taught at the medical school, and taught medical legal issues at the law school. I couldn't grasp the idea that Dr. Morgan had been malevolently murdered and I must have sat there too long thinking about it. Here in Tampa, murder sells for about five hundred dollars, and there are always the freebies. At least, that's the rate for carnies, drug pushers and street people. I don't know about doctors. But Michael Morgan? What could anyone have had against him?

I was so preoccupied with the idea that I didn't really notice when Carly got up, pushed her heavy rattan chair back from the table and left.

After ten minutes, I got up and went looking for her. When I passed the hostess station, she told me Carly had gone out the front door. I hurried outside to check the parking lot. No luck. I couldn't even find the valet. There was no one around. I hustled back into the house, through the restaurant and took the stairs two at a time up to our flat on the second floor. I ran through the den and to the window overlooking the driveway. What must have been Carly's small gray car was driving over the bridge from Plant Key to the Bayshore. She turned left, away from downtown, and I lost sight of her between the palm trees and traffic.

I stood there a while, looking out into the swiftly failing sunlight and took a deep breath. Another. And another. "Breathe in, breathe out; breathe in, breathe out," I repeated my personal mantra as I went slowly back down the stairs.

How like Carly to get herself into a mess and dump it into my lap. I'd been rescuing her from herself most of her life, but this time she may have gotten into more than I could handle. And the timing couldn't have been worse. I couldn't just drop everything and go after her then. For the first time, I noticed there was a lot of activity going on in the dining room, and the temporary staff George had hired to serve at the fund-raiser tonight in his restaurant had started to arrive. I couldn't do anything more about Carly tonight.

I tried to put Carly's news aside. If Michael Morgan was dead, he'd still be dead tomorrow when I could turn my attention to him. And if Police Chief Ben Hathaway hadn't found Morgan's killer in the last three weeks, he wasn't going to be found in the next few hours. Especially since Chief Hathaway, along with everyone else who might be interested in Michael Morgan's disappearance, would probably be right here at George's restaurant for the evening anyway. Carly was gone now, and I had no idea where she went. I couldn't call her back if I wanted to. I'd have to get more information from someone else. Besides, George was so nervous about this party that I had to do my part to make it a success. Rumor had it that not only Senator and Victoria Warwick, but Elizabeth Taylor, the actress and AIDS activist, might be here to show her support. Dr. Michael Morgan, and Carly's involvement with him, whatever it was, would have to wait. But my efforts to forget about it weren't working very well. I'd have to figure out some way not to be preoccupied with it the rest of the night. Given how things turned out, if I had known then that I'd be spending the evening with Dr. Morgan's killer, I don't honestly know whether I would have been alarmed or relieved.

CHAPTER TWO

I drifted back to the Sunset Bar, deciding to retrieve my gin and let the watery liquid relax me. I could feel the tension being chemically erased from my stomach, and hoped the rest of my muscles would feel it soon, too. I was thinking about how best to deal with Carly's problem when George came out of the kitchen, talking over his shoulder to someone. I heard him say, "and make sure all of the flowers are finished. Senator Warwick likes plenty of hibiscus, birds of paradise and other tropicals. Make sure the ones on his table are particularly fresh." He saw me and smiled, came over to my table and bent down to give me a kiss. "I hoped you'd come home early. Would you take a quick walk through the dining room to make sure everything's done?"

George was wearing his usual uniform of khaki slacks, golf shirt and kilted cordovan loafers without socks. Today, the shirt was bright yellow. It set off his deep tan, blue eyes and dark hair like the vivid colors of a Thomas McKnight painting. He looked like the comfortable Floridian he had become about twenty seconds after we moved here. It's closer from Grosse Pointe to Tampa than you might think.

I put my arm through George's and kissed him back. "Just sit down with me for a minute and chill out. I'll walk through, but I'm sure Peter has everything under control." Peter, George's Maitre d', could run the place with his eyes closed. A charity fund-raiser for 500 people would be no great challenge. He'd done it all before.

"I'm sure you're right, but I've had a crush on Elizabeth Taylor since I first saw *National Velvet*. I want to knock her off her feet." He leered and I had to smile, just like he meant me to do. He's not clairvoyant, but seventeen years of marriage have given him an inside track. He knows which buttons to push. I tried to relax.

"You act like all this is wildly important to you when you don't really care whether they have a wonderful time or not," I said.

"That's not true. Every event we have here is important to me. Just because I didn't vote for our democratic senator doesn't mean I want the *Tribune*'s food critic or the *Times*' society pages trashing my party."

This was the male version of fishing for compliments. George's chefs have won the Golden Spoon Award five times and *Florida Trend* magazine has called his restaurant "the best in Florida." The likelihood that the *Tribune* or the *Times* would find anything less than perfect was smaller than the possibility of snowfall.

"Why don't you bring your drink over here? We'll watch the sunset and I'll keep your mind off Elizabeth Taylor." I leered back at him, wiggling my eyebrows, and this time, he laughed.

We moved over to my favorite outside table. The wicker chairs invited one to relax and enjoy the view. In January, sunset is about five o'clock, so there would be plenty of time for George to finish up the final preparations for the party. Being able to sit outside and watch both the sunrise and the sunset over the water is one of the best things about living on Plant Key, even though most of the time I don't care enough about the sunrise to get up for it. Now, if sunrise is the end of a perfect evening, well that's something else.

We sat quietly, words between us unnecessary. The best part of being married is the companionship at the beginning and the end of every day. George has been the best companion I could ever imagine myself having, although when I first met him I imagined romance and lust. Not that I didn't get that, too. This evening, like most evenings, he chattered on about today's events at the restaurant and asked about what had happened in my courtroom. We were both too keyed up to relax, albeit for different reasons.

"I hope you encouraged Kate to come this evening. We'll never be able to keep the senator's wife sober if Kate's not here, and you know what Tory's like when she's drinking," he said.

I had used my best arguments when I saw Kate yesterday at lunch. But Kate is what she is. She'll consult with her inner guidance, maybe cast a rune or three, check with her guardian angel and make her decision. "We'll just have to wait and see," I told him.

"Dammit, Willa. Ever since that woman got involved in Eastern Indian religion, she's impossible. If I'd known she was going to become a Hindu, I'd never have encouraged her to move here." It was a sign of how much stress he'd placed on himself that he was quarrelsome about Kate. My loyalty to Kate, the woman who has been like a mother to me since my own mother died, is limitless. If Kate hadn't moved here, neither would I. I tried to be understanding, just because he's usually worth it, and because I couldn't muster the concentration for an argument.

"Just wait and see. Kate believes the universe is unfolding as it should. Don't borrow trouble." And if she doesn't show up, I thought, God knows what we'll do with the senator's wife. She's ruined more than one event we've attended. Her tantrums are legendary. She drinks, and the more she drinks, the louder and more obnoxious she becomes. Flying Waterford is not unusual. I don't have the same arrested male lust for Elizabeth Taylor that George has, but I don't care for shattered crystal with my meals, either. I had even less interest in Senator Warwick.

One of many subjects upon which George and I seriously disagree is politics. George is a staunch Republican, on top of all the recent issues. He knows who said what to whom and when. He can identify all 100 U.S. senators and most congressmen by sight. To him, because this fund-raiser was sponsored by one of our two state senators (the wrong one, in his view), it was a worthy event.

The sun finally set at 4:58. It was a relatively normal sunset for Tampa: No clouds in the lower sky to give it the spectacular effect it can sometimes have up north.

As I'd promised, I left the Sunset Bar through the archway into the main dining room. It was the ballroom when the house was originally built, so it comfortably held about thirty round tables. Peter had decorated in fuchsia and white, with red and green bromeliads, bird of paradise and other tropical plants that grew in carefully cultured gardens here on Plant Key. The table cloths were white, the napkins fuchsia. Minaret's best Herrend, Waterford and sterling flatware that had come with the house when we inherited it from George's Aunt Minnie was set flawlessly in ten place settings per table. Peter had done something truly spectacular with the ice sculpture on the head table. An eagle, it's wings spread and spanning more than four feet, majestically demonstrated the strength most AIDS patients didn't have. Too bad it would melt before the night was over. Thankfully, it's never cold enough to keep ice frozen in Tampa for long.

I walked all the way through both dining rooms, looking at the flowers and the table settings. If there were any flaws in the presentation, I couldn't see them. I stepped back into the bar and gave George the reassurance he wanted, then went upstairs to our flat.

Our house, Minaret, is a grand old building. George's Aunt Minnie married into it and left it to her favorite nephew when she died. It was built in the 1890's when Henry Plant, Tampa's equivalent of Donald Trump, wanted a family home. Plant was constructing the Tampa Bay

Hotel, now the University of Tampa, which he believed would be a mecca for the rich and famous. When they came to the hotel, he wanted to show off a fabulous home as well. He wasn't going to be outdone by his rival, Henry Flagler, who had done such a magnificent job in Palm Beach.

Before he could build his house, Plant had to build Plant Key itself. Originally, Hillsborough Bay was too shallow for navigation and devoid of land mass. When the Port of Tampa channels were being dredged to allow passage of freighters, Plant persuaded the Army Corps of Engineers to build up enough land mass for Plant Key at the same time.

He made his island oval-shaped with the narrow ends facing north and south toward Bayshore and out into the Gulf. The Key is about a mile wide by two miles long. Plant also built Plant Key Bridge which connected Plant Key to Bayshore Boulevard just east of Gandy. Marine life ecosystems weren't a big priority then. If you had an island, you had to have a way to get there, didn't you?

The locals, and New York society, called the Island "Henry's Ego," but like everything else Plant did, it turned out magnificently. It's hard to fathom sometimes how much wealth could be accumulated in the days before income tax by those who were willing to live just a little bit outside the law. It's also amazing how ostentatious they all were, but that's another story.

Water splashed into the big, old claw-footed tub in my bathroom as I prepared to begin the beautification process. By concentrating carefully, I hoped to avoid thoughts of Dr. Morgan. I put avocado oil bath gel in the water and while it bubbled into snowy white mounds, I turned on quiet, soothing piano music and lit two gardenia-scented candles. When we renovated the house, we had to modernize the kitchen. We expanded the closets, the bathrooms and the bedrooms. We kept the old claw-footed tub, but we did replace the plumbing.

I lowered myself gingerly into the soothing hot water, laid my head back against the bath pillow, stretched out to my full five feet eleven and a half inches, closed my eyes and tried to stay in the present, blissful moment.

No luck. I kept coming back to Carly, catastrophizing her situation and mine. Inactivity is hard for me. My Karmic purpose must be to learn patience. I just couldn't get Carly and Dr. Morgan off my mind, no matter how much I tried the Scarlett O'Hara routine: "I'll think about it tomorrow." Both Carly and I could end up not only unemployed, but disbarred or worse. I wasn't going to be any happier about that tomorrow, either.

The water had grown cold and it was getting late. I gave it up and turned on the seven o'clock news. The lead story was the identification of yesterday morning's body. Or rather, the ongoing non-identification.

Frank Bendler, who had somehow become the reporter responsible for this story, said the body had been in the water too long for a positive visual identification. Dental records would have to be consulted. But the body might be a tourist who had disappeared some months before in what was believed at the time to be a boating accident. The way the body was trussed and tied to cement, the police feared a copy cat killing, copying the death of another tourist a year ago. When they ran the old clips, I realized why the scene had seemed so familiar to me when I first saw it. The earlier killing had been in the news for months, described at length at the time it happened and again at the trial when the killer was convicted last fall. This one was eerily similar. The possibilities were chilling: a serial killer, the wrong man convicted. I shuddered.

Bendler had no hard facts to air, so he resorted to running old clips of interviews with the current missing tourist's traveling companions. I turned down the sound and began drying my hair.

Bent over from the waist, with my head upside down, it was only by accident that I glanced over at the television screen to see Senator Warwick disembarking from a plane at Tampa International Airport. I turned the volume back up, but the point of the story was only that the senator and his wife were in town. Frank Bendler was kind enough to give the fund-raiser and George's restaurant an on-air plug. I didn't see a news clip of Elizabeth Taylor, if there was one.

I was standing in my closet trying to decide what to wear to the party when George came upstairs. "It seems like a perfect opportunity for this Zoran dress. What do you think?" I pulled the cream cashmere shift out of its garment bag, and held it up, looking at my reflection in the full length mirror. It hung there, no shape, no style.

"How about one of your black cocktail dresses?" He suggested, walking through into his bathroom and shower.

I moved back to my makeup. By the third try, my eyeliner looked less like rick-rack on my eyelids, so I left it alone. After a few drinks, no one would notice. Or maybe I'd start a new style. I said "I'm trying to get Victoria Warwick's attention. You know what a status-conscious female she is. But if you'd rather I wore something else, I'd be happy to." Whether he heard or not, he said nothing.

So I put on the dress and looked in the mirror. The wool fabric is fabulous. It felt as soft against my skin as a rabbit's tummy and I loved it. I knew every other woman in the room would, too. Besides, for what it cost, I'd be wearing it the rest of my life. I might as well start now.

George hadn't thought about alternative distractions for the senator's wife if Kate didn't get here, and he didn't want to think about it. He stuck his shaving creamed face around the corner.

"You know, that's always been one of my favorite dresses. You look great in it," He said this with such mock appreciation and sincerity, we both laughed. He tried to kiss me, but I ducked. "You smell great, too," he said. He kept coming toward me, so I dodged the shaving cream by leaving the room. George's fun-loving side has faded somewhat over the years, but a couple of martinis can still bring out the best in him.

I wanted to spend my evening planning how to help Carly, after I found her. But I knew I couldn't. So I asked, "Who's attending this thing?" I shouted into his dressing room from mine while I turned back to my makeup. Minimilism takes more time than you think.

He evaded the question. "All the usual suspects."

"Meaning Marian and the CJ?" I asked, referring to my boss and his wife, who are not my favorite couple.

"Among others," he said. I put down my hairbrush, followed him into the steamy bathroom and confronted him directly.

"What others?"

"All of the offspring will be there, too." He walked into the shower to avoid my outrage.

"George! How could you invite eight Richardsons for one evening?" Four boring, long-suffering, krewe members and their society matron spouses. "This will be insufferable!" I was shouting to be heard over the running water.

"There's nothing that says you have to talk to them and the reason they're coming is simple: $1,000 a plate. Besides that, I couldn't invite Pricilla Waterman and not invite her brother. Now get ready and look perfect, as always." He said as he put his head under the water. The steam was heating me up and wilting my hair. At least I prefer to think it was the steam.

"Don't try to change the subject. Who is Pricilla's brother?" I walked back into my dressing room and picked up my hairbrush to finish my hair. It's so short, it doesn't take much to put it back into whatever shape it's going to have. George pretended not to hear me. When he got out of the shower, I asked him again.

"We've lived here ten years and you haven't even bothered finding out who's related to whom yet?" He was truly becoming exasperated with me. "The CJ, Ozgood Richardson, Senior, is Pricilla Waterman's brother. How could you not know that?"

"The interrelationships of Tampa society don't interest me." Indignation is often the best defense, I've found. "Who else is coming to this thing?"

With exaggerated patience, as if explaining to a simple-minded child, he said "It's a Junior League function. Anyone and everyone willing to pay $1,000 a plate to show up will be an honored guest." He had finished making a perfect bow of his black tie, patted my butt and left the room saying, "If you're really curious, there's a copy of the guest list on the desk."

I went in to look at it. I skimmed over most of the names, which just reinforced how much I was not going to enjoy this evening. About midway down, on the third page, I found what I was looking for—Dr. Michael Morgan and guest. He couldn't very well be dead if he was walking around our dining room tonight, right? I wrinkled my nose and went back to being annoyed with George.

This is the part of being married I don't like—the compromise, the accommodation. If I was single, tonight I'd be out with real friends, or getting some work done or just relaxing with the dogs. My single friends tell me the best part of being single is just doing whatever you want, whenever you want. No holidays with the in-laws, no whiskers in the sink, toilet seats left up, or refusals to eat zucchini. And no interminable evenings spent with insufferable bores just to raise funds for the worthy-cause-of-the-moment.

Like my putative boss, the CJ, for instance. Chief Judge Ozgood Livingston Richardson, Senior—"Oz," to his friends (which does not include me)—is 65 years old, going on 95. Actually, I think the CJ was born old. If he ever laughs, it's politely. He knows which fork to use at eight fork table settings. He married a debutante back in the days when that was important. Each of his three children, two daughters with husbands, and "Junior," (as Ozgood Livingston Richardson, II, is not so affectionately known) are firmly ensconced in society, and they're all just as interesting as white bread. If any of them have ever had so much as a ten-word conversation, the listener had to be hearing impaired.

The CJ's wife is regarded by one and all as a fixture of Tampa society. She'll tell you, each and every time you're introduced, "I'm Marian McCarthy Richardson, and I'm a fifth generation Floridian." If you live in Florida, you recognize immediately how remarkable that is. You're lucky if you can find someone who was born here, let alone a fifth generation resident. This makes her children sixth generation, the equivalent of royalty. The rest of us are expected to kiss the ring, repeatedly. I puckered up and went to do what had to be done.

CHAPTER THREE

The guests were set to arrive at 8:00, but I hoped to have a glass of wine first. I wanted to think about how to unobtrusively gather information on Dr. Morgan, if he didn't show up. I needed to know more to keep Carly and me out of trouble. Someone would know something, I remember thinking. George had closed the restaurant for the evening, dedicating both dining rooms to the fund-raiser. He'd arranged extra valets for parking and I knew we'd have news coverage. These affairs are set for week nights by people who don't work: or maybe by those who do and need an excuse for a late morning or an early night.

Since there wasn't really anything for me to do, I went back to the Sunset Bar for a peaceful quarter hour before the deluge. Maybe a glass of Merlot would improve my mood. I was surprised to see Frank Bendler sitting alone in deep reverie, and I was pleased with the opportunity to talk to him alone.

Ten years ago, Frank Bendler was the new kid in town as far as local television news was concerned. His gimmick was to introduce each of his newscasts with a piece of Florida trivia. You know, like "We're here at Disney World where Richard Nixon once announced 'I am not a crook.'" The idea was that the trivia would relate to the newscast in some way and, of course, distinguish him from all the other television journalist wannabes. He also tried to put a positive "state pride" spin on everything when he could.

The bit was popular with viewers and helped to put him in the NewsChannel 8 co-anchor spot. Like all successful gimmicks, keeping it fresh was the problem. He said he started out writing the bits himself, gathering them from local history books or the newspaper morgue. Now that he's a "star," he has a research staff to do the work. Every night, over 350,000 Bay Area residents tune in, and part of that audience share is due to Frank's ingenuity as a young man.

"Hey, Frank." The traditional southern greeting, just to let him know I was coming into the room. He looked up and smiled with obvious appreciation for the outfit.

"I guess you don't share my husband's disdain for this rather simple dress."

"I guess your husband doesn't understand how fabulous you look in it. If you go to work dressed like that, I may request a transfer to the courthouse beat." He actually winked at me.

"Frank, it's illegal to flirt with a judge," I told him with mock sternness. But I came over and kissed him on the cheek anyway. Frank dated one of my friends for a while before she married someone else. He's always had something of a crush on me, and I've only exploited it once or twice.

"I've seen you on location a lot lately. Run out of cub reporters?" I sat down across the table with my Merlot and he raised his glass to mine in a silent toast. Frank is short. He likes to be with me when we're both seated so he can look me in the eyes. Otherwise, it looks like Boris and Natasha having a chat.

"So it seems. One sign of old age is coming to believe you can do it all better yourself." He ran his hand over his mostly bald head.

"What's the latest?" I smiled as I asked him, hoping I managed just the right amount of curiosity. At least he didn't appear to be attuned to my need to know. Or maybe he was just used to it.

He frowned, fiddling with the plastic stir he'd taken out of his drink. "I'm trying to figure out how a guy can get himself shot, tied up, bound to cement slabs, and stuck in the Gulf of Mexico. And then, after he manages that, to leave no trace of who he is. It just doesn't seem possible, does it, Willa?" I couldn't tell if he was baiting me, or seriously asking the question. A guilty conscience does that. He seemed to be talking more to himself than to me, and I relaxed a little. He didn't know. But he would. Frank Bendler wouldn't rest until he found out who that body was, how it got there and why. I just hoped Carly and I wouldn't be among the wreckage when he figured it out. And where was she, anyway? That thought, at the front of my mind since she left, just kept popping up.

"You know, I was out before dawn doing a human interest piece on the local coast guard or I wouldn't have been on the story at all. I almost wish I hadn't been there. I've never seen such a terrible body. It was bloated, half eaten by fish. Beating up against the Skyway was brutal. If he hadn't been shot before he went into the water, his death would have been even more horrific, if that's possible. How could no one know? Didn't he have any friends? Family? How does a man get that isolated?" He was looking at me intently, focused on my face as if only I could answer his questions.

I tried to stay detached. I knew it was the only way I was going to get through this evening. Then I remembered that Frank is middle-aged and had never been married. No kids or family here. Maybe this was a life analysis issue for him or something. I hoped not. If it was personal, he'd pursue it all the harder.

"You've checked all the missing persons reports, I guess?" Soft suggestion. I sipped my wine to cover my duplicity. Dissembling is not my strong suit; I prefer the direct approach.

"Not personally. But I've got someone on it. Since yesterday morning, nothing's turned up. But if he's a local guy, I'll know who he is by this time tomorrow if I have to question every citizen in the three counties."

The way he said it, I sincerely wished he'd find the clipping on Morgan before he got to questioning me and Carly, recognizing I was getting in deeper with every failure to speak up. Keeping client confidences is easy. Keeping my own guilty secrets was nerve wracking. I told Frank I had to go do the hostess thing, and asked him to keep me informed. I said he'd gotten my curiosity up. Understatement is one of my cultivated southern virtues. I felt better in a way, confident that the authorities would identify the body and begin an investigation by the next day. With Frank on the case, it wouldn't remain a mystery long.

The main dining room was now about two thirds full. I couldn't see Kate, but I circulated through the tuxedoed men and designer dressed women making up the crowd gathered around the foyer. Passing waiters in white tie were serving canapés and champagne, and the room was starting to buzz with a steady level of noise. In an hour, you'd have to shout to be heard.

I made my way to the Maitre d' station where Peter was checking off names on the guest list as people arrived. Dr. Morgan had not checked in yet. But Police Chief Hathaway was here somewhere.

As I stood there, I saw two of my favorite people, Pricilla and Hainsworth Waterman, come in the front door. Their appearance, such a standard for Tampa, was nevertheless startling. Both of them were over 70, formal and regal. But that's where the similarity ended. Hainsworth's full head of wavy white hair and courtly manners suited his position as the chairman and only surviving named partner of one of the oldest law firms in town. He is small and slight of stature, but fit and strong for his age. His wife, Cilla, had to be 5'10", at least. The flowing gowns she favors make it hard to tell, but it's been a long time since her bathroom scale read under 200 pounds. Her freckles and pale skin suggested her blonde hair might have been natural once. A sweeter woman never lived, but she was no beauty. It wasn't the first time I've wondered what had originally attracted him to her, and vice versa. Given their ages, it could have been an arranged marriage. But I thought not. Their's had always seemed to be a love match to me, and it made me nostalgic for a time when values mattered in relationships more than appearances.

I went up to greet them and Cilla, gracious as always, commented on how nicely George had everything set up, how this AIDS benefit would likely be the most successful one the Junior League had ever held and so on. Cilla was chair of the fund-raising committee, and she took her job seriously. I was paying close attention to Cilla, so I was startled when Christian Grover, Tampa's Clarence Darrow, and his current sweet young thing approached us.

"Hainsworth!" He all but shouted from ten feet away. Grover's been playing to the audience for so long, I doubt he can play it any other way. Addiction to applause is a hard habit to break and he'd never tried.

Grover looked like he was born in his tuxedo. It fit him the way my birthday suit fits me, but with a lot fewer wrinkles. The woman who decorated his arm probably worked nights at the Mons Venus or the Doll House when she got out of her high school classes in the afternoon. I thought I could smell Clearasil.

"You're not having ex parte communications with the judge, are you?" Grover framed the question with an inflection that said that's exactly what was happening. I am a United States District Court Judge, appointed for life. I take my responsibilities seriously, whether my "Boss" the CJ thinks so or not. Both Grover and Hainsworth regularly appear in my courtroom and ex parte communications are unethical. Like British humor, if you knew the context, it was a not-so-subtle insult.

Hainsworth, ever the gentleman, hasn't been around law, lawyers and society for fifty years for nothing. He said smoothly, "Why, Christian, please introduce us to your companion. I'm sure she, like Cilla, abhors discussion of business at social events."

I cast Hainsworth a grateful smile. Some wag once said that you'd think a man with such a large name would be a bigger guy. Maybe. But if Hainsworth lacked physical stature, he more than made up for it in what George's Aunt Minnie would have called breeding.

"Actually, we were just discussing how many breast implant customers are in this room tonight. Why, I've never seen so much cleavage—it gives the term 'silicon valley' a whole new meaning." Grover's voice was smooth, snide, sure. And it carried to the rafters. A Shakespearian actor couldn't have done better. Everyone around us was listening and pretending they weren't.

"I'm sure that's something upon which you have a great deal more experience than we do, Christian," Cilla said calmly, deliberately not looking at his date. She turned to me and Hainsworth, took our arms and said, "Oh, look, Senator Warwick is arriving. Let's go and say hello."

With that, she walked the three of us off leaving Grover and his date standing in our wake. "Cilla, you are precious. And Hainsworth, you're one lucky man. It's no wonder you've been married over 40 years." I patted her hand, kissed his cheek and told them I would see them later. Then I did what all women do when they need a break. I went to the ladies' room.

The first part of the restaurant's women's room is a sitting area, tastefully decorated for those ladies having difficulties during dinner with a tendency to swoon, or whatever. I sat down on the floral love seat, gratefully slipping off my heels. Why hadn't I worn my Nikes? I heard two women talking in front of the mirror in the next room, discussing their breasts.

"How long have you had yours?"

"About ten years."

"Have you had any problems?"

"No, I love 'em. After the twins were born, I just had no substance anymore. Dr. Morgan did them right in his office."

"I've only had mine for three years. I haven't had any problems either, but all of this publicity has me scared to death."

"I know what you mean. I told my husband last week that I'm thinking about having them removed. You know, just to be safe. Christian Grover's my lawyer. He said these things are leaking and are poisoning my body every day. Every time I get a little bit tired, I'm scared I'm getting sick."

I got up and walked toward one of the stalls in the room where the women were talking. As I came in, I looked at both women, but I didn't recognize either of them. I confess I looked at their chests and they, indeed, had lovely breasts. They left the room and I didn't hear any more of what their lawyers had told them, thankfully.

When I'd stayed in the ladies' room as long as I could hide out before becoming an official missing person, I went back to the party.

By that time, everyone who is anyone was there. I looked around and saw the CJ and his wife talking in the corner with the Watermans. The CJ and Hainsworth Waterman had been law partners for 20 years when the CJ was appointed to the Federal bench 15 years ago. Cilla and the CJ's wife were standing in the type of absent observation wives affect when their husbands are talking shop. While I couldn't hear the conversation, there was obvious camaraderie between the two men and acceptance between the women. The men demonstrated a genuine warmth for one another and the wives appeared to acknowledge that they traveled in the same circles.

I looked for a family resemblance between Cilla and the CJ, but I couldn't find one. Except maybe in their size and coloring. If George hadn't told me they were brother and sister, I'd never have known it. I couldn't believe such a proper lady as Cilla had come from the same gene pool as the sarcastically dubbed "great and powerful Oz." No doubt about it, I'd have to reassess my judgments about one of them.

While I'd been resting, Kate had arrived, looking perfect in the royal blue beaded Bellini gown she's worn to every formal event she's attended for at least the past ten years. I smiled when I saw it. Kate is so reliable. I walked up and kissed her cheek. "I appreciate your coming. You look lovely in that gown, as always. It makes your eyes sparkle as much as the dress."

"Why should I buy a new gown when this one looks great on me and is perfectly acceptable? I'm long past the point of trying to impress 'society.'" She eyed my Zoran dress pointedly. "Where is Victoria? Has she been here long enough to get into trouble yet?" I could tell by her normalness that she knew nothing about what was going on with her daughter. Carly had not dumped this on her mother, at least, and for that, I was grateful. Kate should have only happiness in her life, I felt. Maybe I cherished her more than Carly because she was not my real mother.

We looked around for the senator's wife. There were small conversation groups here and there, but I noticed a particularly large group under the stairs near the entrance to the dining room like flies at a picnic. "Why don't we try that group over there," I nodded in their direction. "I can't imagine such a crowd coming together around anyone other than the guests of honor."

As we got closer, I could see Senator Warwick with his wife standing next to him. I was startled. "Kate, look at that dress. She looks fabulous," I whispered. Victoria, a woman of some years, as they say, had on a full length gown with a "V" neckline that plunged almost to her waist, showing not just a little cleavage, but most of her breasts.

"I heard she'd had surgery. I thought they were talking about a face lift. Apparently, it's something lower she had lifted." Kate whispered back with extraordinary cattiness.

"Christian Grover said he thought the breast implant manufacturers had a number of customers in the room. I was offended at the comment, but I can see now that he was right."

"Have you ever noticed how humans are creatures of selective attention? It's only after something is brought to our attention, or we have some reason to be involved in it, that we begin to focus on all of the examples of those things that are around us."

"You mean there have always been a lot of women with breast implants around and I've just never paid attention to it before?"

"Attention focused on any thing creates that thing, Wilhelmina."

"So, I've created these implanted women by my imagination, they're not really here, and I have no need to feel we're being invaded by an alien species of amazons?" I teased her.

"Don't mock me, or I'll leave. I didn't want to come anyway. You know what I mean. You're so often in your own world that you don't see what's plainly visible." She said it sternly. Sometimes she still acts like my mother. I like it.

The crowd moved around a little and we were able to see its nucleus. Senator Warwick was speaking loudly enough to be overheard, holding forth on what he proposed to do if the good voters returned him to the Senate in the fall elections. He was talking to Hainsworth Waterman and other members of the party who had gathered around him closest. The Democrats looked like adoring fans—the Republicans resembled sharks to chub.

"Something has got to be done about the product liability crisis in this country. A number of our best corporate citizens have been put out of business by these frivolous product liability suits. When I return to the Senate, I plan to sponsor a bill that will do just that. And when it's passed, America will be able to compete in the global economy without fear of bankrupting its businesses."

There were murmurs of assent and nods of agreement from the faithful. Preaching to the choir. Apparently no one bothered telling the senator that this wasn't a political rally. His wife looked glassy-eyed and I could tell she had been drinking before she arrived; George had given his staff strict orders not to serve her. Kate noticed it, too, and went over to the senator's wife for a private conversation. I was about to leave when Christian Grover's voice rose in challenge.

"Come on, Senator. Statistics repeatedly show that there just aren't that many successful product liability claims brought by victims in this country. At the same time, corporations make billions of dollars selling defective products knowingly, intending to injure consumers. Just because you plan to get elected by big business and they own you, don't try to dress it up as some kind of altruistic crusade." Polite cheers greeted Grover's comments, too. Apparently AIDS really was a bipartisan cause. No self respecting Southern Democrat would side with Grover over Warwick.

The party was about to degenerate into an uncomfortable battle. I saw George across the room and inclined my head toward him. He came over, assessed the situation at once, and spirited Grover and his date off to another crowd. The crisis was averted and it left me to look around on my own again.

Tampa's not Savannah, but it's a southern town and we have our share of eccentric characters, many of whom were presently accounted for. I noticed the medical community was prominently represented tonight. AIDS was their issue, after all. Several Tampa physicians and their spouses were in attendance. I saw Dr. Marilee Aymes, for many years the area's leading cardiologist and still the only woman cardiologist in town, standing alone near the entrance. A few moments later, her most recent escort approached her with a champagne glass in each hand. The speculation around town is that Dr. Aymes is a lesbian and she brings virile young male escorts to all the social events to convince people otherwise. The evidence typically cited in support of this theory includes her extremely short haircut and brassy manner. Tampa women are not abrasive, at least the socially successful ones aren't. Dr. Aymes's graduation from medical school in 1960, when she was the only woman in her class, must have meant she was a little odd. That she wears a tuxedo to black tie affairs fuels the rumors. Besides that, everyone will tell you, she smokes cigars, as if that clinches it. Tampa has never been on the crest of the fashion wave. Smoking cigars here is still something the men retire to after dinner with their port, while the ladies socialize. Oh, the tourists smoke cigars, and you can find trendy cigar bars in Ybor City open until the wee hours. But ladies? It just isn't done.

I saw Grover and Fred Johnson, Grover's partner, himself another prominent plaintiff's attorney here in town, deep in conversation with Dr. Carolyn Young. I certainly didn't want to join that group, so I approached Dr. Aymes and joined her party. She introduced me to her escort.

"My my. I wonder how much of her body is real?" she said, looking pointedly toward Dr. Young. "I've heard that she's actually 65 years old."

Dr. Young looked 35, if that. "You laugh. From here, I can tell those breast implants are at least five years old, the nose has been done more than once, and there've been some collagen injections around the mouth recently. Just think what I'd discover if I had my glasses on and was close enough to actually see her." She puffed on her stogie like George Burns while she talked.

"Marilee, you can't possibly tell all that from 30 feet away, can you?" I asked her.

"Of course I can. First, those breasts look like cereal bowls sitting on a flat board. That's what happens when implants get hard. As for the nose, you can see how small it is compared to the rest of her face. There's no way she was born with that nose. In fact, if you give me a minute, I can probably name the surgeon. It looks like a signature nose to me."

By this time, I was holding my sides and trying not to make a spectacle of myself by guffawing. But I couldn't help it. I had to ask. "The collagen injections?"

"She probably had them done last week. Look how plump the lines are between her nose and her mouth. And when she's laughing, there's not a sign of crows' feet. Probably injected there, too."

She was precious. Tears were streaming down my cheeks now, all thought of my carefully applied makeup a thing of the past. "Couldn't she just be young and a natural beauty?"

Dr. Aymes snorted. "She could be, but I know she's not. How old do you think she is?"

"35?"

"Try 57. Look it up. When she graduated from medical school is a matter of public record. And why do you think she's talking to those two sharks?" Dr. Young was still talking with Grover and Fred Johnson.

"She does explant surgeries for their clients who are breast implant 'victims' at about $5,000 a pop, that's why. Then she talks them into something she calls tram-flap reconstruction surgery for another $5,000."

"How many of those can she do?" I asked.

"I can't get an operating room for my cardiac surgeries two days a week because she's doing explants. And that's just at my hospital. I know she's on staff at three others where she does the same thing. I'd say she does 25 a week. Add it up. Those two guys are going to make her a wealthy woman, and they're just a couple of her sources." Dr. Aymes took another glass of champagne from a passing waiter. At this rate, she'd be more drunk than Victoria Warwick, but I was pretty sure she'd be more fun, too.

I was looking for an opening to ask her what she knew about Dr. Michael Morgan. Tampa is a very small town in many ways. Dr. Aymes had been a practicing physician here for years. I was sure she'd know him and could give me some insight about who might want to kill him. I just wasn't sure how to bring it all up. Before I could figure it out, George had joined the conversation on the tail end of Dr. Aymes' comments about Dr. Young. "You mean to say that Dr. Young is charging $200,000 to $250,000 a week to do reconstructive surgery on breast implant patients? What insurance company would ever pay for that?"

His incredulity was plain. George doesn't particularly care for Dr. Aymes and he doesn't think I should be seen with her. After all, what would people think? I'm sure that's why he came over to join our conversation in the first place, to rescue me, whether I wanted to be rescued or not.

"That's just it. The insurance companies won't pay for it because there's no scientific evidence linking breast implants to any health problem. The lawyers pay for it."

"But where do they get the money? I know those guys have made a lot of money in their lifetimes, but they can't have that much to throw around." He wasn't convinced.

"I don't know, George." Dr. Aymes snapped, annoyed at George's questioning what she told him as absolute fact. She wasn't used to being interrogated. Or disbelieved. "You're the banker, not me. How do people normally finance a business deal?"

"I'm not sure, Dr. Aymes, I haven't been in banking for quite some time. But speaking of banking, Willa," he said as he turned smoothly to me, "I promised Bill Sheffield that you would come over and speak with him briefly. Would you excuse us, Dr. Aymes?" I couldn't think of a quick reason to refuse, and as we walked away, George mumbled "What a most disagreeable woman. How preposterous." George can be as stuffy as my father sometimes. I was still smiling.

We joined Bill Sheffield, a local stock broker, and his wife just as the rest of his group were moving on to talk to others. George and Bill have quite a bit in common since George was formerly in the banking business and now invests heavily in the stock market. They discussed the status of investments and the Dow Jones while my mind was wandering. Then, Bill suggested to George that he consider stock in medical products companies.

"The breast implant litigation has devalued the stock of a number of companies that are otherwise very sound, George. I have no doubt that this crisis will blow over and those stocks will increase again. You can buy MedPro, for example, at $3.00 a share right now. It's a local company and I think it's going to turn around. It went public at $7.00 and it'll definitely go higher."

"I'm investing in technologies right now. Last week I bought DataTech and it's up 15 points already," George responded. They were still discussing the merits of medical versus technical stocks ten minutes later. Both Mary Sheffield and I were long past any ability to feign polite interest. She turned to me and started a conversation about the next Junior League Show House, which I found only slightly more interesting than watching paint dry, so I excused myself.

I saw Chief Hathaway talking with Frank Bendler and I knew they'd be talking shop. They're both too involved with their jobs to do anything else. It took me just a few seconds to decide to join their conversation. But I wanted to overhear it first, so I walked in that direction behind a passing waiter.

"How long will it take to make a positive I.D.?" I heard Frank ask Chief Hathaway.

"It depends. The body is in very bad shape. Finger prints are impossible. Searching medical and dental records might take a while. Too long, maybe." Ben replied.

"Are you sure it's the tourist, at least?"

"No. In fact, we're pretty sure it's not."

Frank saw me lurking at that point and invited me to join them.

"What are you two taking about?" I asked, as innocently as I could.

"I was taking the opportunity to ask Ben about the body we were discussing earlier. I've got to have something to report at eleven besides George's party."

Frank turned to Ben and continued, "Can I quote you that it's not the tourist, at least?"

Ben looked thoughtful for a few seconds and then replied, "I wish you wouldn't do that yet, Frank. We're just not sure enough. There's no point to upsetting everyone until we get a little more information."

"I'll respect that. For now. Can you give me something on the missing Dr. Morgan, at least?" Frank never gives up.

Ben turned to me, then. "Isn't he here, Willa? I saw his name on the guest list and Peter told me he'd been checked off. I was planning to mark that case closed."

I was startled by the direct question at the same time relief flooded through me in palpable waves. Morgan wasn't dead after all. Carly was okay. I was okay. Ben and Frank were still expecting a response from me, so I told them the truth. "I've never met Michael Morgan. But if Peter said he's here, I'm sure he is." Just then two waiters walked by ringing chimes to signal that dinner was served; I was grateful for the excuse to move on.

By the time everyone was seated for dinner, I was ready to call it a night. Kate was seated at the senator's table, as were George and I. Elizabeth Taylor's place remained empty—a no show. The meal passed uneventfully. The senator gave a short speech thanking everyone for their contribution to AIDS research and reminding them of the work ahead. Privately, the senator was campaigning. I heard him tell Kate that it was a critical time for foreign policy and free trade, and the party needed him on the Foreign Relations Committee for another term. The elections were several months away, but early money is like yeast: it's necessary to raise the dough to get elected. From the looks of the crowded room, I guessed he'd made the same pitch to all of them and several thousand packages of yeast would be contributed to his campaign in the next few days. There was no question that the Republican candidate posed a serious threat to Warwick's reelection. I wondered whether the campaign contributions made to Warwick's campaign would really support free trade or just his ego.

The party was over and everyone was gone by 12:00. I left George to clean up, went upstairs to remove my makeup and get ready for bed. I tried calling Carly again to tell her the good news: that Dr. Morgan had been here tonight, alive and in person. There was no answer and I didn't leave another message. George and I usually like to dissect these events and relish the various conversations we've participated in. But tonight, I was just too tired, and went to sleep before he came upstairs. Even though I consume mystery novels like candy, I was new to the investigator game. I had learned what I needed to know about Dr. Morgan without having to inquire. No one acted guilty, whatever that means. So I missed my best opportunity to investigate everyone who had a reason to kill him. In the long run, it would have saved me a lot of pain if I'd figured that out. But ignorance is bliss and that night, I had the last sound sleep I would have for a while.

CHAPTER FOUR

On Thursday morning, I decided to sleep late and have the after party chat with George, over breakfast and coffee, we didn't have the night before. I also decided I wouldn't tell him about Carly just yet. George thinks I have a blind spot where Carly's concerned. He calls it my Mighty Mouse Routine. I'm always saving the day, and he views it as an unnecessary extravagance. I wanted to get it all ironed out before I told him. I didn't get to the office until about 10:00.

I never take phone calls in my chambers. I have a private line which I have given to only Kate, her family and George. If it rings, I answer it. Otherwise, my secretary takes messages or my judicial clerks talk to the callers. It's one of the great advantages of being a Federal judge. A state court judge is elected; they have to talk to everybody. The point is, Carly could have returned my calls on my private line, but she hadn't.

My secretary brought in the message slips for calls I received Wednesday afternoon and Thursday morning through regular channels. I flipped through them quickly: the CJ at 7:45 a.m., a reminder of my hair appointment, Kate, President of the Women's Bar Association and Carly. She'd called yesterday before she came out to Minaret, but I hadn't known it. In addition to making your own hours, a lifetime appointment means that it's not necessary to kowtow to the boss. I put the message from the CJ aside and called Kate. We made a date for a late lunch. I asked my secretary to set up an appointment with the chair of the Women's Bar Association, checked my calendar to confirm my hair appointment, and then sat looking at yesterday's pink slip from Carly, thinking.

While I was still in private practice, I volunteered my time to teach a law school course at Stetson. Despite her two brothers and me all being lawyers, Carly decided to go to law school. Or maybe it was because we were lawyers. Anyway, Carly threw caution to the wind and took my class four years ago. Even if she wasn't my "little sister," I'd have thought she was one of those rare students who understand the subject and have a desire to excel. She became a colleague that year and I found myself working with her to make sure she understood the basics of cross examination, jury selection and evidence. After she graduated, my personal relationship with Carly, always strained, finally achieved an uneasy truce: Carly began to look on me as an available, if not overly desirable, mentor.

She went to work at the prosecutor's office and she would call me from time to time with a particular question or issue. Then, she was asked to leave the prosecutor's office after a year. She wouldn't tell me why and, after a couple of unsuccessful attempts to find out, culminating in one really nasty screaming match, I got the message that it was none of my business.

She asked me to write a recommendation when she applied for a house counsel position with a small medical device manufacturer. That's one thing about Carly; no matter how offensive she's been to me, she continues to act as if she has some sort of God-given right to keep coming back for more favors. Of course, I gave her what she wanted. Maybe because of what she thought of as her disgraceful termination, and maybe because she was still jealous of my relationship with her mother, until yesterday, I hadn't heard from her in over a year, when she was in trouble again. Our relationship is seriously co-dependent. I need to rescue her as much as she needs the help. Knowing that doesn't change it.

My thoughts started to wander down the well-trodden path of my feelings for Kate, who had been my mother's best friend and like a mother to me since Mom died when I was sixteen. I jerked myself back to the present. No point in going over that ground again. Wherever my relationship with Kate's daughter had gone wrong, rehashing history wasn't going to change it. The only reason to relive history is to avoid making the same mistakes. Otherwise, you're just wallowing in the past—an indulgence I know from experience won't get me anywhere. If I had back all the hours I've spent trying to figure out how to make Carly stop acting like a spoiled child, I'd be at least three years younger.

I picked up the phone and dialed Carly's office number. "Good morning, MedPro," the receptionist answered the phone. I asked for Carly Austin and was put through to her office. Carly picked up on the first ring.

"Carly, its Willa."

"Judge Carson! I'm so pleased you called me back."

"Did you think I wouldn't?"

Some hesitation then, cryptically, "I'd like to see you for an hour or so.

Would it be possible for me to meet you somewhere?"

I felt the frown lines between my eyebrows, and consciously tried to relax them. I remembered Dr. Aymes's comments on age lines. No point in getting collagen before you have to.

Carly sounded cheerful, almost normal. No sign of the nervous, timid woman who sat across the table from me yesterday. She'd always been confident and self-assured. Even when she was fired by the prosecutor's office, she hadn't seemed cowed. Yesterday, she did. Now, she didn't. I was confused. I wanted to strangle her and put us both out of my misery.

I started to tell her about Dr. Morgan but she stopped me and said she wanted to meet with me. After a quick review of my calendar to see whether anything I had on today could be rescheduled, I agreed to see her in my office at three o'clock.

Then, I decided to call Frank Bendler to get some more information on the body. If they had identified it by now, I could tie up the whole thing and put Carly's mind to rest this afternoon, too. He answered my call on the first ring.

"Frank, Willa Carson here."

"Willa! How nice to hear from you. So soon, too. What can I do for you?" Frank has a nose for news, obviously. I hadn't ever called him at the station before. I could see I needed to disguise the reason for my call a little more than I had planned, so we talked for a while about the fund-raiser, Senator Warwick, and George's disappointment that Elizabeth Taylor hadn't come last night. Frank was covering the Warwick campaign, and asked if I knew when the senator would be in town again. Finally, I was able to work into the real reason for my call.

"Frank, since our talk last night about that body they pulled out of Tampa Bay, I've been curious about something, and I haven't seen anything on your newscasts about it."

"What's the problem?"

"You said something about the guy being dead already when he hit the water—" I tried to sound tentative, unsure. Not easy for me.

"Yes?" He was going to make me ask the questions before he'd volunteer anything. Rather unlike Frank, I thought. Maybe he'd been told to report anyone asking questions about the body. I wished I'd thought of that before I called him, but there was no turning back now.

"I was wondering how you knew that?"

"It's not really a secret, and I think I did report it the other day. Don't tell me you've been missing some of my reports?" He teased me.

"I guess I must have," I said, trying not to sound too impatient. I wanted to just snap at him to spit it out.

"Well, first of all, he had a bullet hole in the front of his head that blew the back of his skull off. There's not much chance he survived that. And the coroner's report said they found no water in the lungs, which means he didn't breathe in the water and die by drowning." He explained it all patiently, but he seemed to be asking me a question at the same time. I was tempted not to answer the unspoken, just as he had refused to do earlier, but I didn't want Frank poking around in my life trying to find out why I wanted to know about this particular crime. Not until I'd talked to Carly.

"Well, that explains it then." I told him. "George and I were having a conversation at breakfast this morning and he said the police couldn't possibly tell whether anyone had drowned or been killed before they were found in the water. I told him I was sure that even more complicated things had been determined forensically, and I would just call you and ask." Tsk, tsk. A marital squabble. And too much for my pretty little head. Frank Bendler knows me well enough to know I'm not so vacuous, but he accepted the explanation, no doubt for his own reasons. I didn't want to speculate on what those reasons were.

Then, he said, "While I have you on the phone, Willa, let me ask you something."

"O.K." I was willing to be generous.

"I looked around last night, but I never could find Michael Morgan. Then I talked to Peter, and he said he didn't actually see Morgan come in. Are you sure he was there?"

My good mood vanished in an instant. The hairs on the back of my neck tingled. "Like I said last night, Frank, I wouldn't know the man if I saw him."

"Well, ask George, will you? Right now, I'm assuming he's still missing."

"Sure, I'll ask him," I said.

We rung off with the appropriate farewell, and I made a mental note not to ask Frank anything else about the case unless I first checked all other sources. Frank has been an award winning journalist for too long. I knew he had the instincts to bring him back around asking questions, and I hoped I hadn't already sparked his curiosity too much.

I couldn't figure out what to do next without talking to Carly first, so I spent the remainder of the morning reviewing some proposed orders drafted by my clerks, looking over the matters up for tomorrow and next week's trial calendar. Every ten seconds or so, the questions I'd had initially about Dr. Morgan and his murderer refused to stay in storage, and I was looking forward to getting some answers from Carly this afternoon. At one o'clock, I left to meet Kate at the Tampa Club for lunch, happy that I'd put on something besides dockers and a chambray shirt this morning.

I walked briskly to the Barnett Bank building, took the elevator to the 42nd floor and then the stairs up another flight to The Tampa Club. I had joined The Tampa Club when it first opened because I wouldn't join The Tampa Athletic Club. The truth is, the "A Club," as it's known, would not admit women until a few years ago. When they started to admit women and invited me to join, I refused. I'm pleased to report that many other women did the same and now the "A Club" is having difficulty making ends meet. On any given day, however, you can still find the old rich and long powerful at their club. I guess not getting my dues and membership fees hasn't put them into bankruptcy and, in the meantime, all the women who want to be on the inside are still on the outside. If you won't come in after you're invited, what more can they do? That's the trouble with Ghandi's method of political protest; it's so easy for the targets of peaceful resistance to miss it.

As I feared, Kate was already waiting in the Grill Room, the club decorator's idea of a cozy, paneled enclave on the south west corner of the building. I kissed her cheek. "I'm sorry to keep you waiting."

Kate kissed me back, and said "Don't worry, dear. I enjoy the view of the Bay from here. It's almost as nice as the one from Minaret. And I haven't been waiting long. Just long enough to order this glass of Chardonnay. Why don't you join me?"

I took Kate's suggestion and ordered the Chardonnay. It was delicious. After we ordered Greek seafood salads, we discussed yesterday's party.

"I was looking forward to seeing Jason. It's been too long since my oldest son came to see me. I'm disappointed that he wasn't there."

"I was disappointed, too. He called yesterday afternoon, but I didn't get the message until this morning. He said he had to leave for Romania earlier than he expected because of Senator Warwick's trip to resolve the financial situation over there. He left his apologies and said he'd call next week."

Leave it to Jason to disappoint his mother through a message to me. By tacit consent, we both ignored the fact that Jason hadn't been coming to the fund-raiser to see his mother, but rather to support the senator, who is also his boss. Kate has a soft spot for all her children, each for different reasons. Jason she loves as her firstborn and she avoids his shortcomings, just like she does with her other son Mark, and Carly. And me, too, for that matter even though technically I'm not her biological child.

"Well, it was a lovely evening, even if I did have to spend it with the Warwicks. And speaking of Victoria, did you know that her mother has been very ill recently? They think she has Lupus."

"You're kidding! Mrs. Mendel is about the healthiest woman I've ever known. When did this happen?"

Kate smiled. "About the same time Christian Grover signed her up as a plaintiff in the breast implant litigation."

"You mean Mrs. Mendel has breast implants?" I couldn't believe it. "What for?"

"Apparently Dr. Morgan implanted her years ago after she had a mastectomy for precancerous fibroid tumors. Of course, she never told anyone. It used to be that people kept their medical conditions to themselves. Now, I think she's planning to be a guest on one of the talk shows."

This last was meant to be facetious. I think.

Kate's right, though. Health concerns used to be private matters, particularly health concerns over breasts and other semi-sexual body parts. These days, it seems everything is public knowledge.

We exhausted this topic and I was trying to figure out a tactful way to bring up Carly when Kate saved me the trouble.

"You know, I really wanted both Jason and Carly to come last night. It's been a long time since she's seen her brother."

"It would be even nicer if they could both be in the same room without snarling at each other. And you don't have to give me the 'disapproving mother' look, either. Jason isn't the only one Carly doesn't talk to. Have you heard from her?"

I could tell from Kate's expression that she hadn't, and she was trying to come up with some acceptable excuse besides the truth—Carly doesn't talk to any of us. I wouldn't hurt Kate's feelings for anything in the world. So I said, "You know I love Jason and Carly as much as if they were my brother and sister, but they're not perfect."

"No, and neither are you and Mark, as much as you both like to think so."

This wasn't going well. I tried another tack. "Carly called me this morning and left a message. If I talk to her, I'll invite her to Minaret, and you can come over, too."

This got the result I wanted. Kate promised to come, and she was happy. I do love Kate. She's been a great mother to me since my mom died. I love my dad dearly, but he's never around. I haven't seen him in a year. So it was important to me to keep the peace with all the Austins.

We finished our salads, ordered cappuccino and a sinful dessert, and parted half an hour later.

I went back to my office and dictated a few orders on yesterday morning's motions, looked over tomorrow's case load and took care of a few other odds and ends. It was almost 4:30 when I remembered the call from the CJ. While I could have ignored it completely, I decided there was no reason not to return his call and I asked my secretary to place it. CJ hates getting calls through a secretary.

Margaret came back to tell me that the CJ was gone for the day. She'd left a message and he'd likely call in the morning. I smiled to myself. This game of wills I'd been playing with the CJ was humorous. He calls me in the morning because he knows I don't come in before nine o'clock; I call him in the afternoon because I know he leaves early. My amusement evaporated when I realized I'd need the CJ's support to avoid the Justice Department's public integrity unit if I didn't get this thing with Carly resolved soon.

It was then I realized Carly had never showed up for our appointment. I'd worked right through. I picked up the phone and called her again. Her secretary said she'd gone out about one o'clock and never returned. I had no idea where she was. I thought I should just call Chief Hathaway, report what Carly had told me and forget it. It was not knowing what her involvement was that kept me quiet. I couldn't just throw her to the wolves, even though it made me a dog in the road. It was just a matter of time before I got hit by the speeding truck, too.

I was sitting at my desk trying to decide what to do when Margaret came in to remind me that I had a Federal Rules meeting ten minutes ago. Too late to cancel, and too late to spend time catastrophizing. I'd have to leave that for later. But I determined to find Carly and shake the whole story out of her. Then, I'd fix it, just like always. Or so I thought.

CHAPTER FIVE

The Federal Rules subcommittee of the local chapter of the Federal Bar Association, a committee I've been on for a number of years, was scheduled to meet this month at the offices of one of our newer members, Charles Smyth. Instead of taking the time to get my car, I asked Margaret to call another committee member for a ride. It really hadn't registered with me where the meeting would be held until we arrived at the Landmark Tower offices of Able, Bennet & Waterman, where Smyth is a junior partner. Able and Bennet are dead. Elliott Hainsworth Waterman is the senior partner here.

The Landmark Tower building, the most expensive office space in Tampa, sits at the corner of Florida and Jackson and takes up an entire city block. It is one of the newer "A" buildings in downtown Tampa, and it's the most architecturally interesting. The building is over 40 stories high and topped by a white lighted dome. The dome's lights are changed to red and green for Christmas and red, white and blue for the fourth of July. It's easily seen for miles around after dark, and finding your way back to town is not as difficult as it used to be before the building went up.

The walk to the front door is lined with grey granite pillars and in the lobby sits a larger than life size, multicolored metal sculpture of Don Quixote on his horse. This was the first time I had ever been in the building and it certainly had all the indicia of high-priced real estate. The offices of Able, Bennet & Waterman were on the top four floors. As the elevator whizzed up, I was reminded of my lunch. After a 35 second ride, the elevator doors opened onto the lobby—less than one second per floor. I stepped out into the lobby the same way cartoon characters leave an out of control carousel.

I've been in some extravagant law offices but it's not an exaggeration to say that the lobby of AB&W, as it's known around town, was the most ostentatious lawyers' lobby I've ever seen. The floor was granite in three colors, with "AB&W" inlaid under foot. Windows at right angles gave one the feeling of standing on air outside, 420 feet above the ground. Glass walls allowed a floor-to-ceiling view of the

Port of Tampa, Harbour Island, Davis Island, Plant Key and the Bayshore on the south side and the city, the University of Tampa and north Tampa opposite. The office was furnished in museum-quality antiques, the likes of which George's Aunt Minnie would have been proud to own.

The receptionist was a statuesque blonde Barbie look- alike selected for her acting ability. She played the receptionist part perfectly. When we entered the lobby, she greeted us both by name, said we'd been expected and someone would be out to escort us to the meeting shortly.

After about 60 seconds, Smyth's secretary, another exceedingly attractive and briskly competent greeter, escorted us to the meeting in the main conference room.

When we arrived, the meeting was already in progress and we slipped quietly in and sat down. A review of the last meeting's minutes was being concluded. While the familiar recitation droned on, I took the opportunity to look around. This room had a spectacular view of north and east Tampa. The conference table was made in the same shape as the building, of grey granite and various shades of wood inlay. The firm logo was again inlaid in the center of the table. The chairs were mahogany leather and the walls were lined with grey, granite-topped cabinets upon which were perched china cups and crystal glasses in patterns I recognized. Oil paintings of the firm's named partners lined the long wall opposite the windows and above the paintings in large brass script were the words "The Founder's Room." The decorating budget for this room alone must have exceeded the cost of a private college education.

After the meeting adjourned, Smyth approached me and said Mr. Waterman wanted to have a few moments with me if I could stay. I explained my transportation dilemma to Smyth--since I'd caught a ride over, if I didn't leave now I'd have to walk back. Smyth told me that one of the firm's drivers would be happy to take me back to my garage. With any reasonable objections so easily resolved, I accepted Hainsworth's invitation and followed Smyth back to Hainsworth's office.

On the way down the corridors, Smyth gave me a running tour. Each of the wide hallways was lined with original artwork by artists I'd seen before in places like the Smithsonian and the Metropolitan Museum. In several alcoves, vases and other antique pottery was displayed under spotlights.

"I notice you're admiring our artwork," Smyth said. "The firm believes in investing in art. One of our partners is quite knowledgeable and makes two trips a year to the New York galleries. He also attends several auctions a year. The artwork is constantly being bought and sold and it adds significantly to the firm's net worth." He sounded like a travelogue. I was beginning to think the entire firm was populated by the law office equivalent of Stepford wives.

"That's a rather unique practice isn't it?"

"I know some big firms in Chicago and New York invest in art, but I don't know of any other firm in Tampa that does. Here we are." He knocked on a large mahogany door with a crystal doorknob, pushing the door open as he knocked. Hainsworth stood up to greet me and take me off Smyth's hands. The opulence of the office was awesome.

Hainsworth's personal office was on the south west corner of the building, the best view the building had to offer. He had floor-to-ceiling windows overlooking Harbour Island, Davis Island, Plant Key and the Bayshore. I could see our Minaret clearly in the distance. The floors were hardwood, with antique Iranian rugs under the desk, the coffee table and the conference table. Navy and Burgundy leather upholstery covered most of the room. On the credenza and several of the walls were pictures of Hainsworth and Cilla at various milestones: their wedding, their children's weddings, their 45th anniversary party and last year's awards banquet where Hainsworth was named Lawyer of the Year. The opposite wall was Hainsworth with the governor, Hainsworth with our Senators, Hainsworth with our last four presidents.

"Wilhelmina, I'm so pleased you were able to stop in for a few moments. Can I get you a cup of coffee or a glass of wine?" I told him I would take a glass of Merlot and watched him open the door that concealed a wet bar. The wine rack held a selection of red wines, about 20 bottles. The white wines were in the wine refrigerator visible below. As he opened the bottle, I told him how impressed I was with his offices.

He handed me a Baccarat balloon glass, about two thirds full of Stag's Leap and motioned me onto a sofa. While he remained standing, we were eye to eye. "I didn't realize you hadn't been here before. We've had these offices about four years. One of the first firms to lease space in this building. It's been a pleasure putting it together." We raised our glasses in a silent toast. To what?

"How much space do you have, Hainsworth, and how many lawyers have you got?" I might not be a practicing lawyer anymore, but I still know how success is counted in the business.

"We have four floors here, 42, 41, 40 and, just recently, 39. We added ten new lawyers last year, bringing our total to 85." The open pride was uncharacteristic, but unmistakable.

"I had no idea you had so many lawyers in your office. Twenty percent growth in one year must make you about the fastest growing firm in Tampa. What's your secret?"

He smiled, smoothly conspiratorial. "Since you're not in competition with me, I'll tell you. We're strictly a litigation firm. We've been involved in some of the largest litigation in the country over the years. In 1991, when it all started, we were hired by one of the large manufacturers to defend breast implant cases. We've been on their national trial team since then. That's really fueled our growth."

"Didn't that company go into bankruptcy a year or so ago? That impacted your business significantly."

"Fortunately, no. By that time, we had also picked up the defense of another large manufacturer, even larger than the first. I'm sure you've heard of them—General Medics. Because of trial team experience and ground floor work with the first company, we were able to take an increased role with the new client immediately. That assignment has led to additional work from the second company, and others, and the result is what you see." He spread his left arm out, indicting the office, the view, everything.

"Well, I'm sure you're the envy of all your colleagues. In fact, didn't I hear that some of the firms involved in breast implant litigation have gone out of business?"

He nodded. "We've been fortunate, but it's impolite to say so."

I sat my wine glass down, and leaned forward, "Tell me, just because I'm interested. With all the experience you've had defending breast implant cases, what do you personally believe the problem is?"

"There's still a debate among the experts over that subject, and I'm certainly no expert." He looked away.

"I know that, but I also know that good lawyers, such as yourself, learn a great deal about the cases they're defending. I always had my personal opinions, unrelated to what I could prove or not prove, about the facts in my cases. Surely you must have some opinions of your own based on the work you've done." Seeing his reluctance, I added "Which wouldn't, of course be admissible at trial."

He paused with his wine glass held out as if he were about to make a formal toast. His voice took on the stentorian quality he used in opening statements and he started to walk around the room, still carrying his wine glass. "On a personal level, and not as lawyer to judge, I'll tell you that I think this is the greatest miscarriage of justice that has happened in this country since the McCarthy hearings. There is no evidence that breast implants, or any form of medical grade silicones, cause any type of health-related problem whatsoever."

"If that's true, how did we get to the point where there are more than 200,000 claims filed by women around the world?" I was challenging him, and it was clear he didn't like it. He began to get red in the face and his tone took on a sterner quality. I was grateful not to be one of his junior lawyers.

"If my car is wet, does that mean it's raining outside?" He expected an answer.

"Of course not. There could be any number of explanations for a wet car."

"Exactly!" He said, as if I was an exceptionally bright student. "That's the evidence that's been admitted in trials in these cases and upon which juries have been allowed to conclude that a sick plaintiff with breast implants means that breast implants caused the illness. No reputable scientist believes that. And on the basis of evidence no scientist accepts, one very reputable company is in bankruptcy and others have spent literally millions of dollars defending themselves."

"Then how did this all happen?" I asked, almost afraid to push the point, he had gotten so excited. The hand gripping his wine glass was white-knuckled. I carefully moved outside the path of breaking glass.

"It happened the way all of these goddamned products cases happen. The plaintiffs' bar is so organized these days that they can make a mountain out of any molehill."

"I'm not sure what you mean," I said.

The vein over his temple was bulging now, pulsing rhythmically. "Well, they get together and contribute $100,000 or more to a fund to begin litigation in a given area. Then they let it be known that they're the experts with the money and they're planning to launch an attack. Smaller scale plaintiffs' attorneys come along and contribute smaller sums of money until a war chest is developed. They advertise for plaintiffs, stir up public opinion and before you know it, you have Mount Everest created out of an anthill. Look at Bendectin or Phen-Fen. It's disgusting. No evidence to support those cases at all. None."

He was practically shouting at this point. I guessed this was a speech he had given many times before. Maybe he was practicing for the next

Defense Research Institute meeting, or his presentation to General Medics' board of directors. Any good trial lawyer can turn on indignation in a moment, and turn it off just as quickly. We're all actors at heart.

I had the impression, though, that Hainsworth's current display of anger was not completely acting. I decided it was time for me to take my leave before the old gentleman had a heart attack and I had another death to deal with. That old law school brain teaser came back to me—can words alone, if they lead to death, be murder? I turned the conversation to safer topics for a few moments and then said I needed to get back to my office.

We walked to the lobby and Hainsworth asked the Barbie to have the chauffeur drive me back to the federal building. He thanked me for coming and escorted me to the elevator, once again the perfect gentleman.

When I got to the curb at the corner of Florida and Jackson, it was already dark. The only car parked there was a navy Lincoln Town Car and the driver, dressed in a blue blazer with the now easily recognizable AB&W logo on the breast pocket, was standing on the curb. He opened the door for me and asked "Where to?" During the short drive, I asked him if he liked his job. Like every cab driver, he was loquacious.

"Yes, Ma'am. I retired from First National Bank here in Tampa five years ago and Mr. Waterman was our lawyer. I mentioned to him that I'd like to have part-time work and he put me on the payroll. The only thing I do is keep this car clean and drive people around town and back and forth to the airport. If there was an easier job in the world, I'd be ashamed to get paid for it."

"Sounds good to me," I told him.

"It's the only job in town like it. And I get to drive any kind of 4-door full size car I like. I get a new one every year. This baby's only three weeks old. What do you think of it?"

I said I thought the car was very nice and that he did, indeed, have an enviable position. The traffic lights on Florida Avenue are timed, but we hit all the red ones, getting in more quality time together.
"What kind of car did you have before this one?" I asked.

"Oh, man, a beautiful Cadillac de Ville. Black. Prettiest car I've ever had the pleasure to drive. I was sorry to see that one go. I wanted to keep it, but the boss, he said Mrs. Waterman's car was getting old, and she wanted that one. So I gave it to her and got me this one instead."

He dropped me right next to my black opal Mercedes CLK 320 Convertible I called Greta, and I thanked him for the ride. On the way home, my reverie was about the reasons I was no longer working for a firm like Able, Bennet & Waterman.

About a year before George and I moved to Tampa, I decided to get off the "up and coming" merry-go-round. I looked around me and saw the partners in my firm and George's corporate superiors living the life George and I would be living in ten years, and I didn't like it. One of the senior officers at the bank owned five homes, each mortgaged to the point that his $350,000 annual salary fell far short of his payments and his private school tuition obligations for three children. The year he asked one of the bank's secretaries to drive him back and forth to work because his lease car was over the mileage allowance and he couldn't pay the ten cents a mile surcharge, I realized just how precarious his position was. His salary easily exceeded hers by fifteen times, yet she could afford to buy a car, and he couldn't afford to rent one.

Another bank officer divorced his wife of 25 years to marry a service clerk 30 years younger than he. To say the divorce was costly is putting it mildly. His ex-wife was not just bitter, she was vicious. On any given day, he could be seen eating his $2 lunch of hot dogs and cottage cheese in the cafeteria, while telling anyone who sat down next to him just how many more alimony payments he had to make before he'd be able to afford hamburger. When his new bride promptly had twins and quit her job, he stopped eating lunch all together.

The stories were so typical, after a while they weren't even interesting. There was the junior associate in my firm whose husband was in business school. Not only couldn't they make it on his $75,000 salary, they lived on credit card debt that would feed an entire third world country for a year. When they wanted to take a vacation, they counted up their available credit balances to see if they could drive somewhere. A mid level partner, living in a three-story Victorian home in Indian Village couldn't afford a car and had to take the bus to work; another mid level partner had to borrow money to pay the deductible on his health insurance for his newest baby; a third, more senior partner took a loan to pay for more equity in the firm.

All around me, people were working harder, earning more and having less. They were required to work a staggering number of hours just to earn salaries that (while in the top 1% of all salaries in the country) didn't buy even a modicum of time and peace of mind. So I got off the merry-go-round. When Aunt Minnie died and left us Minaret, we simplified our lives, moved to Tampa, cut back on the dollar hunt. But sometimes, like today, when I saw how successful some of my colleagues were who hadn't dropped out of the race, I wondered if I'd made the right choice.

That evening over cocktails, I told George about my visit with Hainsworth Waterman and the splendor of his offices. "It's been pretty well known for quite some time that Hainsworth has had a significant reversal of fortune," he told me as he was turned the page of today's *Investor's Business Daily*. "Five years ago, his house was in foreclosure and he'd been posted at the Club for failure to pay dues on four or five occasions. Now it's quite a different story and I'm glad to know what the explanation is. There've been some very wild stories around town about the source of his wealth. I like Hainsworth. I'm glad to learn his financial reversal is due to good old American hard work and nothing else." Nothing else that marrying money didn't cure, at any rate. That's what I thought at the time.

CHAPTER SIX

Later, I changed into a canary-yellow sweat suit and made myself a drink. I went out to our balcony and sat with my feet propped up, lighting up my first Partaga of the day. It was after dusk, but not dark. The sky was filled with reds and oranges. Tomorrow would be another beautiful day. I was still sitting there, contemplating what to do about Carly's problem when George came out to join me. I was glad to see he'd brought a larger than usual glass of Glenfiddich.

"How do you feel about room service tonight?" he asked me as he sat down in the rocker next to mine. "I can order up some poached salmon over greens with raspberry vinegarette and fresh sourdough rolls. What do you say?"

"Sounds good to me," I answered him, still contemplating.

"I'll give you a silver dollar for your thoughts. They look valuable."

"I was just thinking how really unfortunate it is that the police department never closes." Then, I told George, my partner in all things, about Carly's visit.

"What is it about you that brings everyone with a problem to your door?" The question was rhetorical. It was far from the first time I'd been asked. Nor the first time I'd asked it of myself. For a long time I felt as if I walked into every room with a large sign around my neck that said "bring your problems to Willa." In every crowd, at every party, in every organization I joined, it seemed I soon became the "mother" of the group. Messy divorce? Problems with your children? Out of money? Weight problems? Drugs, alcohol, gambling? Ask "Dear Willa a/k/a Mighty Mouse."

Now that I know myself better, I know I wear my philosophy on my sleeve. You see, I believe all problems can be solved. It's that simple. And most people don't. Most people just want to wallow in it, but they don't want it fixed, especially if the fix requires the acceptance of personal responsibility and personal change. On some level, I like solving problems, other people's problems anyway.

I accepted that was why Carly had come to me in the first place. Not because she had any special affection for me. It's just that I've always been the problem solver. And she certainly had a problem. Where else would she go?

But this time, George was as distressed by Carly's situation as I had been, maybe more. If I try to mother everyone who comes along, George takes in strays, any stray, as long as they're a stray. Because Carly had been estranged from the family lately, George was particularly protective. He'd always liked Carly and he felt protective of her. "Don't you know someone to whom you could entrust this information in confidence? It seems the sort of thing that needs to be disclosed, but I certainly wouldn't want Carly to be arrested just for having suggested the possible identity of a dead man," he said. George still believes in all American institutions.

"I think I'd have to give some reason for my suspicions. Since I never learned why Carly was asked to leave the prosecutor's office, I'm not sure that if I disclosed her name, she wouldn't become a suspect. I can't risk that."

George and I debated the ethics and the practicalities for another hour before concluding that perhaps the tried and true "anonymous phone call" was the best way to go. Since it was scrupulously important, at least to me, that I not be involved, George volunteered to make the call from a pay phone in the local supermarket. I was amused and surprised. Until he suggested it, I wasn't really sure George knew where the local supermarket was, and cloak and dagger is clearly not his style. I'm not sure he even knows who James Bond is. George really is a sport.

We agreed on what he would say and how he would say it. I told him it was important to keep the call to less than three minutes so that it couldn't be traced. After we got everything worked out, he went downstairs to drive himself to the phone.

I waited for what seemed like forever. By the time George got back, I'd already finished three more drinks and smoked two more cigars. One a day is my usual self imposed limit. I saw his car pull up in the driveway and I poured us both another drink. George is not a man meant for intrigue and I knew that he would be at least as shaken as I was.

"Well, what happened?" I pounced on him as soon as he walked in the door.

"It went as well as can be expected. I called the downtown branch instead of 911. I know all 911 calls are taped. I disguised my voice and I said 'I think the body you found yesterday morning in Tampa Bay is

Dr. Michael Morgan'."

"Did they act like they believed you?"

"They asked me to repeat the information. After I repeated it twice, making a total of three statements in the very same words, I hung up. I think the whole call took about two minutes. Then I got back in my car and drove directly here."

"Were you followed?"

"Christ, listen to you! I don't know whether I was followed. I've never been followed in my life except in a funeral procession. I'd have no idea how to find out. Did you see anyone else come up the driveway behind me?"

I told him I hadn't and we both tried to calm down. At the moment, it appeared this was the most we could do. I had called Carly twice after George left. No answer. For all I knew, she could have moved or changed her number. In any event, we'd given the authorities the information we had and, with luck, we wouldn't have to deal with it further. I made a mental note to look up whether obstruction of justice was an impeachable offense first thing tomorrow morning. I was sure I knew the answer, but pretending I didn't gave me some hope.

We had the dinner George had suggested earlier sent up to our dining room and, although neither of us said anything, I knew we were both waiting for the evening news. At 11:00, we turned on the local broadcast. Frank Bendler carried the major stories, including the unidentified body. He recapped the prior reports, the reasons the police had for the conclusion that the victim had been killed before he was dumped in the Bay. The only new information came at the very end of the segment.

"This spot," Bendler said,"just in the middle of the Skyway Bridge, is where the body was found. But there's no evidence to suggest the victim was dumped from the bridge. In fact, it's almost certain that anyone stopping along the bridge, even in the early morning hours, would have been observed by passing motorists.

"Police Chief Ben Hathaway told NewsChannel 8 he believes the body was dumped way back here at the Port of Tampa, and unusual currents related to last week's storm washed the body toward the bridge. This is Frank Bendler, reporting live from the Sunshine Skyway."

Neither Frank, nor any of the other channels carried any information regarding the identity of the man. In fact, by eerie coincidence, none of the journalists even speculated on who the man might be.

George and I went to bed and had a very uneasy night. Every time

I woke up, he was already awake. When the clock finally read 5:00 a.m., there was no way I could continue pretending to sleep, so I got up. George was, finally, snoring. I got Harry and Bess, our two labradors, and went down to the beach for our morning run. For once, I was in the office well before the CJ or anyone else.

I was just thinking it might be nice to take a nap, when I realized it was past time to take the bench. Although judges kept me waiting often enough when I was in practice, I try not to keep a room full of lawyers, at a gazillion dollars an hour, waiting in my courtroom. It's just my little way of reducing the cost of litigation.

I slipped my arms into my robe, zipped it up, took a deep breath for patience and stamina, and walked straight through the back door onto the bench.

As I feared, the court reporter was seated, the bailiff at the door and the room full of charcoal pinstripes and red ties. Everyone jumped up at my abrupt and unannounced entrance: well-dressed jack-in-the boxes. I motioned them to be seated.

I looked around for any women lawyers who might be in the room and, predictably, saw none. Few women lawyers have Federal Court cases. Federal courts handle larger, more sophisticated disputes and crimes. Unfortunately, in Tampa as everywhere, relatively few women have a practice including the magnitude of claims typically brought in Federal Court. Whenever a woman appears in my courtroom, I always call her case first, just so I can give her the preferential treatment I never received as a lawyer. If they catch me at it, I'll find some believable way to deny it.

Calling the court to order is an old-fashioned custom required by the United States Code. But since I was already seated, I just nodded to the clerk to skip it and call the first case; first come, first serve, just like McDonald's.

On Fridays, I hear motions from ten until one. It's perceived to be a waste of judicial time and not worth the energy by most of my colleagues. I'm the only judge in the Middle District who schedules oral argument regularly. On any given Friday, I may hear up to twenty different motions. My colleagues are right about one thing: it takes a lot of time and energy to prepare for these oral arguments and they usually don't change my mind. The Chief Justice of the Supreme Court is wrong about something else—the quality of argument is generally much higher than judges like to admit.

I saw Christian Grover sitting in the back of the courtroom carrying on not-so-quiet conversation with other lawyers waiting their turn. His motion was number four on my docket, but since I detest his style and because I didn't want to give him an audience for the morning, I put his matter at the end. I could tell he was wildly annoyed and he began to speak louder and louder, just to challenge my authority. I made him wait until 12:45, when I finally allowed my clerk to call his case.

"*Jones v. General Medics*, Case No.: 95-57-Civ-T-23E," the clerk called out.

"Ready, Your Honor" E. Hainsworth Waterman, himself. I hadn't seen him come in.

"Ready," Grover said, unable to summon the courtesy to call me Judge. I tried not to smile. It was so easy to tweak him these days. I'm told there was a time when he wasn't so self important, but that was long ago in a galaxy far away. Since then, Christian Grover has been President of the State Bar, President of the American Trial Lawyers Association, President of the Florida Trial Lawyers Association, and on the adjunct faculty of most of the Florida law schools. So many titles, so little humility.

Hainsworth began his argument. "Your Honor, we're before the court today on Defendant's Motion to Dismiss Plaintiff's claims for failure to state a cause of action against us. Plaintiff just doesn't have any evidence that my client has done anything wrong in this case."

Waterman went on for twenty minutes, explaining why Grover had been unable to satisfy the pleading requirements of the Federal Courts to keep his case alive. With every word, Grover was turning redder in the face until he was sputtering. He kept popping up and down, bursting to interrupt. He didn't dare. I run a tight courtroom and I don't allow the lawyers to berate one another or talk between themselves during argument. Grover is well aware of my rules. He didn't say anything out loud during Waterman's argument, but he certainly let me know, along with the few remaining people in the courtroom, that he would sure like to.

After several minutes of long-winded argument, Waterman was finally winding up "and for those reasons, Your Honor, which have been more fully outlined in our papers, we request that the Court dismiss this claim against my client."

Grover slowly stood up to his full six feet, three inches, buttoned his double-breasted jacket, pulled down on the French cuffs of his shirt, smoothed his hair and moved to the podium, poised to begin what I'm sure he planned to be a speech worthy of the congressional record. I held up my hand.

"Mr. Grover, just a moment. Let me talk to Mr. Waterman. Mr. Waterman, you've made an eloquent argument. I'd like to grant your motion. I happen to agree with many of the things you've said." Grover was like a six-year-old who needed to go to the bathroom. He could hardly contain himself. I continued to hold up my hand, preventing him from talking at all. "However, we've thoroughly researched the issues and the cases you've relied upon are not sufficient to allow me to grant summary judgment to your client under Florida law. I'm denying the motion at this time, without prejudice to your right to bring it again. I'll prepare the order Trial Tuesday. Thank you gentlemen."

I stood up and left the bench while the bailiff was still saying "all rise." When my law clerks were back in the office, I could hear them laughing.

"Did you see the look on Christian Grover's face? I don't think anyone has refused to let him talk in 15 years."

"You got that right," the other clerk replied. "I've never seen anybody shut him up before!" At least that would give them something to talk about over dinner this evening and Waterman could go back to his office and profess his victory over Grover, even though he lost his motion.

By some miracle, my afternoon calendar was clear. I tried to work, but I just couldn't concentrate. If I didn't get to the bottom of this thing with Carly, I knew I'd never get any work done. I was tired of waiting around for this thing to go away, and I wasn't getting the answers I needed. I grabbed my purse and headed for the judge's garage. If I dropped in unannounced, Carly would have to see me.

I drove to MedPro, which was across the Gandy Bridge on Roosevelt Boulevard in St. Petersburg. In the parking lot, I pulled into the only empty spot marked "visitors." I'd never been to MedPro before and I was impressed with the aesthetics of the building. There was a small pond out back with a long dock running from the building to a large gazebo. The building itself was pristine white with "MedPro, Inc." in large blue letters over the door. The lobby was similarly clean and decorated in a contemporary style. It continued the azure blue and bright white color scheme.

The receptionist smiled brightly at me as I approached her. Do you need great teeth to be a receptionist? "Good morning. My name is Wilhelmina Carson. I'm here to see Ms. Carly Austin." When she asked me if I had an appointment, I lied.

I heard the receptionist call Carly's office. The receptionist continued to smile at me, but I could tell that what she heard from the other end of the phone was not what she wanted to hear. Her smile faded. Unexpected visitors were apparently not the norm at MedPro, Inc.

When she hung up the phone, the receptionist told me nicely, but with a shade less warmth, that Ms. Austin's secretary would be right down. The secretary arrived less than three minutes later, introduced herself, gave me a visitor's badge to attach to my jacket and asked me to follow her.

It was a long walk back to Carly's office through several corridors. Each time we came to a door, the secretary held up a security card to an electronic reader and the door automatically unlocked. I noticed that the card readers were located on both sides of the doorway, so that it was impossible to travel through the various departments without security access, both in and out.

"Ms. Austin is in a meeting at the moment," the secretary said. "She asked me to make you comfortable in her office and to tell you she'd be with you as soon as she can. Would you like coffee or soda?"

I assured her I would be fine waiting for Ms. Austin until she arrived. She left me alone in Carly's office, which faced the small pond I saw from the parking lot. It was really quite a lovely view, complete with wild life, including a couple of gators sunning themselves on the bank.

Carly's office was pretty nice for a junior counsel. It was about twelve by sixteen feet with a reasonably sized desk and credenza as well as a small conference table, a bookcase and two client chairs facing the desk. The windows covered one entire wall, opposite the door. The office had no personal effects in it: no pictures, no artwork, no desk accessories. Carly had worked here almost three years and if she left tomorrow, new counsel could move into this office without so much as rearranging the furniture. Comforting thought to a young lawyer—you're an interchangeable chair.

Carly's secretary didn't close the door and neither did I. I stood with my back to it, looking out the windows for what seemed like half an hour, but was probably closer to ten minutes. Then I sat down in one of Carly's client chairs and noticed a copy of MedPro's Annual Report on the table. I picked it up and read the biographical section on the company's history.

MedPro was formed in 1980 by three doctors, one of whom was, to my surprise, Dr. Michael Morgan. The other two founders were Dr.

Carolyn Young and Dr. Alan Zimmer. Morgan, Young and Zimmer were all faculty members and research scientists at CFU Medical School in the early seventies when they discovered new applications for silicone technology on a grant funded by one of the major silicone manufacturers.

The report said that, at the time, the manufacturer was looking for a more "responsive" gel for its breast implants, something that would more closely approximate the feel of human tissue. A silicone breast implant is much like Jello in a baggie. The research challenge was to come up with a gel that would be firm enough to resist leaking through the outer envelope and hold up well inside the breast tissue and yet soft enough to approximate the feel of human breast tissue.

At the time, radical mastectomy was the surgical method of choice for the treatment of breast cancer. The procedure was physically and psychologically devastating to the patient and everyone was racing to find an implant that could be used in reconstruction at the same time as the initial surgery.

Study after study had shown that waking up after mastectomy, either bilateral or unilateral, and observing her scarred and flat chest, was more emotionally devastating to the patient than the initial cancer diagnosis. If the reconstruction could be done at the same time as the mastectomy, then the initial shock of the surgery was significantly blunted.

The problem was that the implants available were hard and conical. If both breasts were removed, replacing both with implants would result in a symmetrical appearance. If only one breast was removed, an implant would be obvious.

Even in a double mastectomy case, the harder implants were often undesirable because they were so obviously not a part of the more mature body of a woman likely to have breast cancer. Most breast cancer patients are over 50 and have borne children. Their breasts didn't look like an 18 year old's before surgery, and implants that made the breast look like an 18 year old's after surgery weren't acceptable to many patients. The patients wanted to look and feel just like they had before the surgery, no better and no worse.

Dr. Young became interested in the project after her mother had a mastectomy and was required to wear a prosthesis. Dr. Young, already interested in silicone chemistry, sold her concept to a group of manufacturers at the American Society of Testing and Materials. Three of the manufacturers took her up on the proposal and issued a multi-million dollar grant to her and her two colleagues.

This was a complete paradigm shift for me. I had no idea of the history behind the development of breast implants. It was hard for me to reconcile the chauvinistic product to the altruistic picture painted by the annual report.

After three years, the report continued, Drs. Morgan, Young and Zimmer did discover a suitable responsive gel and all three manufacturers began to make implants using the formula the doctors had created. The new implants were an instant success and immediate reconstruction became the standard of care following unilateral or bilateral mastectomy.

Dr. Young's mother was one of the first patients. A long testimonial letter from her was reprinted in its entirety. A footnote to the report indicated that Mrs. Young had died less than a year after receiving her implant and had granted permission for an autopsy to further her daughter's research. No results of the autopsy were included.

Later, after observing the success made of their discovery and wanting to get in on the money, Drs. Morgan, Young and Zimmer formed MedPro, Inc. They mortgaged everything they owned to get the company started. At first, they manufactured breast implants using their responsive gel. Later, they developed other breast implant products to deal with issues such as hardening of the breasts and rupture of the implants that would sometimes occur a few months to a few years after implantation. After the initial lean years of start up costs, MedPro grew so quickly it went public in 1985.

From my discussions with George about initial public offerings, I knew Drs. Morgan, Young and Zimmer must have become immediate millionaires on paper based on the value of their stock when they went public. What must that kind of money have meant to research scientists used to eating potted meat on a regular basis?

The infusion of capital from the stock sale enabled the company to branch out into the manufacture of other medical devices. They acquired a patent and marketed kinetic therapy products to prevent bedsores in bed-ridden patients. They produced lifesaving silicone catheters and hydrocephalic shunts. By late 1991, their sales exceeded $500,000,000. In 1992, MedPro was listed as one of the top ten publicly traded companies in Florida.

That was as far as I got when I heard Carly come in. I slipped the Annual Report into my purse for further reading at another time. It was a public document. I wasn't stealing anything.

CHAPTER SEVEN

"Wilhelmina, I'm surprised to see you here. Please sit down," she said as she closed the door.

I looked at her closely. She looked in worse shape than she had been Wednesday evening. She was pale, drawn and gaunt. There was an air of desperation about her and I thought she was silently entreating me not to mention our previous conversation. Until I could figure it out, I decided to play along.

"It's been so long since George and I have seen you. I was driving by MedPro and, since I've never been to your office, I thought I'd stop in for a short visit. Would you be interested in giving me a tour of your facility?"

Carly seemed relieved that I'd understood her signals. She flashed a brilliant smile and offered me the tour.

We left her office and turned right, in the opposite direction from the lobby. Carly began a walking monologue, explaining the offices, the plant, the manufacturing practices and the products made here at MedPro. She repeated much of what was contained in the Annual Report, and I got the impression that this was the public story, reproduced in every medium.

In truth, the tour was fascinating. MedPro, Carly told me, was a small manufacturer of silicone-based and other medical products. While going through the manufacturing portion of the plant, we were required to dress in sterile gowns, masks, caps, gloves and booties. During the entire tour, Carly pointed out the precautions taken to follow sterile procedures, packaging, labeling and other FDA related requirements.

When we arrived at the research and development lab, Carly told me about MedPro's latest venture.

"The Company is currently experimenting with natural implants. The process uses a woman's own cells to generate natural tissue inside her breasts. Other researchers are experimenting with vegetable oil and fat filled implants, but our process is different. Within three to five years, if it works, we'll be able to remove tissue samples from somewhere on the body and grow additional cells in a lab. The cells would then be implanted into the breast where they would become real breast tissue."

"Are you saying you're experimenting with cloning humans?"

"Not exactly, but kind of like that. Here's the theory: a tissue sample with cells similar to those in breasts—"

"You mean pure fat?" I joked. I was relieved to see Carly smile, too.

"Not pure fat, but high in fat, yes. Anyway, those cells would be removed from the patient's thigh or abdomen."

"Those other gorgeous anatomic areas." I was trying to lighten the mood, and Carly seemed to appreciate the effort.

"It's surprising Hugh Hefner and Bob Guccione have been able to make so much glamour out of so much blubber, isn't it?"

By this time, we were both smiling, as Carly continued to explain the new process. When she'd finished, I asked her, "How close is this to becoming a reality?"

"Well, there are still a few things to work out, so its likely three to five years away, at least."

"It's got to be a very expensive project. What if it doesn't work?"

"We try not to think about that around here. 'Negative thinking never solved anything' is the researcher's motto."

Carly continued this charade all the way back to her office where she told me how pleased she was that I had come and asked me if I could join her for lunch. I told her I'd be delighted and we went out to my car.

Once we were out of the building and in my car, Carly slumped against the seat and closed her eyes. The charade had drained her.

I drove the few miles from the plant into downtown St. Petersburg and parked my car at the Vinoy, a large art deco hotel right on the water. We went in and were seated in the teak paneled dining room. After I ordered iced tea for both of us, I looked at Carly directly.

"At some point, you're going to have to tell me what is going on. Why did we go through that charade back at the plant? "

Carly seemed no more willing to talk and no less ill at ease than when she first came to the house. Since she wasn't willing to begin, I said "You need to know that George and I told the police who the body was." Her eyes widened, she pushed herself away from the table and started to rise from her seat. I put my hand on her arm to keep her from leaving, or making a scene in a place where both of us were well known.

"We made an anonymous call from a pay phone. All we said was that the body could be Dr. Morgan. Nothing more." She sat back down, slowly, and relaxed a little.

Then, more sternly, I said, "It's time for you to fill in some of the details you left out, or I'm going to have to go to the State's Attorney. This is serious business for me, Carly. I can't have any appearance of impropriety around me or my office over a murder. I want to help you, but you're not making it easy."

"I saw you reading our Annual Report," she said.

"So?"

"What it doesn't say in there, and what you'd know if you read the local papers closely, is that the breast implant controversy came to a complete head and nearly destroyed the company when the FDA ordered a moratorium on the sale of silicone breast implants."

"The report said the company had diversified its product by that time. How much of MedPro's business was breast implants when the moratorium was declared?"

"Over 50%. We had to close one of our plants and lay off a lot of our sales and manufacturing people and we beefed up our other products."

"That just sounds like prudent business, not the end of the world. People get laid off and plants close every day."

"Yes, but the loss was devastating to a young company like MedPro. Dr. Morgan and the other two founders went from being multimillionaires to being in threat of bankruptcy overnight."

"I don't mean to sound heartless, but sometimes wealth easily gained is easily lost. And it's not like any of those doctors are going to starve."

"You're right. And they were weathering the storm pretty well, under the circumstances. Dr. Young's husband had just died, so she was an emotional basket case anyway. Zimmer went to our creditors and restructured our debt. We thought we were going to come out okay.

"But then the lawsuits and the publicity started. The public revilement of everyone associated with the implants was devastating, personally and financially."

"A cynic would say it's the price of fame," I told her.

"You have no idea what it was like. We were under siege. Every day for months, the company was picketed by the Silicone Sufferers support group. We had to hire extra receptionists just to handle the calls. We got two feet of faxes and six feet of mail every day, most of it nasty. Our employees were constantly harassed. A lot of them quit because they were afraid to come to work. Every night for a month, we were the lead story on the six o'clock news." Carly's voice was becoming louder with each sentence. Other diners were looking at us.

"You mean, until a former NFL running back was arrested for killing his wife and the media had something new to report?"

She smiled weakly and calmed down a little. "I know it sounds like a nine-day wonder now, but it wasn't then. None of us handled the pressure well. There were frayed tempers, shouting matches and shoving contests somewhere in the plant every day, and not only on the production floor. More than 1,000 complaints were filed against MedPro and our insurance was canceled. I became a litigation manager. Just answering complaints and discovery requests was more than a full time job. The shunts, catheters and kinetic products were not enough to keep us going. It didn't look like we were going to get out alive."

"So how did it all work out?"

"It hasn't yet. We started preparing our bankruptcy petition, and were close to filing it when the bankruptcy of the largest defendant temporarily halted the litigation and gave us some breathing room."

Carly stopped talking as the waiter brought our lunch and made a major production of arranging it on the table. By the time the bread waiter brought the rolls and the beverage waiter brought refills on our iced tea, a family of four could have ordered, received and consumed a fast food meal, at less than half the cost of our salads. I made a mental note to remind George that not every meal needs to be a dining experience.

Once we were alone, I asked, "What does all this have to do with Dr. Morgan? Are you saying he committed suicide over the business reversal, by shooting himself in the head, then bound and gagged himself and jumped into the Bay?"

"Of course not. But Dr. Morgan had been calling me every day or two for about three months before he died."

"Did he say what for?"

"Oh, sure. Over and over, in fact. He wanted to make a presentation to our scientists at MedPro."

"What kind of a presentation?"

"He wouldn't say. He would only say that it was a presentation that had to be made to sophisticated scientists because lawyers wouldn't understand it.

"He said he knew why women with breast implants were ill and he wanted to explain his theory. He was writing a book about it but, for old times sake, he wanted to give MedPro a preview. He didn't mention what a successful defense would do to the price of his stock, but he didn't have to."

"But that's a fabulous scientific breakthrough!" I said. Her face let me know how wrong that was. "If there's a scientific explanation for women with breast implants becoming ill, then isn't that something everyone would want to know?" I asked her.

"No. I mean, I guess it depends on what the explanation is. If the explanation is related to the product, then the answer is, MedPro doesn't want to know. We can't know. That will put our company out of business."

I was beginning to see the problem. If the women's illnesses were related to the product itself, then MedPro would be at fault.

"Did you set up the meeting he requested?"

"I took it to my superiors. They weren't interested."

"Why not?"

"What they told me, through the proper channels, was that Dr. Morgan is a crackpot. He's a defendant himself in several hundred cases. They believed anything he might have to say would be an attempt to save his own skin, and the value of his stock. They didn't want to be associated with him any more than they already were. It seems everything MedPro does these days ends up on the front page of the papers and on the evening news. If it became known that we were working with Dr. Morgan, we would be the laughing stock of the medical community and he would be forever associated with us in the litigation. They couldn't believe that he had anything to offer that the best minds at the big, well-funded institutions weren't able to discover. They just didn't want to get involved with him."

"But if he was an owner and founder of the company, why did he need you to set up a meeting?" I asked her.

"Dr. Morgan had been removed by the board and only owned his stock. Which, at that point, wasn't worth much."

"Why?"

She looked at me, trying to decide whether to answer. Finally, she shrugged. "This is very hush hush, Willa. If this gets out, MedPro would be in a lot more trouble than it is now, if that's possible."

"Keeping secrets is a lawyer's stock in trade."

"I know, but some lawyers are better at it than others." She eyed me pointedly. I had, after all, made George call the police once already.

"True. All right. As long as I'm not required to disclose what you tell me, I'll keep it quiet."

"Dr. Morgan got into trouble with drugs a few years ago. He went to jail for selling cocaine and he lost his license to practice."

"That makes him a man who's paid his debt to society, not an ignorant incompetent without an intelligent idea."

"Yes, but during the prosecution of his case, it was discovered that he'd been having sex with his patients while they were anesthetized."

"You're kidding! How did they ever prove that?"

"He videotaped the surgeries, and he kept the tapes. The police found them in a routine search of his beach house."

The things you don't know about your own friends and neighbors are amazing. "Then why did he think MedPro would be interested in his presentation after he'd been fired by the other two founders when he went to jail?"

"Because he said his discovery would prove MedPro's innocence and the safety and efficacy of the implants. It was his way of trying to make it up to Young and Zimmer."

"And saving his own ass in the bargain," I said.

"That, too. Since Morgan lost his license, no medical insurer would touch him and no one else wants to be involved. He was begging me to schedule the meeting and, because he seemed so contrite and pathetic, I couldn't turn him down cold. I did tell him that, unfortunately, my management wasn't interested. The last time I talked to him, he told me someone was blackmailing him. He'd run out of money, and the blackmailer had threatened to kill him if he didn't pay. He sounded really desperate. I told him I thought he was exaggerating and he got angry with me and hung up."

"You never heard from him again?"

She hesitated before answering me, took a bite of her salad and washed it down. "No. He'd never given me a number where he could be reached. He always called me at prearranged times to talk. I've tried tracking him down through the Yellow Pages and directory assistance. I even hired a private investigator to look for him. No luck. When I heard they'd found a body in the Bay and about how long they thought it had been there, I just got this weird intuition that it was Dr. Morgan."

"Then why did you call me? Why didn't you just go to the police?"

Carly looked away for the first time in our conversation. Softly, she said, "Who would have believed me?"

"What do you mean? You could have told anyone. Why wouldn't they believe you? You're a lawyer, an officer of the court."

She was impatient again. "I really don't want to get into it. Let's just say that I knew for sure there was no one I could go to with the information. I'm glad you notified the police. With your tip, at least they'll check to see whether it's Dr. Morgan or not. I really want to stay out of it from this point forward. I need this job, Willa, and I like it. There's no one else to take care of me. I don't have a wealthy husband, I don't live on my own island and I don't have a lifetime appointment to the Federal bench. Please," she leaned forward, pleading with me, "don't screw this up for me."

Like the little boy who killed his parents and then complained because he was an orphan, Carly seemed to have no understanding of how much more serious she was making this situation than it already was. She acted like she'd just failed to appear for a court date, when what she had involved us both in was so much worse. Maybe tough love was what she needed now, I thought. "I have no intention of screwing anything up for you, Carly. You seem to be able to do that all by yourself. Do you know what will happen if it turns out this body is Dr. Morgan and people learn you knew or had reason to believe it was him for over a month and didn't tell? Your career as a lawyer will be ended. If you're lucky, you won't be arrested for obstructing justice, or murder." My harsh words seemed to shake her.

"What do you mean? I certainly had no reason to kill Dr. Morgan. I don't even know for sure if it's him, for God sake." She was genuinely shocked.

"Well you were concerned enough about it to come to my house and ask me a hypothetical question. You're concerned enough about it that you wouldn't allow me to talk to you in your office. What do you think, your office is bugged?"

"I know it is" she said.

"How can you know such a thing?" I could hear myself getting shrill and insistent with her, but this was getting to be too much.

She explained with exaggerated patience. "The entire plant is under constant surveillance. Every phone call, in and out is recorded. All of the offices have video camera surveillance. The making of medical products is a highly competitive business these days. The company guards its secrets. Any breach of security and you're out. No second chances."

"Well if Dr. Morgan really had a solution to the breast implant health mystery, why would anyone want to kill him for it?"

She looked at me as if I had just revealed my own insanity. "Have you no idea what you're saying? Do you realize how large a business this breast implant litigation has become? Fred Johnson, for one, is in this thing for millions of dollars. If there's a logical explanation for this, do you really think the plaintiff's bar is going to let go of all that money? And, if there really is a health hazard, do you think MedPro wants that to become public knowledge? The only peaceful coexistence lies in not knowing. As soon as we know, one side or the other loses."

"But what about the women? Aren't they the ones with the most at stake? Don't they have a right to know whether they're going to get sick or not from these leaking implants?" I asked her.

She shook her head. "I never thought of you as naive. Don't you understand the big business of litigation? Believe me, the number of people who would kill to keep such information quiet is limited only by your imagination."

I refused to believe Carly's words, but I decided that I would keep her confidence. At least for now. In turn, she promised to let me know if she heard from Dr. Morgan or if she heard any other information about his disappearance. We finished our lunch and I dropped her off at MedPro before heading back to my office, but only after she promised to return my calls and check in with me regularly. I thought then that I could trust her, but I was wrong.

CHAPTER EIGHT

I intended to go back to the office, but I just couldn't muster any enthusiasm for it. Since I had nothing on my calendar until Monday morning, I decided to play hooky and go home. I pulled over to the side of the road and put Greta's top down. Driving over the bridges, the water on either side, the wind blowing through the car and the top down rejuvenated my spirit, if not my hairstyle.

On the way home, I couldn't help thinking about Carly and what kind of child she had been before she learned *the big secret*. Kate had two sons when Mom and I came to live with her. Later, Carly was born. Since I was ten years older, I learned about the birds and the bees a lot sooner, and I knew Kate had been widowed far too long to have another baby. The boys must have at least suspected, too, but Kate was so happy about the pregnancy and kept referring to the baby as "your brother or sister," that none of us was willing to challenge her on it.

When Carly was born, and as she grew up, it just ceased to be important to all of us who Carly's father was. To us, she was our sister, so it didn't matter. And Carly never questioned it. Until the year she was ten. That year, her science class studied the gestation time for dogs, cats and human babies. She began to ask questions about why her appearance was so different from the dark hair and eyes her brothers had, and finally, the exact date of their father's death.

From that point on, Carly began hounding Kate about the identity of her father. And the boys, being boys, wanted to know with whom their mother had had an affair. Kate refused to say, at least to her children. I don't know what she told my mother at the time. Kate would only say that all her children were hers and they were brothers and sister.

For Carly, it was as if she had lost all perspective. I'm not sure ten year olds are supposed to have perspective, but Carly did. At least, until she decided finding out her father's identity was to be her sole mission in life. She pestered all of us endlessly about it. She made a list of all the men she knew and relentlessly questioned my mother, Kate and the rest of us about them. When did Kate meet each one? How? How well did they know each other? She kept completed questionnaires on all of them, and meticulously correlated their relationships with Kate to her birth date and what she calculated as her date of conception. She'd interview them in circumspect ways, always trying to find out if he'd been around at the right time, if he was the right age. Each time she ruled out someone she considered desirable, she'd go into a deep depression and refuse to talk to any of us for days. By the time I was in college, Carly had filled several looseleaf notebooks of father contenders, viable and rejected.

It was hard to tell whether the serious rift between Kate and Carly resulted from a secret kept too long, or the natural animosity of a teenage girl toward her mother. In either case, Carly was never the same toward any of us.

She went away to college at the University of Colorado and rarely came home after that. None of us knew her, really, since we hadn't talked to her seriously since she was a child. Mark was the closest to her, and she was the most jealous and distant from me. Carly has always seen me as some kind of competition for her place in her family. She knew I wasn't really a blood relative, and she felt she wasn't a full blood relative either. The self-imposed competition made her brittle, even a little flaky.

When Carly secretly moved to Tampa, after her mother and I moved here, we didn't even know it for a long time. I think she did it partly because she was jealous of my relationship with Kate, and partly because she was beginning to grow up. She entered Stetson Law School and became a lawyer like her two brothers and, not coincidentally, me. It's hard to beat the competition if you're not in the same game. Carly wanted a real contest.

Once she moved here, she still saw her mother rarely, but in a typical Carly move, signed up for my class. Even now, she's a bundle of contradictions; independent and rebellious, brilliant but immature. I couldn't really fathom how it must feel not to know who your father was, to feel that rejection and deception. Carly certainly seemed to be struggling with it still, and I wasn't sure she'd ever get over it.

Comparing my childhood to Carly's wasn't really possible.

Kate says that I was a dreamer as a child. I spent all of my time either reading or daydreaming, making up a world far different from the one I lived in. In school, I was always planning the next event, looking forward to activities next month or next year.

After Mom died when I was 16 and Dad left me with Kate and her family, I became even more out of touch with what was going on around me, but I held onto Kate and her family as if I was drowning in abandonment and only familial affection would save me. For her part, Kate took the role of my mother in the same way she mothered her own children. She went to parent-teacher conferences, threw birthday parties, and had her picture taken at my graduations, just as she did with her other kids. She even played the part of mother-of-the-bride when George and I married. Kate is my mother, for all practical purposes, and has been for longer than I knew my real mom. If it wasn't that I'd feel so disloyal, I'd call her "mother." She's suggested it. It's a step I'm not ready to take.

So maybe Carly is right to be jealous of me. Maybe I said or did something those last few years when I lived with Kate's family to justify it. But even if I did, I can't relate to how she treats her mother. Because if my mother was still alive, no matter what she did, I'd never treat her the way Carly treats Kate.

Mom died of cancer. While she was ill, we spent so much time together and I wanted to savor every moment of it. She wanted me to go to school and the truant officers insisted that I go at least half a day. But the last few months of her life, they let me stay home when I promised to test out of the tenth grade after she died.

That was such a glorious time. She taught me how to make bread, arrange flowers, put on a dinner party. She told me all of the secrets a mother imparts to a daughter about dating and dealing with men. Some of what she said scared me. "Never let a boy put his hand on your knee. If you do, he'll want to put it under your skirt." I wasn't sure exactly what she meant by that, but it was advice I followed until I met George years later.

Mom and I had our own little world then. Dad was traveling, as he always had, even at what was clearly the end of his wife's life. On some level, I never forgave him for that. But on another level I was glad for the time it gave mother and me to be together. Maybe that was his present to both of us.

It was while Mom was sick that she told me she'd wanted to be a lawyer instead of a nurse. And I promised her that I would do what she had not done. Eventually, Mom died and her husband, the man I'd called my dad since she married him when I was five, never came home. I went to live with Kate and, as I promised, I tested out of the tenth grade. I graduated from high school at 17 and then went directly to the University of Michigan.

What doesn't kill you makes you stronger. I know now that I was lucky to have loved my mother for 16 years, and to have had her unconditional love while she lived. She sent me off into the world with that, the love, desire and support necessary to make something of my life. Every time I think of her, I think, "I could be better," not just as a lawyer, or a woman, but as a person. She believed that what's important is how you live your life, how you treat others. She taught me always to do my best and to help those who need it. It was a hard lesson to learn at 16, but I learned it, and it sustains me. It also gets me into trouble. Mighty Mouse does save the day, but it's not easy.

Carly was still dealing with Kate from anger and abandonment. I doubt Kate had ever sat her down and asked her to consider the alternative—being born to Kate's family or not at all. But Carly is the closest thing to a sister I'll ever have. She may be flaky and irresponsible and irritatingly self centered, but there's no way I could let her get seriously hurt. Kate would never get over it and I'm not sure I would either. I didn't want to lose anyone else in my life.

About twenty minutes after I left Carly, I was turning onto Plant Key Bridge. I forced my mind back to the present and filled my senses with the approach. Florida is so flat, and Plant Key so far below sea level, that from the bridge, I could only see the top of Minaret. And a spectacular top it is, too.

The house is named after its most prominent architectural feature, a large minaret on the top of the third floor roof. The story goes that Henry Plant had visited Turkey and became enamored of the bulbous onion domes he saw there. He put several on the top of his hotel and one on the top of his home. Ours is shiny steel and the sun glints off of it most of the day, making it shine bright blue with reflected skylight, orange with the sunrise or grey with the clouds. The rest of the house isn't in any way reflective of middle eastern architecture, so the minaret itself is somewhat out of place on top of the southern style home. It's sort of like Jimmy Durante's big nose, something you come to appreciate over time.

As I left the bridge, I drove down Plant Key's version of the Avenue of Palms. Ours are not so old or so tall as the ones at the entrance to Palm Beach, but they stretch for about a half a mile and give one the impression of grandeur an entrance onto Plant Key should have. To show the proper respect to the original, our avenue is unnamed. It opens out to the front lot entrance to Minaret, which is red brick, paved and circular.

Plant copied the entrance from the Breakers Hotel, built about the same time by Plant's great friend Henry Flagler. If you've been to the Breakers, the Ritz in Naples, or seen pictures, you've seen our front entrance, except ours is red brick and not yellow. We have a round fountain in front of the portecochere, and a drive that runs through. In those days, Florida storms were as fierce as they are now, and the ladies and gentlemen needed a shelter from which to leave their carriages. Now, it makes a great valet parking entrance to Minaret, particularly if you're arriving in the summer between four and seven o'clock in the afternoon when we get our afternoon storms.

I drove slowly onto the island and up to the house. I asked the valet to put the top up on the car and I went inside, intending to change into running shorts and a T-shirt and take the dogs out. But when I walked into the lobby, I saw Kate sitting in the dining room with Victoria Warwick and Cilla Waterman. I tried to sneak around to the winding staircase that goes from the main entrance to the house up to the second floor, but Kate saw me and waved me over. I was shaking my head furiously, signaling her that I didn't want to come in, but by this time Victoria had seen me, too. Trapped. I tried to look gracious as I walked into the dining room and up to their table.

"Wilhelmina, please join us," Victoria said, her speech slurred just enough to let me know how many Bloody Marys she'd already consumed in addition to the one on the table in front of her. Kate and Cilla both insisted that I sit down and I couldn't graciously refuse.

Kate and Cilla looked like what they were: middle-aged matrons at lunch. But again today, Victoria had on a bright pink dress suitable for a much younger woman, tight in the bodice with another low-cut neckline. She wasn't wearing a bra. Sunlight illuminates everything: she was no longer 25 years old, or even 55. But she was blessed with a long neck and her bosom did look fantastic. She laughed loudly, put her hands on the sides of her breasts to push them up almost out of the top of her dress. She said, "It's impolite to stare, my dear, but aren't they fantastic?"

Embarrassed to be caught looking, I blushed but I had to agree.

"I had them done in New York about six months ago. I'll tell you it wasn't easy to find a doctor who would do them, even though I offered to pay twice the normal cost. I tried to get Mike Morgan to do them for old time's sake, but he wouldn't return my calls. Men are such assholes, especially the ones you've slept with. They think it gives them the right to be an asshole for some reason."

Cilla's nostrils flared, whether at the crude language or the mention of Victoria's well-known philandering, I couldn't tell. "It's bad enough that you've slept with every man in town, Victoria. Is it necessary to broadcast it, too? It's not like you're the only woman in Tampa to have had an affair with Mike Morgan. Take a number." She was impatient, and snappier than usual. And she sounded too bitter.

More to distract them from Morgan than anything, I said, "I've never known any doctor to refuse to do elective surgery. There's so much profit in plastic surgery. If you agreed to pay twice the cost, why would they possibly refuse?"

Victoria was remarkably coherent, and much more voluble than she likely would have been if she hadn't been drunk. "Well, there's been an FDA moratorium on breast implant surgery for several years. The only way to get silicone breast implants now is to become a part of a controlled study. And, of course, for the controlled studies they want younger, more vigorous women or cancer reconstruction patients. You wouldn't believe all the releases I had to sign and the strings I made the senator pull to get them to do it. But they did, obviously." She giggled, looking down her chest. No kidding.

"But aren't you afraid of the health risks? Tory, really, this is a fairly stupid thing you've done to your body." Cilla was out of patience. She may be a grand dame, but she doesn't suffer fools.

Victoria looked at all of us with open hostility. "I think it's fairly obvious that my body is no temple. It takes years for the ill health effects from implants to develop, according to the doomsday theories. I'm sure I won't live that long, if my darling husband's wishes have anything to do with it. A widower is so much more electable than a man with an adulterous wife, you know. Everyone wants to know *why* she cheats."

None of us had a response to that. Kate changed the subject to some recent charitable activities they were involved in and that gave me my excuse to leave. As I walked out of the dining room, they were still discussing the budget for the next homeless shelter benefit, and I was trying to figure out why discussing Tory Warwick's affair with Dr. Morgan would make Cilla so angry and Kate so quiet.

CHAPTER NINE

When I got upstairs, both Harry and Bess were lying by the door waiting for anyone who happened to come in so that they could immediately lick them to death. Both bounded toward me and wanted to jump on my suit. I made them get down and changed into running clothes. Then I gave in, got down on the floor and rolled around with both of them for a while. Together, they out-weigh me by thirty pounds.

Bess is black and Harry is yellow. Like their namesakes, they're fiercely independent, no-nonsense dogs, thoroughly devoted to one another. We got them originally for protection as guard dogs because so many strangers come into what is, after all, our home. Pricilla Waterman told me once, after Harry slobbered all over her Dior dress, "If you had a gun, and knew how to use it like everyone else in Tampa, you wouldn't need these noxious creatures." But I'm from Detroit. Nothing as sissy as handguns for protection for us.

Of course, anyone who spends five seconds with Harry and Bess realizes what useless guard dogs they are. They do have big barks and that counts for something, at least to strangers. We still pay the alarm company every month, just in case.

After I put on my running shoes, we went down the back stairs, avoiding everyone else who might be in the restaurant, to the beach. I threw sticks and toys into the water for them to chase for a while before we began our run. After fifteen minutes of having wet sticks returned by two ninety-pound dogs, I was as wet as they were. I threw the last two sticks and took off in the opposite direction, counter clockwise around the island. If I don't play with them some beforehand, there's no way I can keep up.

By the time they got the sticks out of the water and came after me it took them, maybe, fifteen seconds to pass me up. It's a little contest I have with myself. I've made it as far as twenty seconds ahead of them, but I have to throw the sticks pretty far out first.

When I'm in good form, I do an entire lap around Plant Key, or maybe two. Other days, I just do half a lap and take a golf cart back.

Because I was feeling guilty about leaving the office early and I had plenty of time before sundown I decided today would be a complete lap day.

A lot of people run just for exercise, hating every minute of it. For me, though, it's a spiritual experience. I love the sand, the water, the sunshine and the companionship I get from Harry and Bess. After years of running, I'm able to get to the runner's high in about three minutes and it carries me the remainder of the run. Sometimes, I have to consciously make myself stop. Otherwise, I might be like the tiger chasing Sambo and run around so long and so fast that I melt into butter. During the summer I feel like I'm melting.

Today I considered what I'd learned on my visit to MedPro and at lunch from Carly. Something about her explanation just didn't fit with the facts. It was nagging me and the more I tried to focus on it, the more elusive it became. I attacked it another way. Why would Dr. Morgan call Carly with his discovery when he could have called Zimmer or Young directly? He knew them better and they had a history together. Why would he pick a young, gullible and inexperienced employee to disclose such allegedly valuable information? It just didn't make sense, unless he planned to use that inexperience for his own ends. Or, and this was more likely, Carly wasn't telling me everything. I worked out a plan for finding out the rest.

As I came up the back stairs after my run, our private phone rang and George answered it.

"It's Marilee Aymes, for you," he said as he handed me the cordless. I wondered how she got the number. Like my office number, it's unlisted and only given out to the family.

"Dr. Aymes. So nice to hear from you." Another lie. To the best of my knowledge, information and belief, as we lawyers say, Marilee Aymes had never called me before.

"Wilhelmina," she said, imperious as usual. "We have a foursome for next Sunday and we've lost one of our group. The handicapper said you're a 10, which would place you at the high end of the group, but he suggested we ask you to fill in. Are you free?"

Kate would say when you want a thing, it happens. I was trying to figure out a way to talk to Marilee Aymes, and she just called. There are no coincidences in life. I accepted.

George and I had a wedding to go to that night. We went, we ate, we came home. I always make Friday night an early one. It's a pleasant end to a long week, and besides, I play golf every Saturday at 6:00

a.m. with my former partner, Mitchell Crosby, out at Great Oaks.

We've tried playing other courses, just to keep our skills up, but there's something about the familiarity of the holes, the fairways and the greens that challenges us to beat our best games. We play best here, on our home turf, but that's not the reason we keep coming out to the same 18 holes every weekend.

I'm not an early riser and I can't make it to the office before 9:00, at the earliest. But on Saturday, I jump up before sunrise, slip on a golf shirt and Bermudas in some wild combination of colors, and sneak out of the house so as not to wake Harry and Bess. For a while there they were on to me, and they'd sleep right next to the bed so I couldn't get away from them. If they wake up, they have to be fed and run before anything else. They know they're the center of our universe and the world revolves around them, not George, although he likes to think he's the Master Cylinder.

So, if I don't get out without waking them up, we can't tee off until 7:00, which doesn't sound like much of a problem unless you're a golfer in Florida in July. If you are, you know what I mean. If you're not, you don't want to hear about it anyway.

On this particular Saturday in January, it was dark at 5:30 when I woke up, and a little too cool. George had opened the windows sometime during the night and the warmth of our Egyptian cotton sheets and down comforter almost sucked me back in for another couple of hours. But I knew Mitch would be on the first tee in 30 minutes. He lost five dollars last week, and whenever he was down in our weekly wagers, he couldn't rest until he won it back. If I skip a day like that, he declares himself the winner and will not back down. Mitch is more than a little obsessive, overbearing and stubborn. Some would say we're perfectly matched.

Once I was washed and dressed, I ran out to the car. Dew on the St. Augustine grass and Impatiens gave everything a crystalline shimmer. As I drove out the circle, the sun was lightening the sky over the Port of Tampa and Harbour Island. By the time I crossed the Plant Key Bridge, the sun glinted on Hillsborough Bay and two dolphins swimming side by side raced Greta and me the length of the bridge. They won. It was glorious. I've always loved morning. It's just that I usually sleep through it.

It's a short drive to Great Oaks. As I approached the large, plantation-style club house, I realized, as I always do, how amazing it is that such a beautiful 36 hole golf course is nestled right in the center of

South Tampa. I parked the car and walked to the pro shop. Since I play every Saturday, the caddies had my cart set up with my clubs. I went into the women's locker room and put on my golf shoes before meeting Mitch at the cart. Of course, he was ready to go, already behind the wheel. On the golf course, as on the road, men do the driving if the women don't get there first.

At the first tee, Mitch hit a drive 200 yards with his Big Bertha driver and was feeling pretty smug, thinking, I'm sure, that he'd be getting his $5 back today. By the end of the first nine, though, I was two strokes under and he was becoming surly. I remembered my mother telling me that I needed to let the boys win; otherwise they wouldn't play with me anymore. She obviously hadn't known Mitch. It's when he's winning that he wants to stop.

We always eat lunch in the clubhouse. Today, Mitch wasn't quite as interested in gloating over his winnings as usual.

"What's up?" I asked.

"Actually, I was feeling sorry for Mrs. Junior. I've always liked her, even if she is rather homely." He said, referring to the CJ's daughter-in-law, his only son's wife, using the nickname we've privately, and derisively, given her husband.

"Why?" I asked, "She has everything in the world. Aside from having to live with Junior, I'd say there are only about fifty million women in the country who would gladly trade places with her."

"Not today. Junior made a complete fool of himself a few years ago and his wife, too. He resigned from our firm yesterday because the scandal broke."

"No kidding! Junior, heir apparent, the anointed one, one day to become the second great and powerful Oz himself? What on earth possessed him to do that?" This was truly juicy news, if only because it would cause the CJ so much consternation. Junior was detested by every partner in my old firm lower on the ladder than he was, and by some who were a little higher up. It's not that Junior was really such a bad guy, it was just that he got his privileges the old-fashioned way — Daddy bought them for him.

To be fair, he probably would have done well enough on his own if he'd been a little more pleasant. But he was one of those guys who always had sand kicked in his face as a kid. He was scrawny, wore glasses, and had a sour personality. In truth, he was one of the reasons I sought a judicial appointment after he came over to the firm a few years ago. Practicing another twenty years with Junior running the show was more than I could bear. Maybe I had to work with his father as the Chief Judge now, but the CJ had no real power over me. Working with Junior as my managing partner was unacceptable. Now, then and always.

"You have to give me all the details. And don't you dare leave anything out." We ordered burgers and beer, our standard Saturday lunch. The beer came in tall, frosty mugs while we waited for the well-done burgers cooked the Jimmy Buffet way: cheese, lettuce, pickles, tomato and onion. Fries, too, of course.

"Well, you know Junior was the rising star in our downtown office." Mitch is like James Michner; he always begins at the very beginning of time.

"Sure, as the saying goes, he came from money, married money, and made a lot of money. All the makings of a successful lawyer, even if he is a twit."

"Willa, that's not very becoming of you," Mitch scolded as he grinned. He doesn't like Junior any more than I do.

"It seems an attractive, sexy, female lawyer was hired in the prosecutor's office when he was over there. And for reasons that can only be attributed to a mental handicap or extreme nearsightedness, she apparently found Junior attractive. Maybe it's the power that turned her on or the promise of future power. I could never understand Lyle Lovett and Julia Roberts, either."

"I'm with you." When the waitress came around with our burgers, we ordered another beer. In addition to the $5 bet, I had to buy lunch and he was making the most of it.

"Anyway, she appears to be attracted to him and he, who never had a date in his life that didn't have to wear a bag over her head, is besotted. Everyone notices. Rumors fly. She's bright and capable and could make it on her own merits, but the favoritism he shows her makes her the target of vicious gossip."

"Imagine that." The drinks arrived, and I settled in for the rest of the story.

"Such sarcasm. Anyway, you know Junior's granddaddy was the President of the First Federal Bank of Tampa, and when Junior's daddy took the Federal bench, Uncle Bishop got the bank job. The largest bank in town, and not coincidentally, one of the firm's major clients, is controlled by Uncle Bish. The CJ and Uncle Bish were afraid Junior had gotten totally out of hand. The scandal would shake his place in society. Uncle Bish, a powerful man himself, can't have that, even if it would otherwise have been okay with Oz, senior."

"This is delicious. What did Bishop do?" I licked the juice off my fingers and dipped a french fry in mustard. Mitch frowned at my poor table manners. He handed me a napkin.

"Uncle Bish called our State's Attorney in to lunch, and, friend to friend, asked him to squash the whole situation by firing the young associate and putting Junior on a big project that would take him out of town for a couple of months."

"A few months away from hearth and home and the floozy and he should start thinking with his big head again, instead of his little head. I can see the logic of it." I smiled, a mouthful of beef, cheese and mustard dribbling down my chin. I picked up the extra napkin so as not to interrupt the story again.

"Right. But the truth is, Uncle Bish is more than a little proud of Oz's sprout. Junior has never before exhibited any traits of real manliness, you see. He's always been sort of a bookworm weeny. Now, at least we know he's capable of manliness. But that doesn't mean Oz wants Junior destroying his dynasty. Junior has four children, after all, and a very respectable wife." Mitch was chewing his burger with gusto. He was really getting into this now.

"How sweet." I said. "A little meaningless dalliance. Well, that's a time-honored privilege of the privileged, but throw away the future the family has planned for Junior on a pair of long legs, even very attractive and smart long legs? No."

"Is this my story or yours?"

"Sorry. It's just so predictable."

"No problem, but watch it." He gave me a mock slap on the wrist. "So, the State's Attorney agrees to the plan because what choice does he have? Besides, he's been totally oblivious to the gossip and didn't even realize what was going on in his own office."

"It's really true that the farther up the ladder you get, the less people talk to you." I waved for some extra napkins again and the waitress brought them over. Mitch took a couple this time, too.

"Right. Besides that, you know the State's Attorney is one of those true blue types. He's been married since he was 25 and he's never even looked at another woman."

"He's never really looked at his wife, either." I couldn't resist. I figured if I was going to be a gossip, I might as well go all the way.

"True, but sex has not been his aphrodisiac. He can't understand how otherwise intelligent men let their dicks do the thinking."

"Amen." I signaled for another round, trying to decide if I should switch to something lighter. I did have to drive home, and I wasn't interested in explaining a drunk driving ticket to the CJ. I could just see it. "Oh, Oz. Junior's story was just sooooo interesting. I couldn't help myself." I decided to stick with the beer for now. What the hell.

"So, the State's Attorney himself calls Junior into his office and gives him the ultimatum," Mitch continued.

"Let me guess. 'This is unseemly. It's embarrassing. It's affecting your future'" I said, covering my sarcasm well, I think.

"In the tradition of the way these things have been handled from time immemorial, he tells Junior to put a stop to 'this relationship' at once, or the young assistant will be fired."

"That's outrageous!" I nearly spit out my beer. "Why didn't they fire him? What he's doing was immoral and illegal. The State's Attorney could find himself on the wrong end of a sexual harassment suit over this."

"Don't I know it. Labor law is my forte, remember? But does anyone ask me? No." Mitch sounds more than a little put out by this. Everyone's got their own ox to gore, every time. Count on it.

"Junior must have been incensed. He is next in line to the throne, after all. Not only the family throne, but Uncle Bishop's throne as well."

"Make that 'was.' The way I heard the story, that was exactly his thinking. So Junior calls Dad and lays it on thick about the lame-brained behavior by the dotty old State's Attorney. But, shock of shocks, Dad agrees with Uncle Bish."

"Junior must have been having a cow! I wish I could have seen it!"

"And you'd have had to stand in line. Anyway, Junior told his cronies later that Dad said 'a piece of ass is nice, Junior, but it's not worth your credibility, your family, and your job.' He wouldn't support him on this one."

"What did Junior do?"

"Junior thinks about it for two hours. He decides to put an end to the affair. He calls her into his office and tries to explain it to her. She cries. She pleads. She sits on his lap."

"So, Junior's little head snaps to attention and he throws caution to the wind." The sarcasm was so thick you'd have to cut it with a chain saw.

"Right. He called the guy I heard this from, really hot. They're not going to railroad him. He'll show them who's boss. And so forth. His pal tries to get him to calm down. No dice. He calls a guy who's been courting him to come over and join our firm for months. He agrees to come if he can bring her with him." The finish was kind of a let down, although the story had been a good one.

"You have got to be putting me on. It's interesting to finally learn how he got to the firm, but why would all this ancient history cause him to resign now?" This was real news. If I ever leave the bench, it actually gives me a place to go back to.

"Because everybody found out about it this week. Uncle Bish had managed to keep the whole thing quiet, but lately there's been some rumblings in our associate ranks that Junior's up to his old tricks. Someone reported him to our managing partner, who called Junior in for a little talk. Junior told him to take this job and shove it."

I don't know if it was the story or the beer, but the whole situation seemed so funny. We were laughing so hard that other patrons in the clubhouse were staring at us.

"I would have paid, paid you understand, to see the look on your managing partner's face when Junior quit. This is precious."

When he could talk again, Mitch said, "Yeah, but the managing partner is really sweating. Now he's really pissed off Oz, Senior, and Uncle Bish, and he knows it. He doesn't know what to do. What will he say? Everyone was planning on Junior to be managing partner when his time came."

"Well, I can't believe many of your comrades are too upset about it. I'm thrilled, although if you repeat that I'll deny it." We signed the check and went out to our cars. Certainly one of the more entertaining golf dates we've had lately, even if it did cost me $50. I had a nice little buzz going. We said our goodbyes and were about to leave the course for the day, when one more question occurred to me.

"Mitch, just out of curiosity, where did Junior's floozy go, anyway? Did she come with him to your firm?"

"No. She left Junior at the same time she left the State Attorney's office and took an in house counsel job for some medical device company in St. Pete." End of buzz. Fifty bucks wasted, but that solved one mystery, at least. How had Carly thought she'd ever keep such a secret? And no wonder she thought she had no credibility with our local authorities.

CHAPTER TEN

By Tuesday, my patience was exhausted and my annoyance level off the charts. I'd spent the weekend alternately in front of the television or the newspapers and trying to reach Carly. The news was all about the upcoming Gasparilla festivities, Tampa's version of Mardi Gras. Carly was nowhere to be found.

Jones v. General Medics started promptly at 9:00 Tuesday morning, as the judge promised, and I was in no mood for nonsense. The case was scheduled for three weeks on my docket, but the way jury selection was going, I was sure it would take three months. Just great. Three whole months of Christian Grover. I couldn't wait. Voir dire dragged on through 12:30, and we broke for lunch.

When I came back to my chambers for the lunch recess, there was a message from Carly. The message said "don't worry I'll be back soon." No number. I asked Margaret, my secretary, whether she had talked with Carly and how she sounded. Margaret said someone else had taken the message and I asked her to find out who. She looked at me quizzically, but knew better than to argue. She said she'd let me know.

As Margaret was leaving my office, she said "by the way, the CJ called. He wants to see you this afternoon when you recess for the day." Interesting. He's staying late to talk to me. This can't be good, I thought. More than that, it promised to be a pain in the ass. Maybe I'd recess early and get out before he came by.

I also had a message from Mark, Carly's brother. Thinking he might have heard from Carly, I called him back. He was out and I left another message. In private practice, I used to bill for telephone tag. Now, it just takes up my time and makes me irritable.

Just before we reconvened after lunch, my secretary came to tell me that she'd asked around and no one remembered taking the message from Carly. She seemed puzzled and promised to keep trying.

Before bringing the venire back into the courtroom, I strongly admonished both lawyers, on the record. "Gentlemen, I've had enough fooling around in this case already. So there hasn't been a breast implant case in the country that's been tried in under four weeks. This one will be the first. When we get started, I will finish voir dire myself. When we have the jury, Mr. Grover, you may give your opening statement. You have twenty minutes. And" . . . I looked at Grover steadily, "there will be none of your infamous shenanigans or I'll mistry this case so fast you won't know what hit you."

I turned to Hainsworth.

"Mr. Waterman," I said, just as sternly, "you'll have twenty minutes for your opening and we *will* get our first witness on today."

I addressed my bailiff before either man could say a word and instructed him to bring in the jurors. Once the panel was seated, I apologized for keeping them waiting and told them that we would finish the case in three weeks. I asked the few relevant voir dire questions I thought had been missed, gave the lawyers their preemptories and finished the selection in ten minutes flat. I instructed the jury, asked them to give the matter their undivided attention and we got down to work. Appealable error be damned.

Grover has a reputation for outrageous behavior in the courtroom, and he doesn't care whether his verdicts get overturned on appeal. I was surprised when he delivered a colorful, but proper, opening in nineteen minutes. As Hainsworth concluded his opening remarks, I could see Grover's mind and attention were elsewhere. I couldn't fault him for that; my mind wasn't on the trial either.

I asked Grover to call his first witness. The trial proceeded quickly through the afternoon hours and we recessed at 4:30. I admonished everyone to be back in the courtroom promptly at 8:30 the next morning and left the bench. I couldn't remember a thing that had been said by either side, and I hoped the jury was paying closer attention.

Because I needed the distraction, I had called Pricilla Waterman during the three o'clock break and asked her if I could come by for a cup of tea and bring over the bill for food service for the AIDS benefit. Cilla is the only woman I know who still has a full tea service in the afternoon. She hesitated just a little too long over the request and I thought for a minute she might actually refuse. But then, gracious as always, she said of course I could come.

I arrived at their Bayshore mansion about five minutes early, and I parked under the portecochere. It was a gloriously sunny day, about 70 degrees, and no wind. The sailors would be unhappy, but for the rest of us, it was the kind of day Floridians live for.

I walked up and rang the bell and Mrs. Smith, the Watermans' ancient black housekeeper, finally got to the door about ten minutes later. She hugged me, and escorted me into the parlor, where Cilla was waiting, her silver tea service set out on the coffee table.

"Willa, dear, do come in. The tea's just ready. You're right on time." I sat down on the antique camel-back sofa across from Cilla, and admired the room, as I have countless times. I don't think there had been a new piece of furniture placed in that room in more than 50 years. Cilla told me once the house had belonged to her parents, and she and Hainsworth had moved into it just as it stood when her father finally died in '64. It was old, but it was clean, and all the pieces were in excellent repair. The rugs alone were worth a fortune. I wondered just how big the Waterman estate would be when their children inherited. And now I was also wondering why her brother, the CJ, didn't live in the house.

Cilla and I spent some time discussing the fund-raiser, how successful it was, and how much the Junior League had Senator Warwick to thank for that. I gave her the bill, ostensibly my reason for coming. She took it as if it was a piece of junk mail, and set it on the side table. I was sure George would eventually get paid, but it's a mark of extreme wealth that Cilla believed it wouldn't matter exactly when the League settled up.

Finally, I was able to bring the conversation around to the real reason for my visit. "Cilla," I said, as if it was, oh, just a little curiosity, "do you remember the other day when we were at Minaret with Kate and Tory Warwick?"

"Of course I remember, Willa. I'm old, but I'm not senile." Just a little edgy. Uncharacteristic of her. Maybe Hainsworth or the grandchildren were misbehaving lately and it was on her mind.

"I wasn't suggesting anything of the kind. It's just that I forget things sometimes, and I thought maybe you did, too." I tried to placate her. I resolved not to get old. Old people are so inflexible.

"No, I remember the day perfectly well. What did you want to ask me about it?" To the point, as always.

"Well," I set down my tea cup and leaned forward, suggesting I'd keep the conversation confidential without saying so. "Tory said something about having an affair with Michael Morgan years ago and you seemed to know about it. I thought maybe you'd tell me what happened."

"You surprise me, Willa. I didn't take you for a gossip monger." She sat straighter in her chair, and cloaked herself in her grand dame persona. I could imagine many an intimidated child had been on the receiving end of the steely look down that long, patrician nose she was giving me now.

"It's not gossip I'm interested in, Cilla, but facts. You know Dr. Morgan is a witness in a number of cases on my docket. I'm concerned about letting him testify because of his background and I thought you might be able to help me." It was a white lie, and the wife of a lawyer should know a judge doesn't investigate a case. But maybe Hainsworth doesn't talk shop at home, because she answered my question, after a fashion.

"Why would you think that?"

"You've been around Tampa as long as anyone. I've heard some wild stories about Dr. Morgan. I thought you might be able to separate fact from fiction."

She considered the question and the explanation. She was wavering. I just kept looking earnest. Appealing to vanity usually works. On that score, Mrs. Hainsworth Waterman was no different from anyone else.

Finally, she said "Just because Tory had an affair with Mike Morgan doesn't mean anything. That was a long time ago. There have been a lot of women in this town who've succumbed to his charms. And, I would bet, a lot of women in many other towns. If you want to talk to all the women he's slept with, you'll have to take a leave of absence to interview them all." She poured herself another cup of tea, offered me a cookie and took three for her plate. I could only imagine the number of calories it took to support her size.

"I don't think I'm interested in all of them, just Victoria Warwick." The cookie melted in my mouth as I mentally calculated how long I'd have to run to compensate.

"Well, I suppose she'd tell you herself if you asked her. Everyone knows about it anyway. It was about ten years ago. She and Shel were having problems again. The way she deals with it is to find someone else to distract her. Mike was the distraction of the moment."

"So it wasn't serious?" What the hell. I reached for another lady finger. Damn, those things are good. But why? Nothing to them, really.

"I don't think Tory Warwick has ever been serious about anything, except Sheldon. She's always been seriously in love with him. He just doesn't notice, or doesn't care."

"Well, what happened to their affair? Tory and Morgan, I mean?"

"She got tired of him, just a couple of minutes before he got tired of her. And it was over. As far as I know, it didn't last long, and it wasn't repeated. They both went on to other things."

"Other lovers?"

She looked at me again, with disapproval and a serious frown in her broad forehead, both of her caterpillar eyebrows coming together over her nose. "Perhaps so."

I decided to push my luck. "Does that mean yes?"

She'd had enough. "It means Michael Morgan is a vile man who has no scruples and no character. I don't know him well enough to know all he's done in his life but enough of my friends have suffered at his hands that I know he's always done whatever it took to get what he wanted."

It could have been just her southern lady disdain for his distasteful affairs, but it didn't strike me that way when she said it. I noticed she spoke of him as if he was still alive. I asked her softly, "What did he do to your friends?"

"You'll have to ask them, and they'll tell you if they want to. The only thing I'm going to say about it is that Michael Morgan has always lived a lot higher on the hog than any other Tampa doctor I know."

It was all she would say. She had some inside information, but she wasn't sharing. And I knew her well enough to know she wouldn't tell what she didn't want to tell.

Through Friday, the trial continued. Every day, I listened to the morning news and both editions of the evening news. I read both local papers cover to cover while waiting for the monotonous scientific evidence to be introduced. Nowhere did I see or hear a report identifying Dr. Morgan as the body in the Bay. By Saturday morning, I was convinced that George's anonymous tip had never been passed on.

Mark called twice during the week, but I missed his calls and we continued to play tag. I was tempted to ask Mitchell what was going on, but I was afraid it would be a breach of Mark's confidence, so I didn't. Neither did I hear from Carly, although I kept trying to reach her. Some days, I would get messages that she'd called, but every time Margaret denied talking to her and couldn't find anyone else in the office who had. By the end of the week, I was exhausted and I fell into bed at 8:30 Friday night. George said if he'd known what being married to a judge was going to do to his sex life, he wouldn't have encouraged me to take the job.

CHAPTER ELEVEN

Since I was playing golf Sunday with Dr. Aymes, I had canceled my Saturday game with Mitchell. I got up and snuck out while George was sleeping to take the dogs for their run.

I tried to work through what I knew about Morgan and Carly. If it was Michael Morgan in the water, who killed him? And why? And why hadn't the body been identified? I was hoping, with my fingers crossed almost the entire time, that it wasn't him. Maybe it really was the lost tourist they had first believed. And if it was Morgan, I knew that both my ethical obligations as a judge and lawyer, and my concern for Carly and her family would keep me involved in this until it was resolved.

I tried to think of all the angles, the reasons someone would want Morgan dead. Who had a motive? Opportunity? My legs started to tire because I was too focused. So I just let my mind soar free. Before I knew it, I had done the entire ten miles and was back at the house.

I went out to the water and jumped in. Harry and Bess were already there. This is the part of our run they like the best because they get to submerge me and each other in the water ten or twenty times before I'm completely exhausted and give up. Then we got out, rinsed off outdoors and I put them in their screened sun porch to dry off while I ran up the back stairs.

I was in the shower, letting the warm water cover my face, inhaling the soothing vanilla fragrance of the bath gel and trying again to think of a way to disclose Dr. Morgan's identity that would actually make someone take notice, when George came into my bathroom.

"Willa," he said as gently as he could and still be heard over the running water, "Carly's here. My God, she looks like she hasn't slept in days. She had dark circles under her eyes, and she looked both exhausted and, at the same time, in a high state of anxiety. I gave her some hot tea and showed her to the bathroom where she could take a comforting soak. By the time she finished, she was yawning and standing in the kitchen with her eyes closed. So I put her in the guest room for a nap. She hasn't regained consciousness."

I turned off the shower with trepidation. I'd wanted her to surface and she had. Maybe I should have been more careful what I wished for. Now what? "Let me get dressed, and we'll see if we can wake her and find out what this is all about." When I came into our small galley kitchen, George was finishing two cups of breve, one of my many indulgences. He carried them out to the veranda along with the Saturday *Times*, talking over his shoulder.

"Come out and have a coffee before you wake her. I think we both need some fortification first."

In the end, we decided not to wake her and Carly slept for hours. I worked for a while in my study and waited. When I walked into the kitchen just after four o'clock, she, too, was making coffee and Cuban toast, wearing an old Key West T-shirt and nothing else.

"Well you look a lot better. I hope you feel better," I told her.

She smiled, albeit slightly, more like a slice of acknowledgment. She didn't act like the weight of the world was off her shoulders. "Do you have any idea what it's like not to be perfect?"

The way she said it, perfection was certainly not an admirable trait. She was snide, almost nasty about it, like being "perfect" was worse than being a child molester. Carly's never been subtle. What you see is what you get.

"Oh, I know you have that little gap between your front teeth and those red highlights in your hair have to be touched up every few weeks. I'll bet it was just really trying to be six feet tall in seventh grade. And George's constant devotion is probably just smothering." She carried her toast to the small table and added skim milk to her coffee making it that sickly shade of green I imagine all waifs must admire. Otherwise, how can they drink the stuff?

"You know, Carly, if I didn't know better I might confuse you with one of my political enemies, not a guest to whom I've been extremely hospitable." I said it lightly, but I was surprised how much her derision of what she viewed as my "perfect" self annoyed me, and I filed away for the moment the serious introspection I should be doing to find out why. I'd been worried to death about her and all she could do was chastise me for not having my life in as big a mess as hers was. Besides, whether one lives a beautiful and privileged life is often in the eye of the beholder, no?

"Look, Willa, all I'm saying is that you don't know what it's like to be less than beautiful in American society. We grew up playing with

Barbie dolls and thinking that our lives would be fabulous if we had perfect measurements, the right nose, and long blond hair. If we had all that, then we'd get Ken, the perfect mate. Most women I know still wear high heels, for God's sake. Is it any wonder that the breast implant industry is booming and has been for almost forty years? Women have put all kinds of things in their bodies to get that 'perfect' look. Who are the real victims in all this, anyway?" She was working herself up into a fine snit, waving her arms around and pacing back and forth in the small kitchen.

Enough. "Although I'm beginning to understand the point, I'm not getting the connection between this enlightened social commentary and your behavior of the last few weeks," I told her.

"Don't act like a judge with me, Wilhelmina. Despite Gloria Steinhem, who by the way is very attractive herself, most women in America just don't feel very pretty. They're constantly bombarded with images of women who are taller, sexier, thinner, more attractive and 'built'," she gestured the "hourglass" figure.

"This is hardly a new or astounding social insight. What does it have to do with you turning up on my doorstep looking like you have neither eaten nor slept since I saw you a week ago?" In my head, I heard my mother admonishing "grace under pressure, Wilhelmina," so I tried to smile at her as I said it, but it took some effort.

She'd run out of steam, just as suddenly as she'd started. She bowed her head and cupped her coffee in both hands. I sat down across from her. After a long while, without looking up, she said, quietly, "Dr. Morgan is dead. If it wasn't for this screwed up insistence on physical perfection, he'd be alive today."

"Tell me exactly how you know that," I said as calmly as I could and in my best judicial voice. She was frayed around the edges, about to fall apart. I needed the information before she cracked completely. I hoped her courtroom training would keep her together until she got it out. She spoke so quietly, and her voice trembled so much, that I could barely hear her over the quiet humming noise of the rotating ceiling fan. She had her head buried in her arms so I couldn't see her face.

"On Friday, after you left me, I went to his house. He wasn't there. He hadn't been there for well over a month. The newspapers were stacked up on the porch and the cat's litter box was overflowing. The cat looked starved. I took him to a vet."

I decided to skip the lie she'd told about not knowing where Dr. Morgan lived, but it confirmed my suspicions about how many other lies she'd told me. "How do you know the litter box was full and the cat hadn't been fed?"

"I went in, of course. I looked around. The place had been trashed." She looked right at me, turned her lips up at the corners in a rueful smile; her hands were shaking, sloshing the sickly green coffee over the sides of the cup. "I don't think the cat did it. Drawers were pulled out, papers scattered all over. Just like on television. Someone slashed all of the sofa pillows and the mattresses. There was no computer in the apartment at all and all the books were on the floor. I don't know what they were looking for, but I don't think they found it."

She set the cup down in the spreading puddle of green coffee, continuing to hold the cup. She lowered her head again. I didn't know if I should wait to hear more or ask a question. After a long time, she looked up and there were tears streaming down her cheeks. Her lip was quivering, her nose red and running.

"I found b-blood and b-brains all over the k-kitchen." She broke down completely. She was hysterical, sobbing uncontrollably, keening as if Dr. Morgan was here in the kitchen with us and she'd just seen him. I went around to her and held her, but she was sobbing hard enough to shake both of us. George came to the doorway, arched one eyebrow at me and I nodded him in.

"Help me get her into the bedroom please, and bring me a Valium from the medicine cabinet." Calmly. Trying not to let her know I'd like to be falling apart, too. She had been such a bubbly child. How did she get like this?

George went to get the Valium and water. I gave it to Carly and we helped her back to bed. She'd calmed down some and I sat with her while she either passed out or went to sleep, I'm not sure which. I closed the door to her room and went out on the veranda, where George was waiting. It was early for drinking, but he'd poured both of us a Sapphire and tonic. I took mine with a twist of lemon and without a twinge of remorse. Three gulps later, I got up for a refill.

"Now, Willa, suppose you tell me exactly what's going on here," George said, "And I'm not kidding around." It was perfectly okay with me. I'd never seen a murder scene and I was pretty sure Carly never had either. Just hearing Carly describe it shook me up. I have a very vivid imagination. I see movies in my head when I think and just her description was enough. Besides that, now she'd have to go to the police and I wasn't sure exactly how to convince her to do it. If she wouldn't, I'd have to do it myself and then there'd be all kinds of hell to pay, with Kate and the CJ for starters. Before, I only suspected a crime had been committed. Now I knew for sure. I'd taken an oath to uphold the law, and I had to do it or face the consequences. I hoped George would have some insight.

We talked for a long time, about Carly and her predicament, and about mine. We poked and prodded the problem, looked at it from all the angles. There was just no way around it in the end. One of us would have to go to Chief Hathaway. I didn't want it to be me, and Carly obviously didn't want it to be her. I knew what my reasons were, but I wasn't clear on hers. If we'd had a different relationship, I might have told the CJ. As it was, I was hoping he'd never find out I was involved. It would be just one more thing for him to ride me about. George and I decided the only thing we could do was to try and convince Carly to call Chief Hathaway when she woke up. If she wouldn't, then I had some tough choices to make.

After we finished our third gin, I decided I'd try to get more facts from another source before pressuring Carly, as I fully intended to do. She'd lied to me at least once that I knew of, and I couldn't trust the rest of her story. There was no way I was going to get any deeper into this; I was afraid of walking right into the middle of something worse that neither Carly nor I could control.

It could be that Michael Morgan's death, if he was dead, had nothing to do with this breast implant business, but the chances of that were really slim. When the largest breast implant manufacturer went into bankruptcy a couple of years ago, I remembered reading in the *Tampa Today Business Journal* that several of the law firms in town had financed the costs of breast implant litigation. One of them was my former firm, some of my former partners having gone over to the "other side" representing women with implants.

I called Mitchell and asked him to meet me for a drink here at Minaret this afternoon. Although he said he was surprised to hear from me since I had canceled our weekly golf game, he agreed to come. If you're a lawyer in a small town, it's not wise to ignore the summons of a judge, even though it may be a purely social call. Knowing this, I try not to use the advantage too often. This was one of those times when it was necessary.

I was waiting for Mitch in the Sunset Bar and when he arrived, I suggested that we take our drinks to a secluded table. The bar was deserted, so I didn't expect any interruptions. The last thing I needed was to be overheard discussing the very cases I'm supposed to be presiding over. I had recused myself from all of my former firm's cases, so it wasn't technically a breach of ethics to talk to Mitch about it generally. Nevertheless, I didn't want to have to explain myself to anyone on the issue, particularly the CJ, who is always looking for something to complain about where I'm concerned. Anyway, if I didn't get this worked out, I was going to have a lot more to explain. Private conversations on privileged matters would be the least of my worries.

"Mitch, didn't I read that your firm is very involved in representing plaintiffs in breast implant cases?"

"Why, Judge, do you want to file a claim?" He eyed my chest speculatively, but with a smile, hoping I wouldn't be offended. He was wrong. I would never look at some man's crotch and suggest anything about the size of the bulge, at least not to him.

"Fortunately, no. I am looking for some information, though, and I was hoping you'd just give it to me voluntarily."

"Well, it's not a secret. Of course, we don't have as many cases as Christian Grover. But he advertised on a billboard and in *The Tribune* for months, so he got a lot more calls than we did. Besides that, his partner Fred Johnson, seems to have some inside track on the Morgan cases. Morgan was the hardest working plastic surgeon in town where breast implants were concerned. I've heard estimates as high as 45,000 surgeries he did. He claims to have made $35,000 a day doing implants in the eighties. We only took what we could get that we thought were sure winners."

"How many cases does Grover have?"

"There's no real way of knowing that. He brags at bar meetings that he's got 3,500 plaintiffs, not including Johnson's cases."

"Really? I had no idea Grover represented so many women."

"Oh, sure. We have about 200 clients, all referred by other lawyers. Grover got most of his cases directly through advertising, but he got a lot of referrals, too."

"Why would one plaintiffs' attorney want to refer cases to another?"

"Well, the thinking is that a particular plaintiff's attorney will learn the science and make it his business to become experienced in handling the cases so that he can maximize the value of each claim. The referring attorney then gets a percentage of the final fee. It's done all the time."

"Doesn't it get expensive to advance costs for all of those claims?" I imagined piles of dollars looking like the ransom money for one of the

Rockefellers.

"Yes, in the beginning it was less expensive because the manufacturers were paying to remove the implants. Now, most of them refuse and the insurance carriers won't pay, either. So, if your client wants to be explanted, which improves her case, you have to make a decision about advancing the costs. It can be as much as $5,000 a case."

"Do you mean to say that Grover and Johnson can have as much as $1.5 million in costs in these cases?" I was incredulous. Tampa isn't Los Angeles. A million dollars is still a rare commodity here.

"Actually, they could have more. That would just be the price of the removal surgery for each woman. There's the cost of experts, getting documents and all the other trial preparation stuff. My firm alone has over $300,000 invested in these cases, and we're a relatively small player. I've heard stories that some of the Texas lawyers are putting out over a million dollars a month."

"How can they afford that?"

He smiled. "Everything's bigger in Texas." Since I didn't return his smile, he said "I can't speak for anyone else, but frankly, we can't afford it. We took out lines of credit and loans with the local banks when we thought the cases would only last a year or so. Now, it's been going on for years and the interest payments alone are staggering." He drained his glass and I offered him another. He got up to get a beer from the bar for himself and Perrier for me. When he came back with the drinks, I'd had time to consider what he'd said. The mathematics were easy, but it was a hell of a way to gamble.

"What will you do?"

"Fortunately, our firm is well-funded. We've had our big successes over the years and we only accepted a limited number of cases. It's not a real problem for us." Sounded like wishful thinking to me, and I was not surprised when he continued a little more subdued. "Although we've all been taking home smaller incomes the past couple of years."

He said this as if it were an afterthought. I was embarrassed for him. He was obviously trying to put the best face on it, but money must have been tight. Another thing I hadn't noticed. Maybe Kate is right and I do spend too much time wrapped up in my own world, oblivious to others.

After a few moments of silence, he said "I hear, though, that Grover is really having a problem. He not only borrowed enough money to fund his cases, but he also has been living off the anticipated settlements, which have just not happened as quickly as we all thought. They may not happen at all."

"He always seems to be fine to me."

He nodded and lifted one shoulder briefly. "The funny thing is that Johnson seems to be flush with cash all the time. I don't know what their financial arrangements are, but it's odd that one partner would be doing fine and the other struggling, when they're both handling the same files."

I thought about it, sipping my Perrier around the lemon wedge. Something was tickling my brain, elusive, but present. I let it go, and it boomeranged back.

"What do you mean, the settlement may not happen at all?"

"Well, in the beginning, when these cases were first filed, the science was unclear and it appeared that the plaintiffs had the better end of the argument because of the common sense approach, you know, 'where there's smoke there's fire'." George had said almost the identical words a few days earlier. Maybe he reads things other than the financial pages, after all.

"And now?" I asked him.

"Well, now scientific study after scientific study is coming out on the side of the safety of the implants. Just like the manufacturers said all along. Even though we can prove they didn't properly test the product, it's becoming more and more difficult to prove that these implants cause any adverse health effects."

"This makes no sense. The last time I looked, causation was an essential part of any plaintiff's case. If you can't prove causation, why haven't all of the cases been dismissed?"

He grinned again, kind of lopsided this time and lifted his glass. "It's the American way. There's still enough evidence to get the cases to the jury. As long as there's no definitive proof that the illnesses these women are suffering are caused by something other than their implants, then the cases still go to the jury and the juries are still sympathetic enough to award damages to the victims in the most severe cases."

Mitch's face changed. He set his drink aside and crossed his hands on the table between us. How sincere he can look when he wants to, I thought. No wonder juries have been so sympathetic to him, giving his clients whatever he asks for.

Mitch said earnestly, "What I'm curious about is why you asked me over here on a Saturday afternoon to talk about this when we could have discussed it any Saturday morning. What I'm telling you is public knowledge, and I'm sure you're going to get most of it from that *Jones* case you're trying right now. Why the rush?"

A legitimate question I'd been waiting for but didn't intend to answer. "It doesn't have anything to do with the *Jones* case, Mitch, but that's all I can say. I do appreciate your coming over on such short notice and filling me in, though. How's Annie and the kids?" Such an obvious change of subject; he got the point.

Mitch graciously let the matter drop, and we talked about his family a while before he said he needed to get home for dinner. I thanked him for his advice and wished him luck with his financing.

When I went back upstairs to talk to Carly, she was nowhere to be found. I searched the remainder of the house, the restaurant and the grounds. Her clothes were gone and when I got outside, her car was gone. She had to have left while I was talking with Mitch. Deja vu, dammit. This is just great. Now what? People think I have no patience, but really, I'm just patient for such a long time that when I finally lose it, they're surprised. I mean, really, wasn't more than twenty years of patience with Carly enough already?

I didn't bother running as I went down the stairs out into the parking lot. I asked the valet if he had seen Carly. He said she had run out to her car and sped off across the bridge about fifteen minutes earlier. Again, I had no idea where she'd gone or how to find her. I went back upstairs and tried the cellular phone in her car, her office, and her house, all with no luck.

These disappearing acts were really beginning to make me angry. Besides that, I hadn't had a chance to persuade her to go to the police. Now what was I supposed to do? It would serve her right if I just called Hathaway and turned it all over to him.

Old habits die hard. So I decided to let it sit through the weekend, and give Carly one more last chance to come back, go to the police, or do something to report what she'd seen. If she didn't do it, I would have to. I picked up some distractions, a glass of iced tea, the Friday *Times* I hadn't had the energy to read yesterday afternoon, and Saturday's *Tribune*, and took them out onto the veranda to try my mind control theory: think about something else. It worked briefly until page three of the *Times*, below the fold, the mention of Morgan's name caught my eye.

> *Dr. Michael Morgan's friends and col-*
> *leagues have been cooperating with Tampa*
> *Police in an effort to locate Dr. Morgan, miss-*
> *ing for over a month. Yesterday, one of the*

> *neighbors reported sighting a woman entering Dr. Morgan's house by the side door. When he was unable to locate the woman, Chief Ben Hathaway obtained a search warrant for Dr. Morgan's home today. Although details of the search have not been released, Chief Hathaway said that he now suspects foul play.*

I dropped the rest of the *Times* and picked up Saturday's *Tribune*, searching all the pages in the first section until I found another small item.

> *Limited details of the disappearance of Dr. Michael Morgan were released to the press today in a news conference by Chief Ben Hathaway. Chief Hathaway said in a prepared statement: "We are trying to identify a dark four door sedan, possibly a Lincoln Town Car or a Cadillac, seen by a neighbor outside Dr. Morgan's home three weeks ago. We are now treating Dr. Morgan's disappearance as a homicide. We believe Dr. Morgan's body was in the car. We identified tire tracks on the grass near the side door of Dr. Morgan's house."*
>
> *An eye witness came forward yesterday. Chief Benjamin Hathaway told reporters that the witness saw the car, saw its lights go on and saw it drive away. Chief Hathaway told reporters that Dr. Morgan's home contained evidence relating his disappearance to homicide.*
>
> *"We found evidence of a struggle, blood soaked tile and other physical evidence consistent with homicide."*

It was getting more and more difficult to protect Carly, not to mention me. George and I struggled with the issues most of the night. We didn't get to bed until 3:00 a.m., and we were no closer to a decision on what to do. I wondered what other careers I might like all through the sleepless night, but I could only see the down sides to all of them.

CHAPTER TWELVE

It wasn't hard to get up for my golf game with Dr. Aymes Sunday morning since I never went to sleep. I was in no mood to play, but it was way too late to cancel. George was more fortunate; he was snoring softly when I crept out of the bedroom. I snatched the Sunday papers off the front porch and searched for further news of Dr. Morgan. I didn't have to look far. While the disappearance of a once prominent surgeon may not command front page coverage, his death did, although still below the fold.

> *No closer to solving the mysterious disappearance of Dr. Michael Morgan, Police Chief Ben Hathaway released further details of the investigation Saturday. He said police found Dr. Morgan's scheduling notebook inside his home and are in the process of interviewing everyone with whom Dr. Morgan had contact in the weeks before his disappearance. Because there are no signs of forced entry or burglary, police believe Dr. Morgan may have been killed by someone he knew.*

And maybe someone we all know, I thought. The rest of the article repeated the information printed in the earlier stories. Incredibly, there was no link, and no speculation, connecting Morgan's disappearance with the unidentified body. How could they be so dense? Wasn't it obvious to everyone? The timing, the disappearance, the homicide? It just didn't make sense to me and I couldn't figure it out. But George wasn't up yet so I could discuss it with him, and the dogs are good listeners but somewhat short on analytical ability. I couldn't wait any longer. I left the paper propped by the coffee pot and dashed out to Great Oaks.

You know you're playing with serious golfers when they have a 6:30 tee time on Sunday. Only a serious player gets on the course at prime time. I was paired with Dr. Aymes. The other two golfers were Grover's partner, Fred Johnson, and another doctor I didn't know. We walked up to the first tee promptly at 6:30 and the men were 240 yards down the first fairway four minutes later.

I thought Dr. Aymes was just being snide when she said my 10 handicap was high for the group. She wasn't. These golfers were going to end up waiting for me, and it put me at an immediate disadvantage. It wasn't until later that I figured out she had deliberately invited me knowing I wouldn't be able to compete, even if I'd had a clear head for the game. In my present state, I was about to get killed. On the golf course, that is.

Marilee hit her first drive from the blue tee about 220 yards. I held my head high, hit from the red tee, and landed just about 30 yards behind her. We got into the cart and she drove.

"Nice shot, Willa. But if you want to play with the better golfers, you've got to shoot from the blue tees."

"Not today," I said.

"No guts, no glory."

"Maybe, but with this group, I'll be lucky if I can keep my head above water." My temples were starting to throb, a dull pounding resembling the beat of a Johnny Mathis tune. I put my sunglasses on as well as my visor. The dim pre dawn light was too much. I was just thrilled with the idea of bright, glaring sunshine in half an hour.

"Just hit 'em straight, and you'll beat these two. I always put them together because they end up in the woods and it saves time." I couldn't tell if she was being sarcastic or just being Marilee.

She zipped the cart over to my ball and we were off. I finished the hole with a double bogey and felt grateful. Marilee missed a par by a five foot put.

By the third hole, Marilee had me laughing with her outrageous commentary, and I'd decided her sharp wit wasn't meant to be malicious. My headache was a slow Bob Seeger tune by this time, but rock 'n roll suits me better anyway. "Who's your usual partner, Marilee?"

"Michael Morgan. But he hasn't played in a month."

"Why not?"

"He's out of town or something. I haven't heard from him. And his substitute is Carolyn Young, but she couldn't make it today."

"Why not?" I felt like a parrot.

"I don't know. When I called her, she just said she couldn't play."

This was an opportunity too convenient to pass up, and I was glad I hadn't just called and canceled. I asked her, feigning nonchalance, how she knew Dr. Morgan and Dr. Young.

"We were all at various stages of our practice at UCF about 15 years ago. We had a foursome including Dr. Zimmer going on then."

"I had no idea you all knew each other so well." Even in my weakened state, I silently blessed the concept of synchronicity. Maybe I'd become a believer yet. Somewhat like Dorothy on her return trip from Oz, I began to repeat to myself "There are no coincidences in life, there are no . . ."

"We were all close until Carolyn stole my project. Then, I stopped talking to them for 10 years. Mike wormed his way into this foursome and then Carolyn started coming. When she plays, I play with Johnson. I certainly couldn't spend two hours in a golf cart with her."

"What did she steal from you?"

"The whole thing. Everything they used to start MedPro. The idea, the grant prospect. All of it."

She tried to act like this was ancient history, but I could tell she was still bitter about it. "We were close once, Carolyn and I. We shared an apartment and we both worked in the research department at UCF. She was younger than I, and she always seemed so vulnerable, some-how. I tried to take care of her, I guess. It was my idea to concentrate on a more responsive gel. I had a grant prospect I thought I could sell to UCF and I was putting together a proposal. It's up to a tenured professor to find enough money to pay at least 60% of her salary, so it was an important prospect to me. It would have covered my salary for three years. I was excited, so I told her about it and she stole it. As simple as that."

We were on the fifth hole by this time. It's a long hole, but it dog legs to the right, and I was trying to figure out which club to hit off the tee for the best position on my second shot.

"Try your three wood," Marilee said. "Your driver will put you past the turn."

I pulled out my three, hit the ball way off to the left and cursed under my breath. "It works better if you hit it straight," she smirked.

"Thanks for the tip." I said, with as much sarcasm as I dared, as she walked up to the tee.

"Carolyn Young never had an original thought in her life." The venom in her words might not have sent the ball that extra 20 yards, but if the ball had been Carolyn Young's head, she'd be in the next county. If it had been my head, at least this damn pounding wouldn't be connected to my body any more.

Marilee must have read my thoughts. "That's how I improved my game. Every time I stepped up to the tee, I imagined Young, Morgan or Zimmer's head instead of the ball. Improved my drives 200%."

On the way back to the cart, I asked her, "How did Carolyn Young steal your project?"

"She told Morgan and Zimmer that she had done the work. She batted her eyes, swished her hips." Marilee jiggled her behind back and forth exaggeratedly as she walked. "Then she fucked Zimmer, so they believed her. He was the leader of our little foursome then because he was the oldest. She didn't care that he was married and had five kids." She waited for me to get my ball out of the rough before driving us over to hers, lying right in the fairway, a straight 250 yards from the green. She hit a three iron and the ball fell about 75 yards short.

"Carolyn convinced Zimmer and Morgan followed along. She gave them all my written work, which she stole off my desk one night when I was out at the lab."

"Why didn't you just tell them it was yours?"

"I did. They thought I was just jealous. They knew she was brilliant and her mother had been diagnosed with breast cancer. Her mother needed an implant. They believed Carolyn had extra motivation. That she'd worked on the idea night and day. Hah!" She hit her ball within two feet of the cup, then walked back to where I was standing and waited for me to make it to the green.

She seemed to want to talk about it, so she just kept pouring out the story. "Later on, I actually started to play with them so I would win every week. We bet. High stakes. I always win," she said as she sank the put easily for an eagle making her five under par for the first five holes.

"What about Johnson? When did he come into the picture?" I set up for my put, squatting down to visualize the line perpendicular to the hole.

"Zimmer had a heart attack last year. Scared him and Matildy. I guess he stared mortality in the face and decided an old grudge match was not the way he wanted to end his days. So he quit. Morgan brought Johnson into the group."

"Was that okay with you?" I tapped the ball lightly, but the green was fast and I over played the hole. Another two putt. At this rate, I'd be lucky to finish last even if the headache didn't finish me first.

"It's a good news/bad news story. The good thing about Johnson is he loses as gracefully as the rest of them do. The bad thing is he's a lousy golfer, although he's better than you." She just couldn't resist. "And he's a less pleasant s.o.b. to be around. He's especially offensive to Morgan. I don't know why Morgan doesn't tell him to kiss off. I've considered it a couple of times myself."

We finished the game in record time. I don't think I've ever played with such a competitive group. My score wasn't worth mentioning when they all settled up at the nineteenth hole. The day's entertainment would have cost me $2,000, but they made it a gift since I hadn't known the rules in advance. The shock killed my headache and I went home, wiser in every respect.

George wasn't at home when I got there, so I decided instead of just brooding about Carly and Dr. Morgan, I'd do something a little more productive. I went upstairs into the den and sat down at the desk where Aunt Minnie had done her household accounts as a young bride. It was a partner's desk; one person could sit at either side and both could work in the middle.

I took out the ubiquitous yellow legal pad and wrote down everything Carly had told me, and everything else I had surmised or discovered about Dr. Morgan's death in the past few days. I put each separate fact on a separate sheet of paper. For each fact, I listed everything I'd like to know about it to determine if it had any significance. I had acquired quite a bit of information, most of it useless. I noticed that I was now calling it Dr. Morgan's death, even though I still didn't know for sure that he was dead. I told you I was no scientist.

I had a lot more questions than answers, but I found some glaring discrepancies, too. Not the least of which was that I knew Carly hadn't told me everything and I didn't know why. She was worried about something, and emotionally keyed up over the whole thing to a much greater degree than I would have expected.

I was still writing, considering and analyzing when George came in with Harry and Bess. They let me know they were feeling neglected, so I put aside my work and we all went for a long walk and then a little afternoon delight, you should pardon the pun. After that, I turned it all over to my subconscious, fell into a deep and blissfully untroubled sleep until early evening.

George and I were going to the Florida Orchestra with Bill and

Betty Sheffield, meeting them just before the baton was raised at 7:30 at the Performing Arts Center. I still had to hustle to get showered and changed, but George was already dressed and ready to go.

I apologized for missing the cocktail hour, and told him I might have time for a quick glass of wine in the car, but George wanted to drive instead of getting a driver, so I left him to drink alone while I finished getting dressed. I quickly did my makeup and was just slipping on my jade silk jumpsuit when George called to me that it was 7:00 and we needed to get moving.

I selected my pearls and black satin sandals to complete the look. Bright red lipstick seemed too flashy somehow, so I selected a deeper wine color, threw a few things into my evening bag and dashed downstairs. George drove the Bentley and we arrived just in time to use the valet and find our seats before the program began. Bill and Betty were already seated. We whispered hello and then fell silent for the program.

At intermission, Betty went toward the ladies' room and the rest of us headed outside so Bill could have a cigarette. As we walked out, Bill asked George how his investments were coming and they began to discuss the risks and benefits of technology stocks during the current bull market. I practiced the art of appearing to listen, and allowed my mind to wander until the mention of MedPro brought my attention sharply back to the conversation. When I tuned in, Bill was still attempting to convince George of the merits of investing in emerging medical products manufacturing companies.

"Which companies do you think are the best buys?" I asked, surprising both men by my sudden interest.

"Well, pacemakers are and will likely continue to be a successful medical product. But the problems they've had with lead failures make investing in those companies risky. I think you need to consider companies that blend medical technology with geriatric science. The graying of America is big business and will continue to be for the next several decades. If you can find a company that makes products used in the health care of elderly patients, and by elderly I mean 55 and over, assuming the company is well managed and not under-capitalized, it should be a sure winner." Like all investment types, Bill talked like the opinion column of the paper's financial section. If you zoned out a second, you'd be hopelessly lost.

"I'm interested primarily in the local economy, Bill," I said. "Are there any companies that make geriatric medical products here?"

Bill looked at me quizzically, too polite to suggest that this was the subject of the conversation I had not been listening to, even though I had pretended I was.

"Well, as I was telling George, I think there are three or four companies like that around here. I've invested a lot of money for our depositors in both Nations' Health Corp. and MedPro in the last six months. The stock has been rising steadily and I've even been able to take profits a few times. Those would be my choices but there are others." He'd finished his first cigarette and lit another off the smoldering butt before he flicked it out into the street.

"Well, George is the trader in our family, but I might be interested in some information on that." Carly hadn't mentioned that MedPro's stock was rising.

"Well, sure. What about if I have my secretary drop the information in the mail to you tomorrow?" I assured him that would be fine, then we heard the chimes indicating the orchestra was about to begin the remainder of the program. We walked back inside and George gave me his "what are you up to" look; puzzled but not concerned. I was hoping he'd stay that way. I was beginning to get an idea about MedPro and Dr. Morgan and I didn't want to have to explain it just yet. It needed time to germinate.

As we were walking back to our seats, Victoria Warwick walked up behind me. "Willa, darling," she said, in a mock whisper, "I hear you've been asking Pricilla Waterman about my personal life. The next time you want to know something, just ask me. A woman with as many secrets as Cilla shouldn't be speculating on the lives of others."

I must have looked mystified that Tory knew about that conversation; I was sure Cilla wouldn't have told her. "Servants, darling. They know everything. Don't ever get any." And she walked on past us closer to the front of the theater.

When we got home, George went down to check on the restaurant and we spent the rest of the evening quietly, upstairs. I told him what Tory Warwick had said to me at intermission. "Maybe you should go talk to Tory and find out just what some of those secrets are, Willa. It could be important. Tory might be erratic, but she's well informed." What an understatement that turned out to be.

95

CHAPTER THIRTEEN

The next day was one of those gloriously convenient Federal holidays that gave us government workers a Monday off: President's Day. I spent the morning puttering around the house trying to put the whole Morgan mess out of my mind to give my subconscious a chance to sort it through. But no matter what I tried to concentrate on instead, I couldn't get it off my mind. Of course, this line of thinking brought me right back to the Carly problem.

Not knowing what else to do, I felt I had no choice but to follow what George and I had decided was the only available Plan B, particularly now that Morgan's disappearance was being treated as homicide. It was what I should have done when she first told me about finding the body—I called the chief of police.

Chief Hathaway's secretary put me right through to him. I asked if I could see him immediately. He said he'd be happy to come out to the house so that I didn't have to appear at the station. He promised to come in the next hour. State employees don't get President's Day off.

Having called Hathaway, I had no alternative but to wait at home for him to arrive. I called downstairs looking for George, but he was nowhere to be found. For a panicky moment I thought he might have gone looking for Carly. But I decided that George was much too level-headed to do that. Besides, if he did go looking for her, it was outside my circle of influence, at least for now.

I wanted to talk to George about whether I should tell Carly's family before I did something that was going to cause such a problem for Carly. I couldn't decide what was best. My internal monologue on the issue resembled a child's seesaw. Procrastination is a wonderful thing. In the end, I waited so long that Chief Hathaway arrived before I'd made the decision.

I invited him into the living room. If I hadn't wanted to be seen talking with a breast implant plaintiff's attorney, I certainly didn't want it getting around that I was having quiet conversation with the Chief of

Police. Hathaway was a big man, not just tall but heavy. Yet, he had the agility of a ballerina, Jackie Gleason like. I invited him to sit down, and he looked around for a chair big enough to accommodate his heavy frame. He finally chose the straight back Louis XVI chair directly across from the couch. I offered him coffee, he declined, and we exchanged pleasantries. I just couldn't seem to get started.

He must have had a lot of experience with reluctant informants, because finally, he said "You know, I think this is the first time you've ever called on me professionally. I'm assuming there must be some very urgent reason for that."

For a moment, I thought I might be making a mistake. Then I remembered Carly's description of Dr. Morgan's house and realized the police had already been there, after she was. They probably had her finger prints already lifted. As a practicing lawyer, her prints would be on file. If we came clean now, it might make her look less guilty somehow.

Besides, in Carly's account there might be something the police had overlooked. The evidence might already be too old to be useful. Although some coroner could probably have figured it out, I wasn't too sure about our local talent. I told Ben everything Carly had told me. When I finished, he looked at me thoughtfully. After a time, he asked me a question I cursed myself for not expecting before I called him.

"How well do you know this woman?"

I answered the question I'd have preferred he ask me, not what I knew he was trying to ask. "I've known her all her life. Why?"

"Well, she seems to have a lot of knowledge about a murder. I'm wondering how reliable she is and also whether she might be a suspect herself."

My response must have been as cold as winter in Alaska, because I saw Hathaway flinch from me as I said it. "Ben Hathaway, there is no possibility that Carly murdered this man. I want you to put that thought out of your mind right now. If you persist in pursuing her as a suspect, I will personally issue a restraining order against you."

He looked shocked but his response was just as cold and controlled. "If you did that, Judge Carson, it would be a gross abuse of your judicial power. There's a limit to your discretion, you know. Interfering with the investigation of a crime was enough to bring down Richard Nixon. It's not something you want to get involved with."

"Maybe so," I replied "but, I'll do it nevertheless." We stared each other down for a few minutes and he must have concluded either that I would be true to my word or recognized it wouldn't get either of us anywhere tonight to test me.

He adopted a much more conciliatory tone. "Okay, let's abandon that line of thinking for now. But consider this: If she's not involved now, she soon may be."

"What do you mean?"

"You said she'd been talking to Dr. Morgan regularly before he disappeared. Then, you told me that when she went to his home, some-one had searched it. If they found what they were looking for, and then killed him, you better hope what they found didn't implicate your little rabbit. As near as I can tell, just about every woman 'of a certain age' in Tampa would have a motive to kill him, not to mention their husbands. And that doesn't even count the business enemies." He ticked off the possibilities like reading a grocery list. No one was above suspicion as far as he was concerned.

"Well obviously, that makes it that much more important that you find Carly, and that you find out immediately if Dr. Morgan is the body in the water and, if he's not, where he is and who is after him."

"I don't need you to tell me how to do my job," Hathaway snapped at me. "I've been doing this a lot longer than you've been a judge. If you'll just keep your nose out of it, I'll take care of my end. If you think of anything else that might be helpful, call me and talk only to me. Here's my private line." He threw his business card down on the coffee table between us. "And then you better spend some time find-ing your friend a good criminal lawyer. She's going to need it. If she doesn't end up dead first."

He got up and walked out. I refused to go after him, and I was more than a little annoyed at the arrogant way he treated me. But I was scared, too. He was right to be pissed off that I had knowledge of a potential crime and, as far as he knew, didn't advise the police. On the other hand, Carly certainly did not kill Dr. Morgan and, if he focused his energies on making her the murderer, he wouldn't be finding Morgan's real killer. If Morgan was dead. I kept hoping he wasn't.

Come to that, how many missing persons reports would he have to consider when he was looking for the identity of a dead body, anyway? There can't be that many people disappearing from the city of Tampa without a trace.

I had one of those "ah ha" moments Kate's always talking about: I realized there was no information on Morgan's identity in the press before Carly went to the house because Hathaway knew who the body was. Morgan didn't have any relatives to notify, so they felt comfortable keeping it quiet, waiting for someone to do just what I did. Identify him.

Hathaway must have believed that the killer would be more likely to make mistakes the longer it looked like the police hadn't identified the body. Now, I had given them Carly and confessed that I'd known about Morgan for two weeks. Carly and I might not need a lawyer, but we needed advice from someone who was thinking a lot clearer than George and I were. I decided to talk to a criminal lawyer tomorrow. In the meantime, I picked up the phone and called Kate. It was time to come clean with her. She wasn't home and I got her machine. Shit! Doesn't anybody ever answer their telephone any more?

I had to find Carly before Hathaway did and persuade her to tell the rest of what she knew. One thing I agreed with Hathaway about; she hadn't come clean with me on her conversations with Morgan and what they had been working on together. Whatever it was, it was enough to get Morgan killed and Carly might be next. Carly's real motivation for keeping her conversations with Morgan secret should have occurred to me, but it didn't. Not for a while, anyway.

I put on my running shoes and got my car keys. I went down the stairs two at a time, racing (decorously, of course) toward my car. I knew where the spare key to Carly's apartment was and I decided to start there. She lives in a gated community and I wasn't sure I'd be able to get in without her consent. A year or so ago I was listed on her limited access list, and I hoped she hadn't changed it. I needed to get to her apartment before Hathaway got there. I knew he would dispatch officers immediately, as soon as he figured out where she lived. He'd left in such a rage he hadn't asked me, and the way he had behaved, I wasn't sure I would have told him.

I drove my car about 25 miles an hour over the speed limit all the way from Minaret to Carly's apartment complex in St. Pete Beach. It's a 25 minute drive under normal conditions, and I made it in fifteen. Because St. Petersburg is outside Hathaway's jurisdiction, I was hoping that it would take more than 15 minutes to get a police car dispatched to Carly's home, even if he could immediately locate the address.

As I pulled up into the guard station at the entrance to her complex, there were four cars in line ahead of me in the one lane driveway. I watched as the security guard talked to the driver of the first car. They were having a friendly chat about the weather, or the last Devil Rays baseball game at the Tropicana Dome or something. What seemed like an hour, and was probably no more than three minutes, passed while the security guard wrote out a visitor's pass for the car and allowed it through the gate.

All of us inched up one car length. The routine was repeated with the second car, and then the third. By this time, I'd waited in line longer than it took me to drive there. Finally, finally, finally, the security guard approached my car. "Good afternoon, ma'am," he said. "How are you today?"

I swallowed my impatience. Everyone else seemed to be on island time, so I tried to fit in by appearing laid back. I don't think he could see my toes tapping, but I'm not sure. "Fine, thank you. I'm here to see Carly Austin. I think I'm on her access list. Please don't call up. It's her birthday and I want to surprise her." I smiled my brightest smile, flirting with him a little. How old was I when I figured out that older men are easily manipulated by a woman who flirts?

"And what's your name, miss? I'll just look it up quickly and then I can let you in," he said with a big, conspiratorial smile. I gave him my name as I looked in my rear view mirror.

I could see no police cars, or at least no marked police cars, either behind me in line or coming up the driveway. There was a satisfyingly long line developing, and I was pretty sure that a police car would have the same difficulty getting through the gate I'd had. Once the cars had lined up at the guard shack, there was nowhere for them to go but through the gate into the complex. The cops would have to wait their turn like everybody else.

Eventually, the guard returned from the shack with my visitor's pass and a smile. He opened the gate and waived me through. He said, "Say happy birthday to Ms. Austin for me. I thought she was out of town. She's one of our most pleasant residents and I haven't seen her much lately."

"Thank you," I sang, smiling and wiggling my fingers at him as I went through the gate, watching the orange and white arm of the gate fall down behind my car.

I drove into the complex, looking all the while for a police car or uniformed police officers from Pinellas County or the City of St. Petersburg. I didn't see any.

When I got to Carly's apartment, I picked up the fake rock out of the planter next to the door. It was easy to find because the flowers hadn't been watered in so long they were all dead. I opened the false slide on the fake rock, pulled out what I hoped was the real key and let myself in.

Carly's apartment complex was on a small peninsula that's particularly vulnerable to hurricanes. Because of the building codes, the garage was on the first floor and the apartment was one floor up. It's a town house style, and the stairway opens into a great room combination of living room, kitchen and dining room. In other words, once you got to the top of the stairs, there was no place to hide except the bedrooms and the closets. I started calling out to Carly as I walked up. I heard nothing. As I came up the stairs and looked into the great room, I could see that the guard was right. Although Carly hadn't been there for quite some time, someone else had been; it was impossible to tell how long ago.

Things were strewn everywhere. The furniture was upended and the fabric bottoms of the chairs and couch were sliced open. The throw cushions were thrown, all right, but they were sliced, too. I looked into the guest room, and the shambles was the same. Just the way Carly had described the search at Dr. Morgan's house. I opened the door to the master bedroom, still calling Carly's name. As soon as I walked in the door, I felt a bowling ball fall on my head. I hit the floor, just like a bowling pin. Strike. They all fall down.

When I woke up, it was dark outside. I tried to raise myself off the floor but the second I lifted my head, it began pounding the way Spielberg showed the footfalls of an approaching T-Rex and I felt nauseous. I laid back down, slowly, slowly, and the room stopped spinning. In fact, it felt so good to lie there, I decided I'd take another nap.

The next time I woke up, faint daylight showed through the mini blinds. I knew I'd been there way too long. I was thinking well enough to understand that George would be worried sick about me and for some reason, no police officers had ever appeared. For that matter, neither had Carly.

I tried once again to get up by raising the top half of my body. No sudden moves this time. Nice and easy. I thought I was talking to myself, but I realized I didn't hear my voice. The thudding in my head sounded like Indian war drums and, while I still felt queasy, I thought I might be able to sit up. I tried it, gingerly, and had to wait a few minutes for the room to stop spinning. But I didn't throw up and I took that as a good sign.

I tried to stand and the magnitude of it nearly knocked me down again. I laid back down. I decided to just wait a few minutes, take it easy, look around. No hurry. After a while, I figured out that I wasn't too far from the bedside phone. I sort of scooched over there on my stomach so I didn't have to actually sit up. After three or four hours, I made it to the telephone. I laid back against the bed, exhausted. Maybe I'd just take another nap, then I'd have enough strength to move forward. That's not such a bad idea, right? No, better call George instead. He'll be worried. Just take several deep breaths and try to stop your hands from shaking so you can dial the phone, and then you can take a nap.

After a while, I was able to reach up and grab the phone. Thankfully, it was a model with the buttons in the receiver. I dialed Minaret first. Evie, the hostess, answered the phone with the voice she uses for callers making reservations. It must have been dusk, and not dawn. How wonderful. I had to clear my throat three times before I could speak.

"Evie." The first time it came out so softly. I didn't recognize my voice and I was sure Evie wouldn't either, even if she could hear me. I cleared my throat and tried again. "Evie."

I could hear her saying "Hello? Is anyone there?" over and over. I tried the third time.

"Evie." I shouted. My head started to vibrate again. My eyes were impersonating Niagra Falls. My voice must have been a mere whisper, but enough for Evie to catch it. I'm going to recommend to George that she get a raise, I thought.

"Evie, it's Willa. Get George. Now." I tried to put as much authority into my voice as I could, but I knew it didn't sound like me. To her credit, Evie didn't ask any more questions, she just asked me to hold on while she got George. A big raise, I decided.

After a few minutes, George came on the line. "Wil? Willa, is that you?" I heard him. I was so relieved. I acknowledged the tears leaking out of my eyes from the sheer effort of trying to avoid them. When I heard George, I began to cry harder. It was several moments before I could answer him. In the meantime, his voice was getting more frantic and he just kept repeating the same thing over and over. "Willa, is that you? Willa, is that you?" Finally, I managed to pull myself together enough to whisper/shout into the phone. "George, I'm at Carly's. Come get me. And call Ben Hathaway."

George kept trying to soothe me over the phone and find out if I'd been hurt. I just didn't have the strength to talk any more so I hung up. Then I laid down on the floor and went back to sleep.

The next time I woke up, George and two Tampa police officers were in the room. Ben Hathaway was there too. George was holding me, helping me to sit up, treating me like a china doll even though my body was behaving like a rag doll. I'm lucky to have George, I remember thinking. George always takes care of me.

Ben Hathaway wasn't interested in how I felt. "Why didn't you tell me where you were going? Why didn't you tell me where Carly lived? We've been trying to track down her home address ever since I left you yesterday!" Hathaway was truly angry. His yelling caused my head to pound harder and louder.

"Compound question," I said weakly as I laid my head on George's chest and closed my eyes. I don't know if they heard me or not. I couldn't say anything else. I heard George ask for an ambulance. When it came, we left.

The ambulance took me to General Hospital (really) where there were no obvious doctor/nurse affairs going on, but our good friend and family physician met us. They did a CT scan of my head and decided there was nothing wrong with it that two weeks rest and ten years of psychotherapy wouldn't help.

At my insistence, they released me into George's custody and we went home. By the time we got back to Minaret, it occurred to me that I had, for the first time in my short career as a judge, and my entire career as a lawyer, missed a scheduled day of trial. I was just too tired and too hurt to care. I didn't call the office or make any excuses. When we got back to Minaret, I fell into bed. George woke me every four hours to make sure I wasn't dead. I might as well have been; I didn't wake up again until the next day.

CHAPTER FOURTEEN

By the next afternoon, I was thinking that in two more weeks I'd begin to feel like a human being. Never again would I believe those movies where the hero gets bopped on the head and jumps right back up for another round. They hadn't found whatever it was I'd been hit with in Carly's apartment, so I was still insisting on the bowling ball theory. If it wasn't a bowling ball, I don't ever want to be hit on the head with anything again.

George brought a tray to the bedroom with some fabulous consomme and fresh bread. Then, looking a little like a new colt with wobbly legs, I walked into the den and sat down. George seemed relieved I was up and about and eating. He made me hot tea and told me that he had called my office, told Margaret that I was ill and asked her to cancel the trial for the remainder of the week. The lawyers and their clients were angry but couldn't very well argue with the explanation. George called the CJ and explained that I had a bad fall and was being treated at home for a concussion. The CJ, true to form, was solicitous of my health. Although we have our little test of wills going, he would never admit to anyone that he wasn't able to control his own team.

Once George figured out that I was going to survive, he released his vivid anger. He went on for quite a while, but I only tuned in to the last part. "Wilhelmina, what in the hell is wrong with you? Did it not occur to you that someone could go with you to Carly's apartment? Why didn't you tell me where you were going? I would have gone along."

"No, you wouldn't. You would have tried to talk me out of it, and you know it. You would have said, let Ben Hathaway handle it." I tried talking calmly the way I've seen television cops calm raving lunatics. It didn't seem to be working.

"So what if I had? That certainly would have been the more reasonable thing to do, anyway. If you'd done that, then whoever hit you might be in police custody now as opposed to you sitting there in that chair just barely able to move around." I can't remember a time when George had ever been so angry with me. In the seventeen years we've been married, we've had relatively few fights. The ones we have had were almost always over my personal safety. I knew his reaction stemmed from concern for me, but it made me bristle nonetheless.

"George Carson, you can just stop trying to boss me around. I don't do what you want me to do or what you say I should, and you know it. I make my own decisions."

"And a fine one this was." He said as he stomped off out of the room, leaving me and my pride to deal with my pounding head, which had returned with the shouting. I sank back on the pillows and closed my eyes.

After he left me with my dignity intact, I had to admit to myself that he might have been right. Unless it was Carly who hit me, which I couldn't believe. And then I realized that I'd heard nothing about Carly or where she was and I didn't know if anyone else had heard from her. I still wasn't strong enough to get up and walk after George, but I could reach the phone.

I called Hathaway. This time, when I asked to be connected, his secretary said he was out of the office. I told her Judge Carson was calling and asked him to call me back. She said she'd give him the message. I had the impression that he'd left standing orders with her that he wasn't to be bothered by Judge Carson. Ben can be so pouty.

I tried reaching Carly at home and at the office, and I tried again to call her car phone. As before, no answer, no answer and no answer. Then, it occurred to me to check my voice mail. When I did, there was a message from Carly. Technology is so wonderful.

She'd left the message on Monday morning. Her voice sounded normal, which made me think she'd called from work where she believed her activities were constantly monitored. "Willa, I wanted to let you know that I'll be going to Minneapolis for a few days and not to worry about me. I'll be checking my voice mail, so leave me a message if you need to reach me."

I replayed it three times because I couldn't believe she hadn't said anything more, and then I saved it so I could hear it again later if I needed to. I hung up the phone softly and tried to think logically about why Carly would be traveling to Minneapolis and when she would be back.

I saw that George had saved the newspapers the last two days and I picked them up to look through them. In this morning's paper, on the front page of the Florida Metro section, was a small article with a headline which read *"Body Identified as Local Plastic Surgeon."*

It was two columns, about four inches long, and after a few minutes I was able to focus my eyes well enough to read it.

> *The body discovered in Tampa Bay near the Sunshine Skyway Bridge two weeks ago was, in life, Dr. Michael Morgan, a local plastic surgeon.*
>
> *The body, following autopsy, contained abnormally high levels of alcohol. Although it appeared Dr. Morgan was a victim of foul play, it also appeared that he was intoxicated at the time of death. He had been plagued in recent years by debts. His estate was valued at less than $10,000. He left several ex-wives, and no children.*

Grover was interviewed. He was quoted as saying that he'd had no contact with Dr. Morgan since settling a 1990 malpractice case against Morgan, and he assumed Morgan was living a quiet life.

Chief Ben Hathaway was quoted as saying that the investigation into Dr. Morgan's death was ongoing and his department was pursuing several suspects.

A similar article appeared in the *Times*. In the *Times* obituary, many of Dr. Morgan's past accomplishments were listed. He had graduated from medical school at the age of 25 and then served his internship, residency and specialty residency all at the Mayo Clinic. He opened his practice in Tampa in 1970. He had been the plastic surgeon to Tampa's stars for several years until he succumbed to drug abuse. A series of malpractice claims followed, culminating in the case which caused him to surrender his license. Dr. Morgan was brilliant. He wrote several major articles and two textbooks. One of the textbooks, on immunology, had made him a millionaire. It was rumored that his will left the continuing royalties from his books to local lawyer Carly Austin. Certain specific bequests and the remainder of his assets went to charity. Ms. Austin had not been available for comment.

I shook my head and blinked several times to clear my blurred vision. That couldn't be right. He left royalties from his books, potentially millions of dollars, to Carly? I read it through twice more. I couldn't believe Carly knew she'd inherited from Morgan, but I knew someone would quickly misconnect the dots and draw a jail cell around Carly's body. I was getting in deeper and deeper. Even a good swimmer can drown if she's too far out in the Gulf.

Morgan's funeral was to be held the next day. Since the autopsy was completed and no family to notify, there was no reason to wait. A closed casket, obviously. We got there just before the service started. Even though it was such short notice, and held in the middle of the week, the church was full. Nothing like the funeral of a locally notorious man murdered in his own home to bring out the curious and the faithful. Then there were the real mourners. Those were the ones I was interested in and why I had convinced George we should go even though I was far from back to normal.

"Michael Morgan may have been a good man at some time in his life, but by the time somebody killed him, he deserved it." Dr. Marilee Aymes said as she sat down in the pew beside me. George frowned his best at her, signifying his desire that she be quiet in church, but she was unfazed.

"He was a thief, and someone stole his life from him. Poetic justice," she said.

The curious couple seated in front of us apparently didn't have George's sense of respect for the dead. They turned around to see just who was making such vivid pronouncements. When they did, I saw she had perfect breasts.

I looked around the church more carefully. Almost every woman in the room was over 55, long past the age for low necklines or see though tight bodiced frocks. But there they were. Only Dr. Aymes and I and a few others didn't fit the profile, as it were.

"Look at all those perfect Morgans." Her voice, still loud, startled me.

"What?"

"Just look around. Have you ever seen so many perfect tits in one room? 'A pair of Morgans' we used to call them. We could always tell."

George glared her into silence just as Dr. Carolyn Young walked by us. She was dressed head to toe in black and had a veil over her face. She walked up to the closed casket and knelt in front of it. From the back I could see her shoulders shaking. She stayed there so long one of the ushers went up to her and helped her to a seat in the front pew—the one usually reserved for family—which was empty.

It seemed all of Tampa society filled Sacred Heart Church for the occasion. Cilla and Hainsworth Waterman were there, Fred Johnson, Christian Grover, Sheldon and Victoria Warwick, even Kate. Probably the first time that many Tampa WASPs had gathered in a Catholic Church since the mayor remarried ten years ago.

The priest who delivered the glowing eulogy was a young man who obviously hadn't known Dr. Morgan. If he knew anything about Morgan's less illustrious accomplishments, he refrained from mentioning them.

After the service, I watched a small group gathered outside around Carolyn Young at the bottom of the steps. "You'd think she was the only woman he ever screwed," Dr. Aymes said with disgust, "instead of just the last one."

"Carolyn Young and Michael Morgan were having an affair when he died?" I felt like the dim-witted straight man in a comedy team. Things everyone else took for granted kept coming as revelations to me. I took solace in the rumor that Tommy Smothers was the smart one.

"Willa, you've got to get out more. Carolyn Young was in love with him for years. Their affair was current, but her lust wasn't. In the old days, you had to stand in line to screw Michael Morgan. I'll bet he slept with every woman in that church." Dr. Aymes turned to look first straight at Kate and then pointedly toward Cilla Waterman.

Cilla hadn't heard the comment, and Kate returned Dr. Aymes' stare, although she blushed deep crimson. Then Kate looked away while Aymes was still staring at her.

"You're just trying to make me jealous, Marilee," George, ever the gentleman, said as he took first Kate's arm and then mine. He started down the steps, pulling us along. "But it's much too pretty a day to dwell on it." We dropped Kate off at home and then went back to Minaret.

Later in the day, I was in the den when I heard voices. I recognized George and I thought I recognized Chief Hathaway with him. I folded up the newspapers and turned on the television.

George and Ben came into the room and Ben seemed less angry with me than the last time I'd seen him. After asking me how I was feeling, Ben sat down in the same chair he'd taken last time and George offered to get us both some fresh coffee, leaving the two of us alone in the living room. Now, wasn't that convenient?

"I'll come right to the point. Someone trashed both Dr. Morgan's and Carly Austin's apartment, in the same way, obviously looking for the same thing. I don't think they found it. Dr. Morgan is dead, but Carly Austin isn't, which is not to say she won't be if I don't find her before the killer does. If you have any idea where she is, you need to let me know that so that I can keep her from getting killed." He spoke calmly, rationally, but not convincingly.

I looked at Hathaway closely. He's probably been a cop too long to betray his true intentions, and I wasn't at all sure whether I believed he was trying to help Carly or arrest her. I knew he was waiting for my analysis to conclude that even if he arrested her, she'd be better off than if her pursuer found her first. The wheels in my head were still turning, albeit slowly. Maybe I would live after all.

"She left a voice mail on my machine saying that she was going to Minnesota and she'd call me when she got back." I could see that this news caused him some serious agitation, but he was trying to control his temper. I didn't tell him I thought the message was another of Carly's lies.

"Look," I said, "Don't shoot the messenger. You asked me if I'd heard from her, I told you what I know. Don't you think I understand she's better off in jail than she is dead?"

I was really running out of patience with this guy. I didn't get to be a Federal Court judge at the age of 36 because I'm stupid. We might be out of each other's jurisdiction, but he certainly wasn't winning any points with me, either.

"All right," he ran his hand over his head, through his thick, dark hair in obvious frustration. His hair looked like it was used to this treatment. It was wavy and constantly messed up. "What would she be going to Minnesota for? What's in Minnesota? Does she have family there, or did Dr. Morgan have family there? You know her. What's she doing?"

I thought I heard preaching in his voice. I hate it when people try to manipulate me. "Don't you think I've been asking myself that same question ever since I got the message? It might help if we knew what she and Dr. Morgan were talking to one another about. Have you been able to shed any light on that?"

Let's just put the burden back where it belongs, I thought. He didn't like it. He was having difficulty conducting a civil conversation. At that point, George walked back in and tried to diffuse the situation.

"Ben," George said, "I think she might have gone to the Mayo Clinic. I read in Dr. Morgan's obituary that he trained there. Carly doesn't have any connection with the Mayo Clinic and she didn't go for business, did she?"

"I checked with her boss. He said she hadn't been in to work in three days and it was most unlike her. He didn't know where she was, or at least he said he didn't. Your Mayo Clinic theory makes as much sense as anything else, George. I'll check it out."

Hathaway got up to leave. "Wait a minute," I said. "What about my question? Have you found out what she and Morgan were working on or why they were communicating with each other?"

He studied me for a long time. "Okay," he finally said. "The only thing that makes sense to me is that they were working on some aspect of this breast implant litigation. Her company, MedPro, derived about 50% of its revenue in the 1980's from the sale of breast implants. They've been selling them in Britain and France following the FDA moratorium here in this country. The lawsuits were threatening to put the company under. I think Dr. Morgan and Carly Austin were working on a strategy to defend the claims."

I let out a long breath of air I didn't realize I'd been holding. "Let's just suppose that's true, why would that have gotten him killed?"

Hathaway looked at me as if the rumors of my intelligence had been greatly exaggerated. "The first rule of police work, Wilhelmina— follow the money," he said as he walked out. I was beginning to hope that he found Carly soon because that would mean I could stop talking to him all together. Maybe forever. I made a mental note to take him off our guest list.

George apologized for getting angry earlier and I promised not to take any more chances with what he called facetiously, my "pretty little head." I had to laugh at that, and the laughter made my head hurt. George is the farthest thing from a chauvinist I've ever met.

After we had the coffee, I decided to turn in for the night. Since he'd already canceled my trial for tomorrow, I thought I'd take advantage of the break.

I skipped my run the next morning. I was beginning to feel closer to normal, but not up to pounding of any kind. I dressed in a denim shirt, chinos and my black Cole Haan flats and, after breakfast, drove myself to the office. Some Federal District Court judges have law clerks who act as chauffeurs, but I really enjoy driving Greta. I've been told she's too flashy for me to drive now that I'm on the bench. If you're from Detroit, cars are the essence of life itself. How could I give up Greta just for a job?

As I went over the bridge off Plant Key away from Minaret, I turned right onto Bayshore heading toward downtown. I was impressed, as I always am, with the view. Hillsborough Bay, particularly along the Bayshore, is truly beautiful. Not many years ago, the Hillsborough River, the Bay and Tampa Bay were completely dead. After a massive clean-up campaign, fish, dolphins, rays and manatee are regularly spotted in all three waters. In fact, the Tampa Downtown Partnership sponsors an annual fishing tournament, giving prizes to the largest fish caught in the downtown area. Thankfully, there are fish to catch. You can eat them, too, if you're brave enough.

The drive down Bayshore, over the Platt Street bridge, toward the Convention Center is one of my daily pleasures. I could feel my mood lightening and I actually felt better physically. Downtown Tampa, once a ghost town, is making a come back. There is the one new office building at Jackson Street, Landmark Tower, where Hainsworth Waterman has his offices. A series of storefronts and Sacred Heart Church make up the four block stretch to the Federal Building housing the Federal Courthouse. But on the other side of Platt Street, the Lightning play hockey in their new arena. A convention hotel is planned, Garrison Sea Port houses cruise ships and the Tampa Aquarium's glass dome lights the sky.

The Federal Building itself is Circa 1920. In 1920, the Middle District of Florida was a much smaller place than it is now that what we Floridians affectionately call "the Black Rat" has moved into Orlando. The building is old, decrepit and much too small for the district's current needs. A new Federal Building is under construction, but for a while yet, we have to make do with small courtrooms and crowded conditions.

As the most junior judge on the bench, in terms of seniority, age and the CJ's affection, I have the least desirable location. It's the RHIP rule; I have no rank and no privilege. My courtroom and chambers are on the third floor, in the back. Getting there from the parking garage helps me keep my schoolgirl figure.

I pulled into my reserved spot and parked Greta illegally across two parking places. Building security got the meter maid to write me a ticket the first time they found my car parked like this, and I smiled remembering that I personally vacated it. I may have no rank with the CJ, but I certainly rank higher than a meter maid. This parking garage was built with the very minimum allowable tolerances. There is just no way I'm going to park Greta where she can be hit by other car doors.

If the building loses revenue, they should have thought of that when they were marking off the spaces. If all the spaces were large enough to hold a Greyhound bus, we'd all have enough room, wouldn't we?

When I got to my office, there was still no word from Carly. I did some paperwork, and rescheduled the *Jones v. General Medics* case to start again tomorrow. Then I went home and went straight to bed.

The next morning, the hours dragged on interminably. My mind was definitely not on the trial and I kept thinking about where Carly could possibly be, when she would return and whether she'd be dead or alive.

By the time I recessed the trial at 4:30, the inactivity was driving me crazy. Off the record, but in open court, I said "Mr. Grover, I want to see you in my chambers. Mr. Waterman, I represent to you that I don't want to discuss anything related to the case with him and I will not hear anything related to the case from him. If you want me to declare a mistrial and you can appeal this ex parte communication, all you have to do is ask."

I could see Hainsworth's astonished face as I hurried off the bench, while he shouted toward my back, "Judge, this is most irregular!" And Grover was simultaneously exclaiming "Judge, you'll create reversible error in my trial." I ignored them both.

When Grover came into my chambers, I had removed my robe and was sitting behind my desk. He came in somewhat gingerly, not knowing what to expect. When he sat down in the ugly olive green client chair across from me, I studied him a long moment before saying anything.

Grover looked worse than I had ever seen him. His sartorial excellence is legendary. He usually dresses like Armani is his personal tailor. He usually looked every inch the successful lawyer and I could see why other attorneys would refer their big cases to him. He was well known, successful and a formidable adversary. I didn't care about any of that.

"Christian, I've known you a long time. We've never seen eye to eye on cases or politics and I don't care. I know you're deep into this breast implant business and you have several suits pending against MedPro. Do you have any idea where Carly Austin is?"

I watched him closely. I didn't expect him to tell me the truth, but I was hoping that I would be able to tell whether he was lying. He was a good poker player. He appeared astonished at the question, with just the right touch of puzzlement. All trial lawyers are actors on some level and Grover was in the top 10% of the local performers.

"Judge, I don't even know *who* Carly Austin is."

"What you don't know, Christian, is that I know Carly very well. So I know that she clerked in your firm when she was in law school. You definitely know *who* she is. What I want to know is whether you know *where* she is. And now that you've lied to me once, I'm not sure I'll believe you no matter what you say. But answer the question anyway."

"I'm not clear just exactly what right you have to ask me this question, Judge Carson. Carly Austin, and any relationship I may or may not have with her, has nothing to do with you. I know she's a friend of yours, but that doesn't give you any right to pry into her personal life." His indignation may have been genuine, but it's hard to say.

"Are you saying that you and Carly have a personal relationship of some kind?" I was incredulous. The possibility not only of Carly having a relationship with Grover, but that she would have a relationship with him and not tell me, was very disturbing. How far was she going to take this rebellious teenager stuff, anyway?

"What I am telling you, Judge Carson, is that it's none of your business. If you have some professional reason for asking me, which I can't imagine in the light of the fact that you told Mr. Waterman you would not be asking me ex parte questions about this case, then tell me what it is. If you're asking me on a personal basis, I don't have the kind of personal relationship with you that would make me answer that. I don't intend to discuss my personal relationships with you. If Carly wants to tell you, she will. Why don't you ask her?" He was belligerent now, feeling he was on firmer ground.

"I would if I knew where she was." I snapped.

"Just as I thought," he snorted. "You're not as close to her as you'd like to believe. If you don't have anything else related to the case, Judge, I do have to prepare for my next witness." We sat there staring across the desk, measuring each other for a few moments until he got up and left. Without my permission.

If I hadn't heard the Junior story, I'd have said it wasn't possible that Carly could be involved in a personal relationship with Christian Grover. Apparently, Carly's taste in men runs from the unsuitable to the unthinkable. As the corporate counsel of a defendant in the breast implant cases, Carly's relationship with a notorious plaintiff's attorney bringing cases against her company would have been enough to get her fired if not disbarred. But then, maybe that's why she hadn't told me about it. Being sexually disgraced in a town where everyone knows everything about you might have snuck up on her the first time. She wouldn't allow that to happen again. She didn't tell anyone about it. And maybe that's why she was so reluctant to pass on Dr. Morgan's theories to her superiors at MedPro. Maybe she didn't want Dr. Morgan to be right.

Poor kid, what a dilemma. If she chose her job, she lost her lover and if she chose her lover, she lost her job. For Carly, who apparently believed she had nothing else, either choice would be an impossible one. I could feel my Mighty Mouse tendencies creeping up again.

If I gave this information to Ben Hathaway, he would believe he was right, that Carly did kill Dr. Morgan. It wouldn't be the first time love prevailed over ethics. His view would be cast in concrete. He'd likely arrest Carly on sight. If she'd killed Morgan either for love or money, her motive wouldn't matter to Chief Hathaway.

And what about Grover? If he knew where Carly was, that would explain his lack of concern over my questions. Of course, that would be true whether she was dead or alive.

I turned it over and over in my head, and I could think of no reasonable alternative but to tell Hathaway. But if I did that, Carly would be arrested and charged with Dr. Morgan's murder. I had to concede, at least to myself, that Carly might be involved in a sexual relationship with Grover. He could be wickedly charming and certainly had enough conquests to prove it. Carly had so little experience that the attention of a rich and powerful lawyer like Grover would certainly have impressed her.

But I knew Carly wasn't capable of murder and the way she reacted when she described the murder scene to me convinced me that she hadn't killed Dr. Morgan. I thought she knew, or at least she believed she knew who had killed him. But what I didn't know was why. Did Carly believe Christian Grover killed Michael Morgan? It was a plausible reason for her behavior. She believed Grover did it and she wanted to protect him. But did he kill Morgan? And, if he did, why? Wasn't Morgan worth more to Grover alive? This is the point where Mighty Mouse is stuffed into the box and thrown into the ocean. Until I could figure it out, I wasn't turning over this piece of information to Chief Hathaway or anyone else. He already had enough incriminating evidence anyway. If withholding this piece, which I only suspected and couldn't confirm until I found Carly, put the final nail in my impeachment coffin, I'd just see how well I could adjust to unemployment.

I recessed the case for the day. I decided the best way to keep my job, help Carly, and confirm or disprove that her lover was a killer, was to do some investigation into the business of breast implant litigation.

CHAPTER FIFTEEN

Follow the money, Hathaway had said. I asked my law clerk to bring me a list of all of the breast implant cases I had currently pending on my docket together with the names of the attorneys and law firms representing both parties. She ran the request through the computer and had it for me in 30 minutes.

I was surprised at how many cases I actually had. The computer list was ten pages long. I asked her to sort the cases by lawyer and defendant. The list I got back reflected the majority of the plaintiffs' cases were being handled by Grover and his partner, Fred Johnson. Only one or two other plaintiffs' firms were represented and then they only handled one or two cases.

On the defense side, there were about five firms listed. The majority of the cases appeared to be against two corporate defendants and one individual, Dr. Michael Morgan. Each of those defendants was represented by E. Hainsworth Waterman. The remaining third of the cases were against various defendants represented by as many defense firms.

Most of the cases had been filed more than two years, and involved a husband and wife as plaintiffs. One case was noteworthy, however, because it was a class action, listing the individual names of more than 350 plaintiffs and the defendants were each of the named manufacturers. In the 350 plaintiff case, all of the manufacturers were represented by one defense counsel, E. Hainsworth Waterman. Plaintiffs' counsel was Grover.

I then looked at the trial calendar. Because 95% of all civil cases settle, I schedule about 20 trials a week during my jury term and 25 trials a week during non-jury term. There were 10-15 breast implant trials scheduled every jury term for the next 12 months.

The class action case was scheduled for trial six months hence. As many cases as were still on my docket, more than twice that many had been transferred to Federal Court in Georgia to the multi-district litigation being handled by my good friend, Judge Franklin. I had no idea what was happening with Judge Franklin's cases, and I decided to call him. Miraculously, he was available to speak to me.

After the pleasantries were exchanged, I asked "Steve, what is the status of the breast implant litigation you're handling these days?"

"We've got a global settlement almost completely negotiated. It's been approved by the plaintiffs and the defendants. I have a couple of motions by insurance companies and Medicare and Medicaid to decide and then I'll make a decision on final approval."

"What will happen to the settlement if it is not approved?"

"I haven't let myself think about that," he laughed. "But, if that should happen, then I guess we'll start having trials on all 440,000 claims. I figure I'll get done about the time I am scheduled to depart the earth, or this will kill me prematurely!"

I laughed politely in commiseration. Judges don't get paid overtime. "And what will happen after the settlement is approved, if it is?"

"After approval, the only step left is for the individual plaintiffs to submit the medical proof necessary to establish their entitlement to payments under the terms of the settlement grid."

"Settlement grid?" I felt like I was learning a foreign language.

"We've worked out a system where women with different types of diseases will be paid different sums of money. The least amount a woman will be paid is $5,000 and the most is $1 million."

I whistled. "That's a hell of a lot of money, especially to the lawyers. How will the legal fees be paid?"

"Well on the plaintiff's side, I want to limit transaction costs to 25% of the total settlement amount. Of course, the plaintiffs are squealing like stuck pigs over that because they're used to 40% fees, exclusive of costs, and the defendants are objecting that it's too high because they're the ones that get to pay it."

The figures he quoted were staggering. Following the money seemed to be the first rule for lawyers as well as murder investigators. "And what about defense attorney fees?"

"Defense attorneys will be paid by the defendants through whatever arrangements the defendants have made for paying them. I haven't gotten into that because the defendants haven't asked me to. I don't see how I could resolve that anyway."

"There seems to be some new urgency in my courtroom by the plaintiffs to get these cases on for trial. I noticed today that I've got ten trials set every jury term for the next 12 months. Do you have any idea why?"

"I think that's happening all over the country, partly because it pressures the defendants to settle and partly because in the last several months the scientific studies that have come out have all been supporting the defense side. The plaintiffs feel they're playing beat the clock. If they don't get their judgments soon, they're worried the defendants will start trying the causation issues and winning. The defendants are pushing the cases to trial because they think they can win or at least they can make the plaintiffs work and then the plaintiffs will get more reasonable. If I don't get this settlement put to bed pretty soon, I'm afraid the whole thing will fall apart."

I thanked Steve for his help, and went back to studying my list. I noticed that Grover had all of his cases set for trial, but none of Johnson's were scheduled. Waterman's cases were all set, but they ran into the next three years, pretty evenly spaced out. The remaining attorneys seemed to be either behind the curve in requesting trial dates or, perhaps, not prepared for trial.

I did some quick multiplication in my head. If each of the plaintiffs Grover represented would settle, it looked to me like just the cases on my docket would net him attorneys' fees of $270 million under Florida's 40 percent fee rule. Of course, he could have made arrangements to accept lower fees based on the volume of business, and he probably owed referral fees to a number of lawyers who had sent him their cases to handle as well. Still, he stood to gain a tremendous sum of money if these cases were all tried and won. Not as much as the tobacco lawyers would get, but certainly enough to keep him and his four ex-wives off food stamps.

More realistically, setting the cases for trial would force settlements and Grover would get the money more quickly. He'd have to discount the value of the claims to settle them now, but he probably wouldn't have to discount them much, considering the costs of defense. It was curious that Grover's partner, Johnson, hadn't done the same math.

And I couldn't see the advantage to the defendants in pushing the cases to trial. Agreeing to prompt trial dates would put a significant amount of pressure on most of the defense law firms. They just didn't have the manpower to do the work required to defend multiple, four-week trials. And even if they did have enough lawyers to put on the trials, their other work would suffer. A defense firm that puts all its eggs in one client basket makes big money while it lasts, but can't withstand the business loss when the cases are over. And why did only two of the plaintiffs' lawyers want to take their cases to trial now? Why not the rest of them? Both Grover and Waterman were in a game of high stakes poker and I wasn't at all sure which one was holding the better hand.

I began looking at the individual plaintiffs' names. I was shocked to find so many I recognized as my friends, neighbors and colleagues. I found myself smiling involuntarily every time I recognized the name of a woman whose cosmetic enhancement had not been obvious to me.

From the defense side, Waterman's two major clients surfaced repeatedly, but there were also quite a few cases against Carly's company, MedPro, and other defendants, both local and national. I recognized some as George's investments. Others were common corporate America household names.

I continued looking at the list and trying to discern patterns within it. I wasn't sure what I was looking for, but I thought something might jump out at me if I just kept looking. It didn't. When I looked at my watch, it was 8:00 p.m. and I needed to get home. I put the list out of sight, but not out of mind.

The other thing I couldn't put off any longer was an extended conversation with Kate. She deserved to know what was going on with Carly, and with me. I stopped by her house on the way home.

I saw Kate standing at her kitchen window when I pulled up in the driveway of her South Tampa home. Kate lives two doors off the Bayshore on Oregon, in an old bungalow type house. It was charming, but it was on a corner lot and the kitchen looked out over a busy side street. Both George and I were worried about just anyone being able to drive up and see her standing in the kitchen, but she said we watch too much television. She wouldn't even put blinds on the windows. She said she had moved to Florida for sunlight.

I sat in the car and watched Kate work for a while before she noticed I was there. She was a beautiful woman still. She hadn't changed that much from the first time I saw her, when I was three. I loved her sparkling blue eyes, and her wide, generous smile. She wore her hair in the same French twist she'd always worn, and if there was a little more grey in with the brown, it looked beautiful none the less.

Kate should be married, I thought, for the hundredth time. She's such a nurturing person. She raised three children of her own, and me since Mom died, without any help from anyone. She'd be a great wife, and a great mother if Carly would just let her be.

Kate eventually looked up from her cooking and saw me sitting in the car in the driveway. She waved me inside. I walked up to the back door and she came to let me in. At least we'd been able to talk her into locking the door when she was home alone.

"Willa! What a nice surprise," she said as she hugged me with one arm while the other held her paring knife. "Will you stay for dinner? Nothing as fancy as you could have at Minaret, but I still make a pretty good veal loaf." I was following her into the kitchen, and she just kept talking without waiting for my reply. I don't remember her doing that when we all used to be around. Maybe living alone was getting to her. I decided to speak my thoughts when I finally had a chance to get a word in.

"Kate, what really happened to your husband?" I hid my face in the refrigerator, ostensibly looking for a bottle of beer, avoiding her gaze. We'd never talked about this, and I wasn't sure she'd think it was any of my business. But she didn't seem to mind.

"He just left one day and never came back. He didn't even have enough originality to come up with a good story. He said he was going out for cigarettes." She had pulled out three potatoes to peel after she put the veal loaf in the oven.

"When he didn't come back from the store, you must have been frantic." I took up the green beans, washing them at the sink and cutting off the ends so they could be steamed.

"Oh, sure. Crime in our neighborhood was as bad as anywhere for 1975. I called all the hospitals, the police department. No one had seen him."

"How do you know he wasn't injured or killed or something?" I asked her, putting the beans in the sauce pan with a little water, salt and the steamer.

"Here, let me season those. I put rosemary in them. Gives them a nice flavor." She took the pot out of my hand and emptied the water in the sink. She refilled the pot, added rosemary instead of salt, and put the beans back in the steamer. She turned the burner on under it, and moved back to the potatoes.

"He wrote to me, about ten years after he left. He'd found another woman he wanted to marry, and he asked for a divorce, which I gave him, of course. He never asked about the boys." She was putting the potatoes on to boil, adding whole garlic cloves to the water, and then moved to the refrigerator to get out salad greens.

"That must have been enough to sour you on men for a while," I said, sitting down at the table. It was apparent she didn't want any help, so I decided to stay out of the way.

She nodded. "For a long time, I didn't understand it. I thought there was something wrong with me. Since I never told the boys I'd divorced their father, I couldn't very well tell them I planned to date. And for a long time, I just wasn't interested."

"Well, at some point, that must have changed."

"Because of Carly, you mean? Yes, but that was years later, and quite unexpected, really. Would you open that red wine, Dear, I think I'll have a glass with you while you have your beer." I opened the bottle as she got a wine glass out of the cupboard for each of us and began to set the table for two, even though I never said I'd stay. She lit tall green candles in pewter candlesticks that I knew, from long familiarity, she'd inherited from her mother. I went to call George and tell him I wouldn't be home for dinner.

When I came back into the kitchen, the potatoes were done and Kate was mashing them, drinking her wine and adding large dollops of butter. Tomorrow, headache or no, back to my running or I'd soon weigh as much as Pricilla Waterman.

When the veal loaf was done, and Kate had made the burgundy gravy to go with the garlic potatoes, green beans and salad, we sat down to eat with another full glass of wine each. The intimacy, and the wine, gave me the courage to take up our conversation again.

"How did you meet Carly's father, anyway?" I tried to make it sound casual, as if I knew, but had just forgotten. Nothing could be further from the truth. Kate had never told any of us anything about him. In fact, this was the first time I'd ever had the nerve to suggest we all knew Carly's father was not the same man who had fathered the boys. With Kate, somehow, we'd known the topic was tabu.

I'm not sure if Kate was more surprised that I'd asked, or that she answered, but eventually she said, "Your mother was responsible for that, actually. She had a party and she invited him. We met. We danced. I let myself go. I woke up in his hotel room. We had a lovely breakfast, and I never saw him again. Except for every time I look in Carly's eyes."

She was trying to keep it light, but her voice became very soft and I could tell that, whatever she thought now, she had loved him then. I sensed she wanted to talk about it, finally, this thing that had made her so happy, but had caused her daughter so much pain.

"Carly looks just like him, you know. His hair was curly and red like hers. And her flashing, deep blue eyes. People think she got those from me, but she didn't." She paused, remembering.

"When I found out I was pregnant with Carly, my first reaction was pure fright. Single mothers were not anything like accepted the way they are today. And it may have taken Carly ten years to do the math, but my family and my neighbors figured it out right away." She was recalling bitter words, now, I was sure.

"But what could I do? I had two sons at home and I was divorced and pregnant. That was the reality of it. There was no choice. I could be pregnant and unhappy or pregnant and make the best of it. Your mom was great. She'd wanted another child after she married your dad, but she just couldn't get pregnant. She was so happy she'd be Carly's godmother. Your mom really helped me through those days." She emptied the Merlot bottle into our glasses and we sat quietly while she remembered that far away time and tried to decide how much to share with me.

"And then something curious happened. I started to be really happy. I was smiling all the time, looking forward to the baby coming. I don't think I'd ever been quite as happy before that time, and I'm not sure I've ever been that happy since." Her face lit up now with the memory.

"Just the pregnancy hormones, you think?" I was staring at the flickering candle flame, almost hypnotized.

"It was partly that, but something else, too. You see, Wilhelmina, I believe in the affluence of the universe. I believe you make your own life. You decide what it is that you want, and then the universe gives it to you. It's not that you don't have to work for it, but the law of least effort applies more often than not. If it's too much trouble, it's usually not worth it. Happiness is first, seeking happiness is the most important quest, and achieving it is life's best goal." Philosophy often comes in a bottle of wine, I've found, and it was no different with Kate.

"I don't mean happiness from a pill or a syringe. I mean real happiness that comes from obtaining your life's desires. It's hard to achieve happiness because real happiness is so often confused with things. You look for a new house or a new job or a new relationship, because you think those things will make you happy. Really, the opposite is true. If you're happy, you'll enjoy your job or your house or your relationship, and all good things will flow to you." She took a deep breath. I waited, afraid to break the spell.

"And when I was pregnant with Carly, I finally accepted that I had wanted another baby, and I had gone to that party looking for just such an available man as I met, and I got what I wanted. For all Carly's angst over her paternity, she was the most wanted baby ever conceived and certainly one of the most loved."

I went over and gave Kate a big hug. I blinked my tears away, but Kate wasn't crying. To her, this was an old story and she remembered it with obvious, almost ethereal joy.

We were having such a wonderful evening that I didn't want to spoil it by telling her what I'd come to say. But I couldn't let her hear about it from one of the town wags, either. Fortunately, Kate never read the newspapers or watched television news. She said they only reported bad news, and she wasn't interested. So, after we put the dishes in the dishwasher and sat down with our coffee, I gave her a very abbreviated version of Carly's situation. I omitted my own troubles. I felt I had gone into this deal with my eyes open. No point in blaming it on Carly or putting the burden of my decision on Kate.

She didn't seem at all dismayed, and I couldn't quite understand why. After everything she'd told me tonight, I knew she loved Carly as her chosen child, maybe even more than the rest of us (although before tonight, I'd always thought that particular honor belonged to Jason, her first born).

"Kate, you don't seem very worried. Carly is in serious trouble. You understand that, don't you?" I was beginning to think she'd had more wine than she could handle, but I'd underestimated her again.

"Willa, there's no chance that Carly killed Michael Morgan, or anyone else for that matter. As to where she is at the moment, I'm sure she'll turn up with some reasonable explanation. There's nothing I can do for her until she comes to me with the same questions you've asked tonight. Carly has to get over being angry with me for keeping her father from her, and start being grateful she's had such a wonderful family. Until then, there's nothing I can do for her except love her, and trust that she'll be all right. The same thing I do for all of you."

So, in the end, I gave her a hug, told her I loved her and left, uneasy in the knowledge that I'd underestimated her again.

CHAPTER SIXTEEN

My conversation with Kate left me with a lot to think about. Finding Carly before she got hurt and solving the relationship problems she had with Kate shouldn't have been my mission but somehow it was. I was sure the connection between Carly, Dr. Morgan's murder, Grover and Johnson had to be related to the breast implant cases. Hathaway had said to follow the money, so I tried piecing the puzzle together with the money in mind. Carly said Dr. Morgan had been conducting research and believed he'd found the scientific explanation for the occurrence of symptoms in some women with breast implants. Something like that would have to be worth a lot of money on the legitimate market, not just to the interested parties to the litigation.

The most obvious place to start looking for Dr. Morgan's theories were the two places that had already been searched, his home and Carly's, but only if you knew the two of them had been talking about it. And who knew that besides Carly? Grover? Probably. Who else? Putting aside the "who," the thoroughness of those searches convinced me that I was looking either for some type of paper document or some type of computer stored information, and that whatever it was had not yet been found. I could only hope that the killer believed Carly had it and that he wouldn't kill her until he found it.

I went back to the office from Kate's house and spent the evening pouring over the court file in the *Jones v. General Medics* case. I read the complaint, the answer and other pleadings. I read the deposition transcripts of the experts. One thing I was surprised to find was Dr. Morgan's name on Grover's witness list. I looked for Dr. Morgan's deposition transcript in the file, but it wasn't there. Then I looked for deposition notices indicating that his deposition had been taken. There were several notices of his deposition, but no proof that the deposition had actually taken place.

I checked out the dates of the deposition notices and the date on the witness list. Dr. Morgan had been named as an expert early in the case. The notices for his deposition were sent at intervals as the case proceeded. The last deposition notice scheduled his deposition two days before he died. The curious thing was either that he was deposed and explained his theories, in which case why kill him; or that he wasn't deposed and, in that case, how did Grover explain the failure to produce him and why hadn't Hainsworth filed a motion to strike his name from the list if he couldn't be produced for deposition? Every angle I tried left me with more questions than answers.

I left my office and went down to the courthouse library. Using the online computer services, I pulled up all of the newspaper articles relating to breast implants in the past five years. The computer listed 1,765 articles, so I tried to think of some way to narrow my search. I started by narrowing the date range. Articles printed after the largest manufacturer's bankruptcy and before Dr. Morgan died numbered 432. Still, too many to read one at a time. I arbitrarily excluded articles about the bankruptcy itself, although I felt the risk in doing that was substantial. That left 142 articles.

Knowing that articles reprinted in the local papers from *The New York Times, The Wall Street Journal, The Washington Post* and the major wire services might account for duplicates, I printed a list of the last search. After eliminating the duplicates, I was left with 68 recent newspaper articles on the subject. I sent all 68 articles to the printer and began to read them as they came off.

Some of the articles just weren't helpful. They discussed individual cases or individual medical studies being conducted. I scanned them quickly and moved them to one side. None of the articles dealt with MedPro, which was somewhat surprising since it was a small but significant player in the market. Only a few articles dealt with Dr. Morgan and they were all related to his death and his obituaries.

After all 68 articles printed, and I had read through most of them, I rubbed the back of my neck and looked at my watch. It was 11:30 and I was really tired. I signed off the computer, took the articles back to my chambers and called George to assure him everything was fine. I put the articles in my brief case and decided to read them more thoroughly at home.

George was already upstairs and had run the dogs before I came in. He'd ordered a cold snack, but I was still too stuffed to move from Kate's dinner. So he made me a Sapphire and tonic with a twist. I held the frosty glass against my forehead.

I told him about the day's events and, while he reluctantly agreed with my conclusions, he didn't like the idea of keeping information from Ben Hathaway. George thought it was Ben's job to catch killers, not mine. Ordinarily, I would agree with him. In this case, though, I wanted to be sure Hathaway caught the right killer. I'm enough of a liberal to believe that *some* innocent people are convicted, although I certainly admit the odds are against it.

I spent the rest of the evening poring over the newspaper articles. At 3:00 a.m., I had read them all four times. I sorted, diagramed and thoroughly digested each one. I flipped through the pages of my yellow pad, looking at all the facts, trying to see the connections. If there was a connection between anything printed in those articles, Dr. Morgan's death and Carly's disappearance, I couldn't find it.

By the time I wearily went to bed, tossed and turned, and thought about what I'd read, it was 5:30 before I finally went to sleep. When the alarm went off at 7:00, I cursed my promise to keep this case moving quickly.

We began trial again promptly at 9:00. If possible, Grover looked like he had spent a later night than I had. For that matter, Hainsworth and his associate didn't look very well rested either. I remembered well the days of preparing long into the night for trial, and attributed the defense team's weariness to that preparation. As for Grover, I couldn't believe his ego would have allowed him to spend the night in grunt work. I found myself studying him, looking for signs of stress or mental strain caused by waiting to be arrested for murder. If he felt any, he certainly covered it up well.

The afternoon session was taken up with the playing of video depositions, always a boring part of any trial, and I nodded off a couple of times. These depositions were plaintiffs' national experts, doctors who were making a killing testifying around the country in breast implant cases. It was rumored that some of them charged as much as $25,000 just to review a patient's medical records, $10,000 for a deposition and $50,000 to testify in court, if they would even come live to trial.

One of the articles I'd read last night said that many of the experts were making a much better living as professional witnesses than they'd ever made as doctors. The legitimate medical community was appalled, of course, but the experts were doing nothing illegal, or even novel.

This afternoon's witnesses were experts on the surgical techniques for implanting and explanting the breast prostheses. Their testimony was a lot of diagrams and charts and videos of actual surgeries, which left most of us squeamish.

Plaintiffs' final video of the day was the deposition testimony of an expert immunologist, a doctor specializing in the human immune system. This doctor testified that implants cause the immune system of an implanted woman to turn on itself and destroy her own cells. The doctor likened the process to AIDS. He said it was just as debilitating and likely to be progressive and degenerative. Although Waterman glowered at the testimony, I had overruled all of his objections to the evidence in pre-trial motions. At the conclusion of the video tapes, the jury seemed more sleepy and bewildered than impressed.

I dismissed the jury and then the parties. I returned to my chambers at 4:35, hoping to sneak out before the CJ arrived. Like a high school principal, he had been the victim of this ploy before; he arrived early and was reading a magazine in my waiting room. I pretended to be pleasantly surprised to see him and invited him into my chambers.

"Wilhelmina, you know I think the world of you and your husband." He knew, and I knew, he thought no such thing and, even if he did, what was the point? I smiled and nodded and waited for the punch line.

"Wilhelmina, I'm concerned about you. You were off last week after you were, as I understand it, attacked by a mugger. Today, you look like you haven't slept. You know, this position is not really all that hard. You have some control over your schedule. You need to pace yourself." He tried hard to sound genuine, but I could tell by that tic at the corner of his left eye that it was stressing him out some. And, I was quite sure we hadn't gotten to the point of the visit yet, so I just thanked him for his concern.

He cleared his throat and finally spit it out. "I've been asked to tell you that your conduct is being perceived, by some, as well, not what we'd hoped for. It's true you have a lifetime appointment, but you can be impeached. It doesn't happen often, but it has happened before. I suggest you leave the homicide investigations to Ben Hathaway, particularly when the deceased is someone as disreputable as Michael Morgan. I doubt there's a person worth knowing in Tampa who's sorry to see him dead. You want to be careful who you make your enemies." Now, he had my full attention.

Ever since I'd mistakenly taken his parking place my first day on the job, the revered first spot next to the door reserved for the Big Guy, the CJ, Oz himself, he'd been on my case. I thought his reaction was more than a little bit strange for such a minor infraction. I got the worst case assignments, the smallest chambers, the most meager courtroom redecorating budget. At meetings, he ignored my suggestions and just generally made it known, without saying so, that I was far from his favorite. But this was the first time he'd ever said anything overt to me. It was so out of character, so inappropriate and so unjudicial, that I wasn't sure I'd heard him correctly.

"Are you threatening me, CJ? And if you are, are *you* threatening me or is this a message from someone else?" I asked him coldly.

"Don't take that tone with me, Wilhelmina. I'm trying to give you some good advice. If you don't want to take it, the risk is yours." He got up, and slammed the door on his way out.

I wasn't sure if the CJ was warning me because he thought I was disgracing his precious court, because he held me somehow responsible for Junior's recent loss of face, or if one of the groups who used to contribute heavily to his reelection campaigns when he was on the state bench had asked him for the favor. I know he has aspirations to higher office. Maybe it's a black mark against him if he can't keep his junior justices in line, and he won't be considered for the Court of Appeals. If so, that would be most unfortunate. The only chance I had of getting rid of him was the Peter Principle: get him kicked upstairs. It was quite a while before I figured out the real reason for his warning, and I had to be hit over the head with it even then.

Since I was already in such a fine snit, I picked up the telephone and called Ben Hathaway. He was as cool to me as I was to him. I asked him what news he had of Carly and he told me that an ongoing police investigation was none of my business.

"If you want me to keep out of it, you'll tell me what you found, if you found anything," I snapped back.

"You'll keep out of it if I tell you to keep out of it, Federal Judge or not!" and he slammed down the phone. I slammed down my receiver immediately afterwards. What a shame he couldn't hear it.

On the way home, after I thought about it, I concluded that Hathaway must have nothing to report. If he'd found Carly or knew where she was, he would have been only too happy to tell me. In fact, she'd probably be in custody if he knew where she was. It was small comfort that he didn't.

I don't know if it was because of my fight with the CJ, or with Ben Hathaway, or just that I was getting tired of not knowing what the hell was going on. I wasn't conscious of it, but somehow, Greta just decided it would be a good idea to drive by Michael Morgan's house instead of going immediately home. I found myself driving down Kennedy to Westshore, and into the exclusive, pricey Beach Park subdivision, looking for the address that had inexplicably imprinted itself on my memory.

The house itself was old and fairly small, a typical Florida ranch. It had a Beach Park address, but it wasn't one of the more glamorous homes in the neighborhood. I pulled up in the driveway, all the way to the back of the car port. The house was on a typically small South Tampa lot. The side door and the side of the house were visible from the street and from the house next door. Anyone could have seen a black car in the driveway, just as the witness told the police. The killer must have been cursing his luck that Dr. Morgan's house, like so many homes in Florida, didn't have an attached garage.

When I tried the door, I discovered that one of Tampa's finest, or someone else, had left it unlocked. It took me about two seconds to decide. I knew my car was distinctive, and someone would notice it, but I was already here and Morgan was already dead and I was already obstructing justice as well as in trouble with the CJ. What more could I risk? So I went in.

The side door opened into the kitchen. I had to duck under the crime lab's yellow plastic tape to get inside. The kitchen was on the left of the doorway, and it was large enough for a small drop leaf table and two chairs. Splattered blood and grey matter was still on the wall behind the chair facing the door. Had the killer stood right inside the door and pulled the trigger? Or had they been talking at the table when he did it?

I looked at the door jamb, and it didn't look like anyone had forced the locks. No marks on the door or the jamb. There was black finger printing dust all over the knob, but it wasn't there before the murder.

I walked into the dining room, off to the right of the kitchen. Chair seats had been slashed, but the china cabinet seemed untouched. The doors were open, but the dishes looked fine. Had they been dusted for prints? Had the evidence vacuum been run over the floors? I couldn't tell, but they didn't look particularly clean. Hell, I wasn't even sure if the Tampa police had an evidence vacuum.

The living room was through an open archway from the dining room. It was a total shambles. Seat cushions and seat backs were ripped to shreds. The chairs and the love seat were turned over, and the bottoms slashed, too. Books were strewn everywhere, their bindings cracked and open.

I quickly walked through the rest of the house. Every room was a shambles. I went outside and looked around the grounds. It was hard to tell if Dr. Morgan's car port had always looked like a cyclone had been through it, or if the mess was a result of a search, too.

Since no one had shown up to arrest me yet, I went back into the house, and tried working out the particulars of the murder. If Dr. Morgan was already seated at the kitchen table with whoever killed him in the chair opposite, the body must have fallen to the floor near the wall. From the chair to the back door was about ten feet. From the back door to the trunk of a car was another fifteen feet.

Logistically, getting the body to the door shouldn't have been too hard. You could drag it along the floor. I looked in the grout between the Spanish tiles, and although it was already a dark brown, something had stained it in the right location. Hard to tell if it had been blood or just some cooking accident. The police probably had some sophisticated test for finding out.

The hard part would be getting the body from the kitchen floor into the trunk of the car without being seen. It would have to be done at night. The area was much too open to get away with it in the daylight, although this was an affluent neighborhood. Maybe none of the neighbors was home during the day.

In any case, it would have to be done fairly quickly. A car trunk is at least three feet off the ground. With the advent of weight lifting as a national pastime, most people could probably lift 175 pounds three feet off the ground, even without the extra adrenaline flow you'd have to have to kill him in the first place. But it wouldn't be easy and it had to be fast.

After he got the body into the trunk, the rest could be done in the relative privacy of the killer's garage, assuming he had one. It's the only way he'd be able to do it in absolute confidence that he wouldn't be caught.

So where would you get the concrete and the clothesline? I looked around the house again, and then I went out to the back of the storage shed. Eureka. Some broken patio stones under the trash cans, and a few were missing. They'd be small and light enough to be easily handled, and heavy enough to weigh down the body. But finding patio stones of just the right size that wouldn't be missed is a lot of luck to count on. The killer had to be someone who knew he'd find those materials easily available, so it had to be someone familiar with the house.

I felt sure I'd found out just about all that was knowable from the physical surroundings. But I didn't think I'd get another chance, so I went back inside, just for one more look around. Something was bothering me about the scene. It was such a mess, but there was something not right about it either. I just couldn't put my finger on what it was.

I went to Greta and pulled out the disposable camera I kept in the glove compartment. I took pictures of the kitchen and the living room, master bedroom and den. I knew the pictures would distort the scene, but I didn't trust my memory for the details. Something wasn't right here, and I resolved to let my unconscious work on what that something was. I left before some nosy neighbor decided to call the police about me, too. I dropped the film off for overnight developing on the way home.

CHAPTER SEVENTEEN

I'd decided somewhere along the way that I wanted to talk to Dr. Carolyn Young. My instincts told me there was some reason for her behavior at Morgan's funeral beyond her affair with a man she knew to be incapable of faithfulness to any woman. I hadn't tried to contact her up until now because I couldn't figure out an approach that would convince her to talk to me. But, after my golf game with Dr. Marilee Aymes, I thought she might agree to a round of golf with me, to "help me improve." I was right. She didn't know me, and she was curious to see why Dr. Aymes had invited me to play. She'd accepted my invitation for a game this Saturday afternoon.

I had invited Carolyn to Great Oaks, since it was so much easier to play close to home. We met at the clubhouse at 2:30 Saturday, when the course would be nearly empty. I stopped by to pick up the developed film I'd dropped off, and I stuffed it in Greta's glove box with all the other essential junk I had in there.

Carolyn Young might have been 55 years old, but like Dr. Aymes had said, she sure didn't look it. If her smooth skin, firm breasts, and great legs were the result of modern medicine, I wanted some. I suspected her patients felt the same way. A perfect advertisement for her plastic surgery practice.

We walked out to the cart and she immediately took the wheel. Her "I'm in charge" attitude was apparent in every movement. Nothing about her was tentative. When we arrived at the first tee, she told me to take the first shot so she could "check your swing." After my tee shot, she started giving me "tips" on how to improve my game.

"You know, Willa, your swing isn't bad. You're just too tense. Let the club swing more. It's not baseball. Watch me." She walked up to the tee, and hit the ball a good 20 yards farther than I had. Until that moment, I thought maybe she just played with Dr. Aymes every week to salve a guilty conscience. With her swing, if it was true that Aymes always won during their games, some of the time, Carolyn must have let her.

After the first three holes, Carolyn had given me enough suggestions. Some of them were simple and did improve my game, but most of them were pure harassment. I decided to start the conversation I'd come for, if nothing more than as a distraction to her constant harping. If she'd been like this with Morgan, I was more than willing to believe he'd dumped her. Life is too short!

"It was a pleasure meeting Fred Johnson when I played in your place last week. I've heard about him, of course, but he gets overshadowed in his partnership with Grover, I think." I watched my ball sail right over the creek and onto the fairway on the other side. Carolyn was waiting for me in the cart.

"Grover has a big personality. It's too bad he's not as good a lawyer as he fancies himself." She drove the cart at breakneck speed across the bridge over the creek. I had to hold on to the side rail to avoid falling out.

"He gets some awfully big verdicts, and he always seems to have the most high profile cases in town," I shouted over the wind whistling and the protesting whine of the cart's battery.

"Maybe. But Fred is the successful one. He picks the winners. You only have to be around them both to figure that out." She drove right up to her ball, jumped out of the cart and grabbed her nine iron. She set up, took her shot, landed on the green and jumped back in the cart, all in less than two minutes. She stepped on the accelerator and sped over to my ball, mashing the break and throwing me forward.

"Do you think they make these things with seat belts?" I asked her as I got out of the cart slowly, and tried to shake myself out before having to concentrate to beat her lie.

"Sorry," she said. In a pig's eye. I took pleasure in getting my set up just right, and I could see her fidgeting while I looked at the angle of the ball to the pin. I laid my club on the ground, and walked back to check the direction of the ball, something I hadn't done in years. Speed was her ally. If she could get me frazzled, she'd be on her best game and I'd be off mine. I needed to slow her down.

You can learn a lot about a person by the way they act on the golf course. Polite? Play by the rules? Short temper? Clubs in the lake? Like a trial, it's a microcosm of life. Carolyn Young was impatient, fast. And good. After I hit, I strolled back to the cart, wiped the dirt off my club with my towel, and took my time putting it back in the bag. Then I climbed in, hanging on.

She stepped down on the accelerator before I got settled in the seat, and drove about 20 miles an hour toward the green. I began to wonder if this was a specially jazzed up cart just for her. "I've known Christian Grover for years. He has always been an insufferable chauvinist."

"Is he old enough for that?" I asked her.

She laughed. "It's not the age, it's the mileage," she said, over her shoulder as she walked up on the green. I was still getting out my putter, and could barely hear her.

"The biggest problem he has," she continued, talking right through her put, which rolled seven feet, curved left and fell into the cup, "is how many law firms he's worked with. He stays with each one as long as they can stand each other. Your turn." She picked her ball out of the cup and stood to one side. Just to tweak her now, I stooped down, laid my club from the ball toward the hole, took a couple of practice swings. I could see her tapping her foot and fidgeting, getting more annoyed by the second. Some people just have no patience.

She continued to talk while I took my time with the shot. "Generally, he gets asked to leave after enough young lawyers have complained about the way he treats them or the firm has been sued enough times for one or another of the types of discrimination and malfeasance law firms get sued over these days."

I finally hit the ball and I could almost hear her saying, "come on, come on," but she kept quiet. My ball rolled ever so slowly right toward the hole and stopped about six inches short. She wanted to give it to me, but I insisted on putting it in, and I went through the whole procedure again. I didn't actually believe I was going to teach her any patience, and I knew she'd never play with me again. I wanted her off balance.

"But he has the magic touch with juries and whenever he loses one position, he gets another. For some reason, as offensive as he is in what George would call 'polite society,' juries love him," I told her. The ball rolled the last six inches smoothly and dropped in.

"Maybe," she said as we sped off to the fourth tee. "If you're a cynic, you can say that's because jurors are stupid. Or, if you're a realist, you can say it's because he's so highly manipulative he's able to talk a banana out of its peel. A few million dollars from unsophisticated polite southerners is easier for him to get than a winter cold." Again, she jumped out of the cart, set up and hit her tee shot a country mile on a par five, 509-yard hole, almost before I could get out my driver.

"Whatever it is, it works. The rumor is he's a millionaire many times over." I walked over to my ball, slowly, taking my time, admiring the wildlife preserve, the tropical plants, anything that would slow down the play. As I set up, I was getting used to her constant chatter. I tuned it out.

She asked, "Have you ever heard the story about how he got his first million?" I had, but I wanted to hear her version, so I denied it.

"In 1975, Grover was just three years out of law school. He had taken a plaintiff's case, without the knowledge of his senior partners, because the prestigious law firms in those days didn't do plaintiffs' work and had refused to even discuss accepting the file. He handled the case at night, on weekends, behind their backs. When he couldn't get a quick settlement of a million dollars, he took the case to trial. The jury gave him what the defense attorney wouldn't and awarded five million dollars to the family. Grover got fired, and made the headlines as the youngest member of the million-dollar club, all in the same instant."

She didn't say any of this like she admired him for it, and in the meantime, she'd hit her second shot off the fairway another 200 yards with her three wood. Maybe she's never heard that women like it slow. After I duffed my next shot, I'm sure I heard a snort from her under her breath.

I figured she didn't know that Grover didn't hold on to that first verdict. He had to settle the case at a substantial discount, but his reputation was made as "the people's lawyer." The next day, he hung out his shingle at the corner of Kennedy and Himes and attracted more business than he could handle. He joined the Florida Trial Lawyers' Association and rapidly became its rising star. He took on case after impossible case and won every time, or so it seemed. Speculation is that those cases he didn't win, he quickly settled, and kept quiet.

Back in the cart, whizzing along the fairway, holding on for dear life, I was beginning to feel like I'd be glad to get out of this game alive. I shouted to her over the wind to slow down, but if she heard me, she didn't act like it.

By the age of 30, Grover was a multimillionaire. And then he decided he needed respectability, which he couldn't get from a jury of six men and six women taken from the voter registration rolls.

He joined another prestigious firm and married the daughter of a Democratic state senator, in a splashy wedding at St. John's Church and then a splashier reception at the Tampa Yacht Club. They promptly had four children and he seemed conventional for the first time, perhaps, in his life. And respectability proved too much for him. I don't

135

know if it was the burden of it all, or the fish bowl, but he began using drugs and traveling with a fast crowd. By the time I came to Tampa, he'd been divorced for the third time, his children wouldn't talk to him, and he was in the process of building back his fortune in the same way he built the original one, taking on lost causes. I didn't know how much of this Carolyn Young knew or cared about. Her antipathy originated elsewhere, I felt sure.

"Is that why you're taking referrals from him on explant surgeries?" By this time, I didn't care whether she thought I was being polite or not. I wanted some answers to my questions, and then I was calling it quits. I felt a sprained ankle coming on, from a twist somewhere in the next three shots.

If I thought she'd be offended by the question, I misjudged her. "No, I take referrals from him because I'm a surgeon and his clients are patients. I suppose Marilee Aymes has been talking about how much money I get for the work." She snorted again. Not a particularly attractive habit, I suppressed myself from saying.

"She mentioned it."

"I'll bet. Marilee seems to think a doctor should donate her talents for the good of mankind. Making money on the practice of medicine is sinful in her book. If I'd inherited money, maybe I'd agree. As it is, even Michael Morgan didn't leave me his shares in our company. I'm not going to apologize for making money while I can."

"You look pretty healthy to me. I'd say you've got a few years to make money yet," I told her, looking around for a convincing place to stage my minor accident.

"True, but this explant business won't last forever and I'm planning to make all the hay I can while the sun shines." She sunk another fifteen foot put, and I decided the sand trap to the right of the green was a good spot. It was well below the green and she couldn't see if I actually hurt myself or not. I deliberately hit my ball over there, and when I went to retrieve it while she was walking back to the cart, I fell down and yelled. Of course, when I was making up this plan, I forgot she was a doctor. She didn't buy it for a minute but she seemed glad to go back to the club house anyway. I told her I would drive, forgetting I was supposed to have turned my right ankle.

"Does Grover have a lot of explant referrals?" We were cruising along now at a respectable speed, so we could talk. And I was in the driver's seat, literally.

"Yes, but not as many as his partner, Fred Johnson. I could make more if I would take his."

"Why don't you?"

"I wouldn't do business with Fred Johnson if I was starving to death. That man is a snake and anyone who doesn't believe it should have talked to Michael Morgan." I backed away from the venom, in case it could somehow enter my bloodstream through her breath. She really was a ruthless bitch.

"Carolyn, you've mentioned Dr. Morgan several times today," I said, trying to act like I'd just noticed. "Did you know him well?"

"I knew Mike Morgan better than anyone did. We were planning to be married." She said it quietly, fighting for composure. Her chin quivered and her eyes filled. She took a couple of deep breaths and wiped her eyes. Theatrics? I didn't think so.

"Really? I didn't know that. Then let me offer my condolences." I said, with real sympathy. If she had loved the man, maybe everyone was being too harsh with her. But I knew this would be my only chance to ask her.

"Do you have any idea who killed him?"

"I'm sure Ben Hathaway will tell you that there were enough suspects to fill the Tampa telephone book. But for myself, I'd think it was a woman scorned."

"I've heard Dr. Morgan had a number of affairs," I suggested. "Do you know of anyone in particular who should be considered?"

"I've thought about that a lot these last few days, actually. I've got it narrowed down to a few real possibilities, yes. If I was a betting woman, which we know I am, I'd look for one who stands to gain the most now that he's gone, and that obviously wouldn't include me."

Not a bad suggestion. Ben Hathaway had said the same thing. Trouble was, the way I was beginning to figure it, Carolyn Young might be the only woman who knew him who didn't gain by his death and I wasn't sure whether she orchestrated that or not.

CHAPTER EIGHTEEN

When I got home, George had the newspaper articles I had pulled off the computer spread out all over the living room floor. They made a carpet about twelve by sixteen feet in the center of the room. He had moved the cocktail table and some of the furniture to accommodate his giant mosaic of newspaper made from the computer printouts.

"I started laying these articles out chronologically on the table, but I ran out of room, so I moved them to the floor. After awhile, I had to start moving the furniture. But what I have is a chronological map of everything you pulled off the computer." He said this with more pride than the situation seemed to call for.

"I can see that, but the question is, so what? I've read those articles until I can practically recite them, and I can't tell that they say anything that would solve a murder or tell me where Carly is."

He smiled. "You may be the lawyer, Willa, but you have no head for numbers. You had these articles all mixed up. If you read them in the order they were written, they give you a more accurate picture. You can also see that one reporter is responsible for more than half of these stories. And guess who that reporter is?" He was grinning so broadly, I was sure it must be at least a Pulitzer Prize winner.

"I give up."

"Robin Jakes," he smiled, looking like the cat after he'd had a large helping of canary for lunch. Robin Jakes is a good friend of ours from Detroit. She had dated Kate's younger son, Mark, for a while before he married. George was always sorry that hadn't worked out. I think he's secretly attracted to Robin but he denies it. If Robin had been writing on the breast implant litigation for some time, she was a resource that never would have occurred to me.

"That's not all. Look at the development of these articles," he pointed, coaxing me down to the floor with his enthusiasm and an insistent pull on my leg.

"George, I looked at the 'development' of those articles until 3:30 in the morning. Obviously, if I could see some 'development' in them, I would have noticed it already."

"You don't have to be so testy. Drink your gin. I'm only trying to help you. Look, early on, the articles are very sympathetic to 'the plight of the women victims of our male-dominated society which makes breast implants a desirable commodity'. As time progresses, the articles get less sympathetic and more scientific. In the next group, they're discussing recent science and point out how that science supports the manufacturers, not the victims."

He had my full attention. I leaned over his bent knee on the floor so I could read the computer print more clearly. "I see what you mean. At the same time, the global settlement is about to fall apart and the major manufacturer and contributor to the global settlement goes into bankruptcy."

He nodded like a teacher with a dim pupil finally catching on. "Exactly, finally, there's hardly a supportive article on the plaintiff's side. Instead, the articles are about the financial woes of the plaintiff's bar and the limited amounts being paid to 'victims'."

"And, it's only in the end that Michael Morgan's name is prominently mentioned," I pointed out. "What do you think, George? Do you think Dr. Morgan was about to disclose a definitive connection between breast implants and auto immune disease that would run the manufacturers out of business?"

"Or was it the opposite? Was he about to disclose that there was no connection and the whole house of cards would come tumbling down? Either way, a large group of disappointed people would be lining up to keep him quiet."

"I think a call to Robin is in order." I said as I headed toward the phone.

"Put her on the speaker," George replied, as he leveraged his creaking knees to push himself up off the floor.

We spent an hour and a half on the phone with Robin. She told us she had been on the breast implant story since 1992. She had a special interest in the material, she said, because she'd had implants after cancer surgery and had never had a moment's unhappiness with them. She covered the story from a variety of angles as it unfolded and she had written more than 75 articles in the past four years under her own byline. Some had been picked up by the wire services. We didn't have them all.

She confirmed George's observations regarding the progress of the controversy. She told us of the hardships the corporate defendants had suffered at the hands of the plaintiff lawyers. She had interviewed several dozen defense attorneys who, while happy to have the work, consistently proclaimed that the science didn't support the causation theories offered to explain the women's injuries. Robin's view was that breast implants were in the same category as other products wrongfully accused as unsafe. Time would prove the implants' safety, she said.

Finally, Robin confirmed that Dr. Morgan had been studying the phenomenon. He claimed to be the most knowledgeable plastic surgeon in the country on breast implants. After he surrendered his license, he followed the controversy both academically as an expert witness and as a defendant himself in many cases. Robin had interviewed him several times. She said he was often intoxicated and incoherent. Other times, he was quite lucid and convinced that he knew why some women developed autoimmune symptoms and others did not. He maintained the symptoms had nothing to do with the breast implants but neither were they related to random occurrence in the population, which was what the defense believed.

Robin told us that Dr. Morgan had recently approached a number of the manufacturers and defense attorneys seeking to disclose his conclusions to assist the defense. Because of his background, all of the defendants had refused to be associated with him, preferring to rely on more "legitimate" research.

Robin told us she'd had an appointment with Dr. Morgan just before he died. He told her his theory and gave her a video tape of the presentation he wanted to make to the medical device companies. As a freelance writer, she'd written a feature article for *The New York Times*, Sunday Edition. It would be published this weekend, but she offered to fax a copy of the article to me tonight.

After reading the fax, I wanted to talk to Robin in more detail and see her video interviews of Dr. Morgan. So I made a plane reservation for a six thirty flight the next morning. Then, I called Kate's son, Mark, to tell him I was coming to town so we could meet for an early lunch. He was busy and couldn't make it but I couldn't reschedule the trip.

I awoke to another glorious day, with the sky just beginning to light up and the early morning temperature already about 55 degrees. I dressed and ate quickly, then drove my car to Tampa International Airport, only a short drive from Plant Key, a fact that has come in handy more than once. Today was no exception. There was no traffic going toward the airport, and I made it to the short term parking lot in about eight minutes from my driveway.

I parked Greta, reached into the glove box for the photographs, took the Amelia Erhardt elevators to the third floor and Airside D to the Northwest Airlines gate, where I flashed my first class ticket. One of the benefits to being in private practice for as long as I had been was an unlimited supply of frequent flier miles, entitling me to membership in the executive lounge and upgrades to first class whenever I traveled. It was a little extravagant to travel first class for the two hour and fifteen minute flight to Detroit, but I wasn't in the mood to sit next to a returning vacationer, a screaming child or a chatty businessman in coach.

As the plane lifted off, I reclined in my seat and closed my eyes. George can never sleep on planes, but until a few years ago, I'd always been able to drop into immediate REM sleep on take off. Since the crash of flight 255, I've been unable to sleep until we're in the air for more than seven minutes. That was how long after takeoff the 255 went down.

In that seven minutes, I imagined the 255 passengers as I actually watched the passengers on my flight getting settled, pulling out their blankets and pillows, opening their books and magazines. I saw mothers comforting children and nervous fliers relaxing their grip on the arms of the seat. I imagined the passengers on flight 255 doing the same things, looking forward to a four-hour flight to Phoenix. In the eighth minute, the 255 went down and crashed into the I-94 expressway.

There were no survivors except a four-year-old girl who had been traveling with her parents. For days afterward, stories in the *Detroit Free Press* and *The Detroit News* described every conceivable detail about the "miracle child of flight 255."

That was years ago and I had heard nothing further about the girl, after she'd been reunited with relatives. But from that day forward, I thought about her and every one of the passengers who died on that flight, and I couldn't sleep until after my flight passed the seven minute mark. If my plane ever goes down in the first seven minutes, I want to be in full possession of my senses.

Today, I didn't spend that first seven minutes reviewing all the high points of my life, like I usually do. Instead, I kept prodding and poking at the riddle I couldn't seem to solve: Who killed Michael Morgan? At this point, the possibilities seemed endless, even if you discounted all my personal acquaintances. Any lawyer involved in the breast implant litigation, on either side, would certainly have a motive to keep Morgan's threatened great solution to the health issues from ever being published, if Carly's theory of the litigation were true. Ditto, the "victims," manu-facturers and the doctors making bundles on expert fees. Somehow, though, I thought the murder a little too vicious for that, a little too devious. It seemed to me the murderer went to a great deal of trouble to keep the murder itself secret. It was only luck, and the tide, that caused the body to be discovered at all. If the tide had been different, or the Skyway bridge in a different place, Dr. Morgan would never have been found. The police would eventually have inspected his home, but without a body, who could be charged and convicted? Just killing Morgan had been the goal. Bad luck, not stupidity, seemed to be this killer's real enemy.

Methodically, I considered each person I knew to have an axe to grind with Michael Morgan. I took out my yellow legal pad, filled now with notes, facts, thoughts on the case. I wrote down each of the possible suspects that I knew about. It took two pages, leaving room for notes after each name. I forced myself to consider each one in turn. It only took seconds to eliminate Carly. I was determined that she didn't kill Morgan, and I wasn't willing to consider the possibility. If she found out the products her company made were at fault in the litigation, she could always get another job. It wasn't her company, after all. She was a difficult woman, but even though I subscribed to the nature theory of childhood development, I would never believe one of Kate's children was a murderer.

Which led to MedPro's two remaining founders: Dr. Zimmer and Dr. Young. Zimmer was too old and frail to kill Morgan in his home and spirit his body off to the gulf by himself. An accomplice? Maybe, but I just couldn't see a man who had given up something as trivial as golf to be with his family after a threatened heart attack, risk giving himself another one to avoid the potential financial ruin of a company in which he held only a partial interest. I checked him off my list.

Carolyn Young was another matter. By all accounts except hers, Morgan had used her and discarded her like so many others and she hadn't gotten over it. Besides that, in addition to her ownership in MedPro, (which, if Marilee Aymes was to be believed, she was willing to commit a theft to obtain in the first place) she had her very lucrative explant scam and expert witness fees to protect. The end of the litiga-tion would make a sizeable dent in her earning power. But murder? Of a man she supposedly loved to the point of making a public spectacle of herself at his funeral? It's been done before, and I couldn't eliminate her. But I didn't believe it.

I kept going down my list, considering the strengths and weaknesses of each suspect in the same way. I covered Marilee Aymes (very angry, capable of lifting the body, a good shot?), Victoria Warwick (woman scorned?), Sheldon Warwick (reelection bid tainted by Tory's affair with Morgan? Nah. Everybody knows Tory's a flake. If it never affected him before, could it affect him now?) Christian Grover (a definite possibility), Fred Johnson (the same motive as every other plaintiffs' lawyer on the planet), Hainsworth Waterman (ditto on the defense side), even Cilla Waterman (you've got to be kidding), Kate (now you're really getting silly). I still had several names to cover, but the flight attendant was asking me to put my seat up for landing, and the captain slowly lowered the L1011 onto the runway at Detroit Wayne Airport.

One major advantage to flying first class, besides more interesting flying companions and more comfortable seats, is that first class is always at the front of the plane and you can get off and on your way before waiting for every other passenger to accumulate the various overstuffed duffel bags they've brought on with them and waddle up the aisle to the exit. I was the first passenger out into the frigid jetway when I realized I'd forgotten my coat. January above the Mason Dixon line. How absurd.

Instead of renting a car, I turned up the lapels on my pink tropical wool blazer, made my way to the taxi stand and got into the first available cab. "The Renaissance Club, please," I told the driver, trying to keep my teeth from chattering. He looked at me like I'd have to repeat myself in Arabic before he'd comprehend anything I said. After a time, he did pull the taxi away from the airport and start east on I-94 toward Detroit.

About twenty-five minutes and $45 plus tip later, he dropped me off in front of the Renaissance Center, but not before I'd had another chance to wince at Joe Lewis's black fist positioned right in the middle of one's first view of downtown Detroit.

The sculpture wasn't meant to symbolize the black power movement of the seventies, or to warn visitors of the city's inhospitable crime rate, but every visitor's first impression was one of those two options. Joe Lewis was a great native son, but why the artist couldn't do a more flattering and welcoming sculpture of the man was a mystery.

The Renaissance Center was the brain child of Henry Ford II, built to revitalize Detroit's river front in the 1970s. It was designed by an Atlanta architect and resembled a collection of giant silver cans of various heights. It was remarkable for two things: being so impossible to navigate indoors that new signing giving internal directions was designed and implemented several times; and it was the subject of the first lawsuit I ever worked on. Fourteen years later, I'm told the case is still not settled.

The Renaissance Club is on the top floor of Tower 400, and as I took the glass elevator facing the Detroit River and Canada up 45 floors, I was almost nostalgic for the city I'd practiced in for eight years. Almost, but not quite. I shivered again in the cold.

Robin was waiting for me in the club lobby, and gave me a big hug when I came in. After we were seated and discussed the "what have you been doing with yourself since I saw you last" stuff, I asked her about Dr. Morgan.

"Dr. Morgan was a curious guy, Willa. Brilliant, arrogant, but so charismatic that it's easy to see why he'd had so many lovers. He used to ask me why women particularly, more than men in our society, latch onto every idea that comes along for improving appearance.

"He raved for hours about how women will not only spend billions of dollars on makeup and clothes to enhance their outer appeal, but will spend billions more on drugs, creams, injections and more serious surgical procedures just to look more attractive. Volumes have been written on the prevalence of eating disorders and preoccupation with excessive thinness in American women. Famous women have died of these conditions. And yet, nothing deters women from their quest for physical perfection.

"Health is one thing, he'd say. Exercise and proper nutrition for health reasons is sound thinking. Prolonging the joy of living is everyone's right. But bulimia, anorexia, plastic surgery, removal of ribs, tattoos, body piercing. These are abominations, mostly preying on women, primarily frivolous and some seriously harmful.

"And the men. What are they doing? They wear oxford cloth button down collar shirts from the time they're eight until they're eighty. If you look in any man's closet, you'll find the same wardrobe from the time his mother dresses him until the time his undertaker does, with brief respites in the teen years for purple hair and middle age for red bikini underwear." She chuckled at the image these last two apparently conjured up.

I was half listening, and half thinking that I'd heard a variation of this same speech not too long ago from Carly. Did she get it from Morgan? There are no coincidences in life. It came from somewhere.

"Isn't that just a little disingenuous coming from a man who made more than one fortune performing plastic surgery on wealthy matrons?" I asked her.

"And sleeping with them all before, during and after? Sure, but that's what made him interesting to interview. It's an endlessly fascinating topic. Haven't you read the best seller list lately?" Robin teased. We ordered more coffee, and she looked at the desert tray. I lit up a Partaga. I think better when I'm smoking.

"The point is that what Morgan said got me to thinking about the issues, and that's how I sold the piece to the Sunday *Times*. Whatever causes this situation, it is perhaps nowhere more prevalent than in the context of breast implants. A more chauvinistic product has never been conceived, manufactured and marketed.

"Yet millions were sold, and most of them were not just beloved, but worshiped by the women who bought them. Even when the potential side effects of breast implants became known, intelligent and otherwise serious women have manipulated the FDA rules to get implants. Why is mammary fat worth all that pain and perhaps death?"

"You're right that it makes a great piece. I'm sure you'll at least be nominated for a Pulitzer for it. But what's on the video tapes?" I asked her, trying not to be too obvious about looking at my watch. I had a 3:00 plane back to Tampa and I was running out of time.

"The video of my interview with Morgan is running on *Dateline* Thursday night, and I brought you a copy that you can take home," she reached down and handed me a shopping bag filled with blue plastic boxes, each with a video tape inside. "One of these is an edited version of about twenty hours of interviews with Dr. Morgan. I talked to him on every conceivable subject, and the interviews are really astonishing."

"And the other tapes?"

"There are copies of the unedited interviews. I thought, for your purposes, you might want to see all the tapes. I'm planning to use more of it for a book, but I wanted you to see the clips *Dateline* found interesting for the show, too. Of course, you'll have to call your friend Frank Bendler to get him to let you look at them. The tapes are commercial and can't be viewed on your home VCR."

She paused, sipped her coffee, and then delivered the bomb. "The red box holds a copy of the taped presentation Dr. Morgan wanted to make to the manufacturers. He gave it to me in confidence, but now that he's dead and because of our relationship, I decided to share it with you. I haven't disclosed it to anyone else yet, so I know you won't spread it around. I wouldn't trust it to just anyone and I'll take your word that you won't either."

"Putting that in a red box was certainly a good idea. Red alert, for sure. Do you really want to give it to me?"

Robin laughed, "It's a bombshell, all right. It's too bad he's dead, because it certainly would have given him the spotlight, if nothing else. We've known each other a long time, Willa. I'm sure you won't disclose it without my permission. If I can't trust a judge, who can I trust?"

Indeed. She didn't know the CJ. "Do you agree with his theory?"

"I don't know. I've been on this story so long, I've heard enough theories to fill the Library of Congress. Suffice it to say Morgan believed in it, but I don't think it'll be what he liked to call it."

"What was that?"

"'The Silicone Solution.' He thought it would end the litigation. But it won't. It's just a theory."

I agreed to keep all the tapes, and especially the tape in the red box confidential, and Robin agreed to let me use my discretion as to when, where and to whom to disclose all of them except the red box. She'd kept her copies, and already sold her copyrighted stories. She told me I could let Frank Bendler see them all, though. She and Frank have been working the Michigan/Florida connection for years.

"One last thing, Willa, that might be important. Now that Morgan's dead, I've been feeling guilty about not reporting this sooner but he didn't want me to, so I respected his wishes. I'm not even sure it's true or that he would want me to tell anyone." She sounded unsure, tentative. Very un-Robin like.

After some cajoling, and more promises of confidentiality, she said, "You'll see on the tapes that Morgan and I got quite friendly after a while. He was coming on to me, I think more out of habit than anything else. But because of that, he started to tell me things about his life that I don't think he would have told me otherwise. You know, how many affairs he'd had, how he wished he'd had children, things like that. They're all on the tape. One of the things he said was that he'd been being blackmailed for over ten years."

I remembered he'd told Carly the same thing. "Did he say why?"

"Yes. He said it started when he settled that first wrongful death case years ago. There was a confidentiality agreement, and he didn't admit liability, but he knew he'd killed that patient."

"I take it someone else knew it, too?"

"Right, and Morgan paid for it. To the tune of about a million dollars over the years."

I whistled, low and slow. A million reasons to kill someone, but only if Morgan had been the perpetrator of blackmail, not the victim. Why would the blackmailer kill the golden goose? Unless Morgan was threatening not to keep paying. Then, maybe it made sense.

"Did he tell you who the blackmailer was?" I asked her.

"Yes, but I didn't recognize the name and I can't remember it right now. It's all on the tapes. I know you've got to run but just be careful, OK?" I gave her a quick hug, promised to keep in touch and ran back to the taxi stand to catch a cab to the airport.

CHAPTER NINETEEN

On the return flight, I got my list of suspects out again and I had more to think about. If Morgan was being blackmailed, and he'd paid over a million dollars over the years in what the novelists call "hush money," where did he get it? He was a successful doctor, I'm sure he made a good living for his time, and he had written more than one successful textbook. But he'd had more than a little trouble with lawsuits, drugs, and high living. He made some money from his ownership interest in MedPro. Still, a million after tax dollars would be hard to come by.

I pulled out the photographs I took of Morgan's house. I looked at the kitchen, the blood on the wall, the position of the table and the door. I looked at the living room again, examining the strewn furniture and books. I remembered that something about the house bothered me when I was there and I tried to look at it again in my memory, with the pictures to help. I visualized the scene, then looked at the picture of that part of the house. I kept looking at the pictures and visualizing the rooms. Suddenly it came to me. I had it. It wasn't what I'd seen, but what I hadn't seen that had bothered me.

I thought about every private home I've ever been in, including ours. Had I ever seen one so obviously lived in as Michael Morgan's with absolutely no personal photographs at all? I couldn't think of one.

So where did Morgan's personal photographs go? And why? Did they include the killer? Or the reason for the murder? Too many questions, and too little information. But it was an angle I hadn't considered before, and I knew Hathaway hadn't either. I wrote the word "Pictures" in capital letters on the top page of my yellow pad.

Another thing was the blackmail. Everything I knew about Morgan's finances would fill a thimble but I just couldn't make it add up to a million extra dollars to pass to a blackmailer after taxes, or even more unlikely, outside the IRS. Where did the money come from? Maybe he got the money the same way he paid it out, in blackmail. I liked the idea, but I had no evidence to support it; unless it was in this bag of video tapes I'd practically had handcuffed to my wrist since Robin gave them to me. I wrote "Blackmail" on my legal pad, too, as if I'd forget it.

I got back from Detroit about 6:30 at night. I hadn't had a chance to call George to tell him about my conversation with Robin, so he didn't yet know about the tapes. When I got home, the first thing he told me was that Grover was being held for questioning in the murder of Michael Morgan. George had called Ben Hathaway and told him we believed Grover had some knowledge of Carly's whereabouts, so Ben agreed that we could come down to the station and observe him question Grover through the one-way mirror. Grover had refused a lawyer. What did he need one for? And even if he did need one, he'd never admit it.

Ben believed Grover had been blackmailing Morgan. Morgan's bank statements showed several large payments to Grover's partner, Fred Johnson, over the last four years. Ben wanted to believe the money went to Grover but if Grover knew, he wasn't saying.

George drove us to the Tampa Police Station at about 10:30 p.m. Grover was in the interrogation room and we could both watch and hear. He consistently denied any knowledge of Dr. Morgan's new research conclusions. He knew Dr. Morgan was working on a solution to the breast implant autoimmune disease issues and, he claimed, that's why he refused to allow Morgan to be deposed in any of his cases.

He said he had not seen Dr. Morgan for several months before Morgan died and had no idea that he had reached any definitive conclusions. Grover admitted to being under financial pressure over the loans he had taken out to finance his breast implant cases, but he denied any involvement in Morgan's death. He said he was going to be an even richer man when his cases settled. Why would he need to blackmail Morgan?

After an hour, Ben Hathaway came out and told us he would be keeping Grover for further interrogation the rest of the evening, but, unless something new came up, there wouldn't be enough to arrest him. George and I went home after Hathaway promised to call us if an arrest was made.

On the way home, I told George what Robin had said about the blackmail. "What I can't piece together," I said, "if Johnson was getting the payments, as the bank records showed, why didn't Ben detain Johnson instead of Grover?"

"Too simple, I guess. We'll have to watch the tapes. The more interesting question is, where did Morgan get the money to pay Johnson?"

"I've been thinking about that. The only thing I can figure is that

Morgan blackmailed someone else to get it."

George seemed to consider that for quite a while before he said, "Yes, and there are so many possibilities. All those rich women with their secrets. Any evidence that Morgan kept a record of what they all told him? And what they might have paid to keep him quiet?"

It was an issue I hadn't considered. What if whoever trashed Morgan's apartment was looking not for "The Silicone Solution," but for a record of blackmail payments? Wouldn't that put a different spin on things? Things are not always what they seem, I had learned over and over in this investigation. But this time, I thought we'd been the victims of deliberate misdirection.

When we got back to Minaret, we walked into the lobby and there was Carly sitting on the couch. As soon as she saw us, she ran toward us, sobbing hysterically. She kept saying, "You've got to help me, you've got to help me" over and over and over.

We took her upstairs and managed to get her calmed down. Between sniffling and hiccuping, she managed to tell us the problem. "Christian's been arrested. They think he murdered Dr. Morgan. You've got to help me get him out."

I shook her, hard. It startled her into a less histrionic pose, but only for a moment. "What do you mean?" I asked her. "Grover's not been arrested, he's being questioned. Maybe he killed Dr. Morgan. And if he did, he'll be charged."

"Oh, Willa!" and she began to sob all the harder. "Christian didn't kill Dr. Morgan. We can't let him be charged with murder."

"How do you know he didn't do it?"

"I know him. He couldn't have done it. Anyway, I know who did. That's why I've been hiding. It wasn't Christian," she said while tears continued to pour from her eyes at about the same water volume as the Naguchi fountain in front of the Convention Center.

"Then who did kill Dr. Morgan?" I asked her, fully expecting her to name Johnson or Young or even Aymes.

"Hainsworth Waterman."

"But that's not possible!" I said.

"That's preposterous!" George said simultaneously. We both sat down heavily on the couch.

"Maybe," Carly hiccuped, "but true. I saw him outside Morgan's house that night. I went to see Morgan. I had convinced MedPro that he'd found The Silicone Solution and it was good news for us. I wanted to tell him they'd meet with him. It was what he wanted, and I knew he'd be happy." Her nose was streaming at the same rate as her eyes and George gave her his handkerchief. George might be the only man on the planet who still has a freshly washed linen handkerchief at all times.

"I circled his block a couple of times because there was a car pulled up on the side of the house and I didn't want to meet anyone there, or" and she looked a little sheepish, "interrupt him if he was busy. Anyway, on about the third pass, I saw Mr. Waterman leaving the house, pulling off a pair of surgical gloves and dropping a gun in his pocket. I left before he could see me, too. But I've been afraid he did see me ever since my apartment was trashed."

I was dumbfounded and, apparently, George was too because neither of us said anything for a long time. I didn't believe her or that Hainsworth had committed murder. Nor was I ready to have her accuse him, probably just to divert attention from Grover, who wasn't out of the woods himself, not by a long shot. "Why didn't you tell me this before?" I asked her, quietly.

She looked down at her hands and seemed to have difficulty answering the question. She had twisted George's handkerchief into a thin rope, and then pulled it as if she could shred the linen into pieces the way she'd done with her paper napkin that first day. The neck of her shirt was wet with her tears.

"I told Christian. We've been secretly living together for about a year. When I got back from Dr. Morgan's house, I told him. Not about Dr. Morgan's research. He didn't know about that. But about Mr. Waterman. He said no one would believe me if I accused Mr. Waterman. Mr. Waterman's reputation is impeccable. I'm a nobody from nowhere and I'd had an affair with his nephew, which he disapproved of. Why would they believe me? I thought Christian was right. So I didn't tell. And we both thought that the body would be found quickly and forensics would prove Mr. Waterman did it." She started to cry again, but this time the tears flowed silently. We waited while she blew her nose again.

"But then, they didn't find the body and when they finally found it, they didn't know who it was. The time dragged on and on. I just got so stressed I couldn't function. Christian, too. When my apartment was broken into, I went to Christian's and I've been staying there ever since."

"What was someone looking for in your apartment?"
For the first time that evening, she smiled, albeit weakly. She reached in her pocket and pulled out a floppy disk. "I'm not sure, but I think he

151

was looking for this."

"What is it?"

"I haven't read it, but I think it's Dr. Morgan's solution report. I think it lays out all of his data and conclusions. He gave it to me the last time I saw him because he said someone was trying to kill him. He wanted me to have it encrypted at the plant and I did. If it checks out, and I've convinced MedPro to analyze it, it vindicates all of the defendants and will put an end to this litigation once and for all. We may be the evil empire," she smiled, "but in this case, to quote George Lucas 'the empire strikes back'."

It was already after midnight, and I was dead tired. I wasn't in the mood to go traipsing down to the station again and I wasn't sure they'd just release Grover on the strength of a statement from his lover. Besides, I wanted to watch Robin's tapes and to think about this a little before I accused Hainsworth Waterman, Tampa's most prominent legal figure, of something I wasn't sure could be proved. If the CJ was on my back over a parking place mixup, imagine what he'd do if I accused his brother-in-law of murder. No, I just couldn't act on this without some more serious thought. And I didn't have the strength to think any more.

I admit there was some ego involved, too. I'd been with Hainsworth Waterman almost every day during the trial, and never guessed he might be a criminal. He seemed much less distraught than Carly did now. In fact, his defense of his client had been excellent. And he believed in the manufacturers' cause. I didn't think he would try to suppress evidence that his clients were right. But then I remembered his temper in his office the day of the Bar meeting and the opulence of his surroundings. Maybe it was that money corrupts absolutely. But for Hainsworth, the code of honor he lived by was strong. I couldn't believe he would kill for money, no matter what Carly thought she saw.

I told Carly we'd go with her to Chief Hathaway in the morning, but not tonight. And I told her why. She agreed to wait, but she wasn't happy about it. I told her she knew where the guest room was, and George and I fell into bed.

During the night, I was either dreaming or hallucinating about Morgan's murder. I just couldn't see Hainsworth Waterman killing Morgan. I couldn't visualize it. Hainsworth was small and slight, not to mention old. If he shot Morgan, how could he have gotten the body into the trunk of his car? And besides, I've seen Hainsworth's car. It's a white Cadillac, not a dark blue sedan. I couldn't make it add up. When

I stopped trying, I must have finally dozed off. But I got up in an hour or two and went into the kitchen. Once again, George was already there with the coffee.

"I just can't make the facts fit. Even if he *would* have done it— which I don't believe—he *couldn't* have done it. Hainsworth couldn't have shot Morgan, put him in the trunk of his car, tied him up and dumped him into the bay. He's just not big enough or strong enough. I know they say adrenaline can do that to you, but I don't believe it. The effort would have killed Hainsworth, too." I sat with my head in my hands, bleary eyed, and wired. George didn't look any better, but he was thinking along the same lines I was.

"Unless he had help. He could have done it if he didn't do it alone."

"A conspiracy? How could he trust anyone to keep quiet about such a thing?"

"It would have to be someone with a common interest, someone he trusted. But maybe it's time to look at those video tapes Robin gave you."

George set up the VCR in the den. He put the red box tape from Dr. Morgan in first because it was the only tape Robin had copied on a format that would play in our home VCR. For the rest, we'd have to go down to Channel 8 and ask Frank Bendler to let us use his editing booth.

I went out to the kitchen to refill our coffee so I could manage to stay awake. When I came back into the den, the television screen was filled with an older, male version of Carly Austin's face. And I dropped both mugs of coffee all over George's favorite of Aunt Minnie's wool antique rugs.

"God Damn it, Willa! What's the matter with you?" George jumped up to get some wet towels to soak up the coffee before the stains got too dark to be removed, but I just stood there, transfixed by the screen. George had pushed the "mute" button on the remote, so no sound was coming out.

Morgan's blue eyes did sparkle, like Kate had said, just like Carly's. And his red hair was just as curly. His complexion was ruddy where her skin was flawless, but that might have been from age or drink. His smile was hers, and so were his teeth. Even the nose, although he could have afforded a more substantial one. Why didn't I know it earlier? Morgan as Carly's father was the only logical explanation for her fixation on him. Anything else just wouldn't have captured Carly's attention to the extent he had. There were so many clues. Why hadn't

I figured it out?

George finally came back in the room and noticed that I was still staring at the television. "What the hell?" he started to say.

I grabbed his arm and pointed him toward the screen. "Look, George. Look at him. Who do you see?" I whispered.

"Michael Morgan, I presume," he said, mocking the old "Dr. Livingston" routine. "But if he upsets you that much, I'll turn him off." He went over to the remote and did just that. George still didn't see it. I guess if you didn't know, it wasn't obvious, and I felt a little less like the loser in the old "I spy" child's game: One child picks out something in plain sight and the others try to find it. Having a good grasp of the obvious is a positive character trait. I'd always thought I possessed it.

I sat down with my coffee, silent for a time. I'd seen photographs of him, certainly, but they were always black and white. I had never met the man, and I guess the idea of Carly actually finding her father had long ago ceased to impress me. I began thinking about what Kate had told me about Carly's father, and what I had already known. I told George the entire tale. He didn't believe it possible at first, but after we had rejected all the other explanations, we turned the video back on and he agreed the resemblance was uncanny. It had to be him. Otherwise, why put Carly in his will?

Did Carly know? She must. But if she didn't, should we tell her? Or should we confront Kate? We finally agreed that the first thing to do was to watch the tapes. Then, we would decide. Carly had already seen Morgan, and, at a minimum she knew what he looked like. Interesting that she hadn't ever mentioned the resemblance.

Even though it was the wee hours, and Frank isn't normally an early riser, I called him anyway. Maybe, if he hadn't had that crush on me, he would have refused. Once a news man, always a news man, though. He said he'd meet us at the station in fifteen minutes.

We decided to leave Carly alone in the guest room. Where would she go, after all? And, wherever she went when she left us, she kept turning up again anyway.

When we got to the station, Frank met us there and set us up in the editing booth, with a minimum of questions or fuss. Frank knew when to accept a gift horse. He stayed in the booth with us, though. He wasn't that altruistic.

We started this time with the edited tape that would be aired this week on national television. On it, as the guest journalist, Robin's interviews with Morgan were interspersed with commentary about him and his theories, as well as history of the "breast implant crisis." (If it wasn't a "crisis," it wasn't worth reporting, apparently.)

His voice was deep, resonant, and commanding. I could picture him crooning in the ears of countless women, and I could see he had a certain charm. He looked in good physical condition. It would have been hard to kill him if he suspected his killer, so it must have been someone he knew, someone he would sit down with at his kitchen table and talk to. Until now, I was hoping that part at least, wasn't true. There were several shots of Robin walking around Tampa with Morgan; down the Bayshore, in front of the University of Tampa, outside his home, having coffee con leche at Cold Storage.

He told Robin he'd found an answer to the medical question of why some implanted women developed nonspecific auto-immune symptoms, such as rashes, fatigue, joint pain, memory loss and the like, and others didn't: The Silicone Solution. He'd considered and rejected the allergy theory and the random occurrence theory, as well as other theories that had been brought up in the past few years.

But he wouldn't disclose his "answer" because he was planning to use it in the litigation "at the right time." In an eerie bit of foreshadowing, Robin said on the tape that Morgan had told an unidentified third party his theory and given her a sealed video taped presentation, "in case something should happen to him before he has a chance to present it in the right context." Had he been threatened, as Carly had said? If he said so to Robin, it wasn't on the edited version of the tape.

In all, the report was fair and complementary, but was primarily a chance for the regular *Dateline* staff to rehash the breast implant controversy and give a new twist to the story. Aside from revealing Carly's paternity to me, it hadn't told us anything new.

I put in the tape of unedited interviews that Robin had told me contained the blackmail conversation. It looked to be about six hours of tape, and she'd said the conversation we were interested in was about half way through. While I was setting it up, Frank went out into the news room and came back with cappuccino, bagels and cream cheese.

I started the tape in the middle of a question by Robin, so I rewound it and played it again. It wasn't what we were looking for, and I continued moving the tape around until I got the segment I believed she was talking about.

Robin and Morgan were seated in his living room. I recognized it from my visit to the house, and from my pictures. But I was disoriented because in the video, all the furniture was upright and the room was arranged as it should be. I moved the tape around until I got a wide angle shot of the room. I stopped the tape, frozen on the picture.

On the piano, to the left of Morgan, were three photographs in frames. I couldn't make them out well, but they were all pictures of Morgan, each with a different woman. One looked like Carolyn Young, and the other two were nudes. A fourth picture looked like Morgan between Cilla and Hainsworth Waterman and they were all dressed in formal wear.

Someone restarted the tape, not seeing what I thought I saw. Robin was speaking. Angrily. "Mike, during that malpractice case, didn't you know you had been negligent? You operated on a patient while you were drunk and the patient died. How could you possibly think it wasn't your fault?"

Morgan was angry right back at her, and I could see even more similarities between him and Carly. Nature or Nurture? The old debate. But if anyone looked at this video tape and knew Carly at all, they'd know he was the sperm donor, without a doubt.

"Look, the woman died. It happens. There was no proof whatsoever that I did anything below the standard of care. Causation, causation, causation. If I'd operated with my feet and she lived, no one would have complained. Besides, I've paid for that mistake. About a million times." He snapped it out.

I don't think he realized what he'd said, but Robin did. She followed up quickly with the next question. "What do you mean? The settlement to the family was only $50,000 and it was paid by the hospital, not you."

He was responding rapidly now. "That's what the hospital paid her husband, not what I paid the lawyer."

"You mean, the lawyer's 40% fee?" Robin was puzzled, but she knew she was on to something, and she was going with her instincts.

"No, I don't mean the goddamned fee. I mean the money I paid that bloodsucker Fred Johnson over the years to keep quiet about it." Fred Johnson. Grover's partner. The one whose bank records showed he got the blackmail money. "I spy" again.

We watched more of the unedited interviews, trying to get a feel for Dr. Morgan. George sat down beside me and watched the rest of this tape. Frank was glued to the screen. I knew he was calculating how to get me to agree to let him put this on "Live at 5" tonight, but I just didn't have time to worry about it right now.

Robin never asked Morgan where he got the money to pay the

blackmail, but there could only have been one source. He must have been blackmailing the women he'd had affairs with. At least the married ones. But how did he do it? What leverage did he have? And would it be enough for murder? All this time we'd assumed Morgan was murdered because he knew something about the breast implant controversy that his killer wanted to keep quiet. What if that wasn't the motive? What if it was one of Morgan's other secrets the killer was concerned about?

We tried to leave without Frank, but he wasn't having it. Now that we'd involved him by using his studio, he was stuck to us like glue. We were finally able to shake him by telling him we were going home to sleep, but we'd call him the second we woke up or if anything at all happened. That would keep Frank at bay for about four hours. After that, we'd have to come up with trained Dobermans.

CHAPTER TWENTY

When George and I got home, Carly was still down for the count. We decided to put Morgan's report in the computer and read it before we did anything else. Carly had unencrypted the whole disk so we could view the document. The Silicone Solution report was long. It was an interesting theory, but enough to kill for? And wasn't it just a little too simplistic? I read through it a couple of times, skimming most of the medical jargon and the scientific recitations. They didn't mean much to me anyway.

Morgan said he had been a member of the medical staff at University of Central Florida hospital in Tampa and on the faculty for several years back in the 1970s and 80s. Later in his career, the University allowed him to return to teaching after he'd lost his license to practice medicine, mainly because he promised to bring in grants and do a great deal of research. They made him promise to teach medical ethics and responsibility, as a lesson from one whose career in that regard should not be emulated. The catch was that like all faculty members, he was required to raise at least 60% of his salary in grants every year.

Grants for the study of the effects of silicone on the human body were easier to get than any other kind. When the FDA declared a moratorium on breast implants, several of the larger manufacturers immediately donated money for research grants to prove the implants were safe and effective. The FDA, and the plaintiffs' groups, called it too little too late, but for professors at the nation's top medical schools, the money was a welcome relief from other long, tedious and unfruitful grant applications.

Morgan got his grant from the National Institute of Health, but the funding came from MedPro. His initial hypothesis, which he proved wrong, was simple — certain women were allergic to silicone in their bodies and developed immune system responses in a way similar to reactions to bee stings or hives.

He immediately requested and easily received 200 volunteers among women with implants to undergo controlled observation and provide epidemiologic evidence of a "typical" implant population. The report explained the mechanics of how a registry was set up to follow the volunteers and they were all given fictitious identification. Extensive medical histories were taken, including family and social histories. Each volunteer was subjected to a battery of tests at the outset, and then at regular intervals thereafter.

Following the scientific method, it was a tedious trial and error process. But in the end, he found nothing. None of the women had documented evidence of any disease caused by implants. The report contained more facts on the volunteers, the period of time they'd had implants, what type of implants they'd received, onset of symptoms and so on. But the bottom line was that, at least as far as the allergy theory went, the research established only that no such connection existed.

However, like the accidental discovery of the glue that didn't stick leading to the invention of those ubiquitous sticky notes, Dr. Morgan said he found something else of significance while looking to confirm the allergy theory. He called it "Morgan's Syndrome" and claimed it was the clear explanation for the reported nonspecific symptoms among certain implanted women, based on the relatively new psychoneuroimmunology work being done by one of his colleagues.

Morgan said it's only been within the last century that the immune system has been recognized as the single major determinant of health and disease. His scholarly and scientific explanation seemed to boil down to this: the immune system's task within the body is to determine what is the body, and what's foreign to the body. In effect, it's a sophisticated scanning system, searching out and eliminating foreign materials. The immune system's most famous issue these days is AIDS. When the immune system is compromised or absent, it fails to detect and destroy bacteria that attack the body, causing diseases that allow the body to attack itself, which can be severely debilitating.

In studying women during the height of the breast implant hysteria, Morgan described how he began to follow the most interesting new work being done in psychoneuroimmunology–the relation of the mind to the body's immune system. Recent scientific studies prove conclusively that the brain and the immune systems talk to each other and are interdependent. In short, emotional conflict undermines physical health and absence of stress promotes health.

Oversimplifying, Morgan's conclusion was that the "victimizing" of breast implanted women by their own lawyers and the media, coupled with unscrupulous doctors willing to make a mis-diagnosis without scientific support and to prescribe treatment and the hysteria around the supposed ill effects of free floating silicone in the body, has resulted in a psychoneuroimmunologic illness: Morgan's Syndrome.

"In other words," George said, "Dr. Morgan's great Silicone Solution is that they think themselves sick. You get what you expect to get." He got up, stretched and went out to the veranda, just so he could see some daylight.

Psychoneuroimmunology–the scientific study of the mind/body connection. So much of the last century had been devoted to the study of how the human brain works that theories abounded. From Freud's study of "hysteria" and psychological dysfunction to Csikszentmihaly's studies on human happiness and optimal experience, an astonishing number of theories had been explored. Physical examinations of Einstein's brain have been going on since it was retained for study after his death. Goal setting and visualization are now de rigueur not only for athletes, but for salesmen, doctors, even day care providers. Our popular culture has intuitively believed that attitude can cure cancer, although it's never been proved.

Imagine the impact on all of society if Morgan's theory had been proved by the scientific method. This would not only be The Silicone Solution, it could be the beginnings of a solution to all illness and all achievement. Man could truly control his own destiny. It would stir more moral debate than cloning, put physicians out of business, cause the gross national product to soar. And the theory would make the scientist who popularized it immortal as well as rich.

Morgan's solution was so simple that like the concept of ulcers caused by virus, and colds caused by germs, it would take years before the world would accept it. It would be controversial and next to impossible to prove empirically. But, if what I'd learned was true, it wouldn't likely end the implant litigation. Too many had too much at stake for that.

Thinking it through, The Silicone Solution itself was worth killing for, but it just didn't feel right to me. Trust your intuition, Kate says. Greed is a well accepted motive for murder, but this murder was done for passion.

I was about to pull the disk out of the computer when I decided just to look at its directory to see if there was anything else he'd stored on there. I pulled up the directory structure, and tried to decipher it.

Everybody has their own way of naming computer files, and some of his I could figure out. "Rpt.dr1," "Rpt.dr2," were easy: drafts of his reports. "Cronin.pat" and "mem.pat" were a little tougher, but when I called them up on the screen, they turned out to be lists of patients participating in the study who had received Cronin and MEM type implants. "Cronin.rup" and other similar files turned out to be the names and data on patients who claimed their Cronin type implants ruptured, and so on.

I went through the whole disk, calling up the files I couldn't figure out by their names. They all had to do with the report, and once I figured out his system, I almost didn't look at them all. But I decided to be thorough rather than impatient, just this one time.

As much as I like to believe in divine insight, or brilliant flashes of genius, I'm sorry to report that thorough, like slow and steady, wins the race. About three o'clock, my neck screaming with the muscle pain of computer work, I found it, buried in the sub directory containing files with the extension "pay": A list of all the women who had paid Morgan money over the years, the amount they'd paid and when. His very own accounts receivable system.

The total was staggering: enough to pay Frank Johnson's blackmail, and then some. What was on the list were the names of most of the women in town who were old enough to have known Morgan in the biblical sense. Some had paid only a few hundred dollars in a one time deal. Others had paid what looked like installments for longer than a home mortgage was amortized.

The amounts didn't seem reflective of the net worth of the women or their families, so they must have paid more or less depending on how valuable the information was to them. Even a home mortgage gets paid off eventually, but Morgan's blackmail scheme seemed to be as perpetual as Foucault's pendulum. At least, as long as he was alive to collect it. I doubt it could be an asset of his estate. That is, unless someone planned to take up where Morgan left off.

I copied the disk twice, and hid the original and one copy in my locked box of diskettes. Then, I erased the "pay" files from the copy I put in my pocket to give Chief Hathaway.

I didn't think there was any reason to splash their names all over the *Times*. If Tory Warwick, Carolyn Young, Cilla Waterman and even Kate had paid to keep their affairs with Morgan quiet and never complained, I couldn't see that any valid purpose would be served by disclosing it now. The amounts they each paid were curious, though. You'd think one of the wealthier women would have been the biggest contributor. She must have hated him for years as he slowly drove her into poverty. I could imagine her rage, her embarrassment, the scandal of it all. I'd been right. This was a murder of passion. But how to prove it, that was the question.

As I walked out of the study, the house phone rang again. I figured it would be Frank, no longer content to talk to the answering machine, like he had the last three times he called. But the hostess said Chief Hathaway was here to see us, and I told her to tell him to come up. I invited him in and offered him a drink. Once again, he sat in what George has started calling "the Hathaway chair." I went out to the veranda to get George, and I checked on Carly. Unbelievably, she was still sleeping.

Chief Hathaway came to tell us that he had released Christian Grover because there wasn't enough evidence to charge him with murder or blackmail. He planned to keep looking. In the meantime, he wanted to know if we had learned anything about Carly. Just as he said it, she walked into the room. Hathaway gave us a look that said we might all find ourselves down at the station in a few minutes, if we kept hiding suspects.

"We might be able to help you there, Chief," George told him, dryly. When you're caught with your hand in the cookie jar, it doesn't help to claim you're looking for the vacuum cleaner. "It seems Carly has been hiding at Christian Grover's house because she believes she saw the man who murdered Michael Morgan."

I braced myself for the explosion, but it didn't happen. I don't know if Grover had said something to get his own ass out of trouble, or if the chief just took one look at Carly and realized that she could never have lugged the dead weight of Michael Morgan's body from his house and lifted it into the trunk of a car, let alone done all of the other things necessary to put it in the bay for three weeks. I knew he was speculating whether she and Grover could have done it together. It might have been too much for one slight woman, but I already knew two people could have managed it. Morgan himself wasn't that big.

Before Hathaway could get too worked up, George said, "Why don't you tell the chief who killed Morgan and how you know that, Carly." And she did. Then, I gave him the copy of the disk in my pocket, along with a short course in its contents.

Neither George nor I believed it, and neither one of us said Carly was wrong. I believed Carly saw Hainsworth at Morgan's house that night. The scene of the crime, as it were. But I didn't believe he killed Morgan. He was just there to help the killer dispose of the body.

Ben said Carly could leave, for now. I've seen slower moving jets than her exit. True love was a powerful motivator, I thought sourly.

After she left, I laid out my plan and they both liked it. We decided to do it tomorrow. I didn't say my plan would get us a valid confession from the killer. Both Hainsworth and I knew who had killed Morgan. It was my arrogance, and too much television, that made me think that under pressure, he would name someone who would never be charged otherwise. If I hadn't been too tired to recall his elan ever since the murder, I might have avoided the final scene.

I set it up pretty carefully. If I was correct, I'd be spending about half an hour alone with a man who was at least an accessory to murder. I don't know whether it's easier to kill when you've got nothing more to lose, but I wasn't interested in testing the hypothesis. Unlike Dr. Morgan, I've never had the patience for science.

I had my clerk place the call and schedule the meeting for 5:30 in the afternoon, after the trial day. If I needed help, my bailiff would be close by. Security in Federal Buildings is tight since the Oklahoma City bombing. I was sure he wouldn't be able to bring in a gun or a knife, and I also thought I could probably take him if I didn't let him sneak up behind me again. Long enough for the bailiff to arrive, anyway. Just to be safe, I scheduled Ben Hathaway for 5:45. Clever, eh? That's why they pay me the big bucks.

Hainsworth arrived about ten minutes early. I made him wait until past his appointment time. Then I had my secretary show him in. Business as usual.

When he walked in the door, he looked around the room as if he was expecting someone else to be there. "Hello, Hainsworth. Please, sit down." I waved toward one of the green leather chairs across the desk from where I was seated. I didn't need the elevated platform under my desk to enable me to tower over the nervous inhabitants of the client chairs. But I took the office just the way my predecessor had decorated it. He was only about five feet tall, and I'm sure you've got your own ideas about little men with a little power.

In this instance, though, I confess that I felt more confident being about a foot taller than I otherwise am. Hainsworth looked up at me from his chair. It put him a little more off balance, unsure.

"Judge Carson." He nodded. Was he that cool, or just reverting to forty years of training? "Good of you to see me. What can I do for you?"

Smooth. But I had no intention of allowing him to take over this time. Put two people in a room who are used to having complete control over their lives sometime and watch what happens. It's a little like two male lions in the same cage. Right now we were circling. He was watching for clues. He hadn't dared to ignore my "invitation" with a case currently in trial in my courtroom. But he wanted to know why I'd summoned him here and he wasn't going to ask twice.

I let him simmer a while longer. "Excuse me just one minute while I finish reviewing this order, Hainsworth. I'll be right with you."

One of my former partners used to sit in a room with one other occupant in complete silence. Nature abhors a vacuum, he would say. Pretty soon, most people will start to talk, just to fill up the silence. Hainsworth Waterman was too old and too crafty a player to chatter without purpose. But the silence was having its effect. He was starting to perspire, just a little film over his upper lip, but it was definitely there.

"Too warm in here for you, Hainsworth?" I asked him, just to let him know I'd noticed.

"I'm fine, Judge. Thank you." He clearly wasn't fine. I was winning round one, and we both knew it.

"Hainsworth, I asked you here because I need a little advice." I said, after ten more minutes of silence, putting the order I'd been working on to one side. He visibly relaxed. He crossed his legs and put his arms on the arms of the chair. Giving advice was a role he was all too familiar and comfortable with.

"I heard a piece of information and I'm wondering what I should do with it. I thought you might be able to help me." Ah, the irresistible damsel in distress.

"I'd be delighted to help you in any way I can, Wilhelmina. What kind of information?" Gallant, chivalrous Hainsworth asked me. He smiled. He struggled to look as normal as I'd ever seen him. But he wasn't.

"I know who killed Michael Morgan." I looked right at him as I said it. I don't know what I expected. Tears? A breakdown? He didn't flinch. His poker face was perfect. Not a twitch. He didn't say anything either. He wasn't concerned about whether I knew who the killer was; he was calculating whether I could prove it. To a lawyer, if you can't prove it, it didn't happen. His face was covered now with a fine sheen of perspiration. I kept silent, waiting him out. Finally, he cleared his throat and said, "Are you sure?"

Up until that moment, some part of me had doubted Carly's word, doubted Morgan's blackmail story, doubted those damn pictures on the piano. I wanted Hainsworth Waterman to be what I had thought he was. An honorable gentleman, an ethical lawyer with a lovely wife and beautiful family. Like I told Carly, some "perfect" lives only seem that way to outsiders. Now I knew he was none of the things I had believed him to be, and it saddened me. He was at Morgan's house that night. He did put the gun in his pocket, and he was driving a large, dark sedan. I could feel it. But I was also right that he wasn't a killer. He couldn't be. My judgment just couldn't be that wrong again.

"Yes, I'm sure. I've had testimony from an eye witness."

"Who's the witness? Are you sure he's credible?"

"She. I believe her, and I've had quite a bit of experience with prevaricators." I kept a steady eye on him as we talked. He was starting to squirm, but you'd have to know Hainsworth to notice it. He slowly pulled out his monogrammed linen handkerchief and wiped his brow. I guess George isn't the only man who still carries one. He recrossed his legs and held onto the handkerchief in his left hand, settled himself more evenly in the chair. He was stalling, testing me. How much did I know? The best defense—deny, deny, deny.

My intercom buzzed. "Judge Carson, Chief Hathaway is here," my secretary said over the speaker, right on cue and loud enough for Waterman to hear it. "Ask him to wait, Margaret, thank you." I continued to look at Waterman.

"What should I tell him, Hainsworth?"

He cleared his throat, twice, before he got it out. "I'm sure your witness is lying, Wilhelmina. Why don't I volunteer to represent her?"

"I've always admired you, Hainsworth. When we first came to Tampa, you sponsored us at the club. You supported me when I was nominated for my appointment. It was largely because of you that the other big firms in town endorsed me. Your work with the bar has been exemplary. You have been 'Mr. Ethics' to every young lawyer in Tampa." It was one mournful moment and I said it as sadly as I felt. Not an accusation, but a realization.

He started to fold into himself, diminished by his guilty knowledge. I'd reminded him of what he'd thought he was. He was remembering the plaque the Hillsborough County Bar Association gave him just last fall naming him Lawyer of the Year. His ego wall covered his entire office. Forty years of life in the law, all gone now. In the end, his training didn't desert him. He sat up, tall and proud, held his head high, and said, "Please invite Chief Hathaway in, Judge Carson. I'd like to surrender myself to his custody."

It wasn't enough for me. I needed confirmation. "Sure, but just one more thing I'd like to know. Why did you search Carly Austin's apartment and what did you hit me with?"

"I have no idea what you're talking about. I've never hit a woman in my life, including you." He could still be regal when the occasion demanded.

So we called in Ben Hathaway, and Hainsworth surrendered. But he still hadn't confessed, and I knew he wasn't Morgan's killer after he was arrested any more than he was before.

Then, feeling like I owed him something, I called Frank Bendler and told him Hainsworth had surrendered. He could cover the story in time for the 11:00 news. Maybe now that Carly was out of trouble, I could leave the investigating to the professional investigators.

CHAPTER TWENTY ONE

A few days later, George was working on next week's menu, and I was staring at the Bay, trying to figure out who had hit me with that bowling ball in Carly's apartment and why. Ben Hathaway walked into the Sunset Bar, ordered Ybor Gold on draft, and came over to sit down with us.

"Good evening, Ben."

"It's evening, but I don't know how good it is" he said, sourly.

"I know what you mean," I said. "I can't tell you how sad I am that Hainsworth Waterman's in jail." And I was. Learning your heros have clay feet might not be the most disappointment one can experience in life, but its right up there. Truth to tell, I was more disappointed that Christian Grover wasn't in custody instead. Not just because I liked Grover less (a lot less), but also because Carly seemed to like him so much. I had visions of Grover causing me indigestion at the Thanksgiving Dinner table for years to come.

"It would be even worse if we could prove Waterman actually killed the guy. I expect him to walk, if we even indict him."

"What do you mean?" I asked him, with what I hoped was just the right touch of curiosity. I thought he'd get to this point eventually, but I wasn't expecting big things of Ben Hathaway in the crime solving department. I made my mistake in misjudging Hainsworth Waterman. When I set him up, I thought he'd eventually give up the killer. I was wrong then, and more cautious now.

"Well, we can't find any trace of a murder weapon, although we've checked the house and his office. He drives a white Cadillac, but his wife drives a black one. It has no traces of physical evidence in the trunk or anywhere else. And we just can't figure out how he'd have physically been able to move the guy, tie him up, and dump him in the gulf. Dead bodies weigh a lot more than you think. Then there's no physical evidence linking Waterman with the body. It just goes on and on. The big problem is now that Waterman's dead, we'll never know."

"Dead?" George and I said simultaneously.

"Suicide. In his cell a couple of hours ago. I thought you'd want to know."

"How did it happen?" George asked him softly. I was speechless, feeling guilty and responsible.

"He'd investigated too many cases over the years himself, I guess. He knew what to do. He tied his socks together and stood on the sink. He tied one end of the socks to the bars on the windows and the other end around his neck and stepped off the sink. If he'd been a bigger man, he would have pulled the bars off. But he was so slight, they held."

I could feel tears in my eyes. George reached over and took my hand. "He was a proud man, Willa. He'd never have been able to live with the shame of it. Tampa is such a small town that way. He'd have become a total outcast in a town he once owned."

George was trying to comfort all of us, I know, but it wasn't helping me much and I was very sure it wasn't helping him, either. If it hadn't been for my bright idea, Hainsworth probably never would have been in jail in the first place. I was trying to rationalize my guilt. Now two men were dead and the killer, I believed, still free. Although I wasn't so sure it mattered anymore. Eventually, enough has got to be enough. Carly was out of the woods, I had dodged the impeachment bullet, I needed to let it go.

Ben sat there a few minutes, his head bowed over his beer. Then he looked at us both.

"I hate to ask you this, but would you come with me when I tell his wife?"

"Pricilla doesn't know yet?"

"No. She knows we arrested him, but not that he's dead. I thought someone she knows should go over there to tell her. She's bound to take it hard."

I definitely didn't want to tell Cilla that Hainsworth was dead, and I could tell by looking at him that George didn't, either. It was such a waste. Why did he do it? Finally, George stood up. "Let me get my jacket, Ben. Willa, you'll want to wash your face. We'll be right back."

George took my hand and we went upstairs to make ourselves somewhat more presentable. I don't know why we felt we had to look calm to deliver such terrible news, but we did.

We took separate cars and Ben followed us since we knew where we were going. George and I held hands for the three-mile trip to the Watermans' Bayshore mansion. I was remembering happier visits, balls and cotillions, old-fashioned parties, Cilla's southern charm and hospitality and Hainsworth's courtly manners. I know George was, too.

We pulled into the driveway, George parked and we got out of the Bentley just as Ben Hathaway drove up. No matter what happened before, I knew from this point on Ben Hathaway would be counted among our friends. We walked up the long driveway to the front door together and Ben rang the bell. The Watermans' housekeeper opened the door, as she had a thousand times before. Ben asked to see Mrs. Waterman. The housekeeper invited us into the parlor to wait.

"Mrs. Waterman will be right down" she said, as if we were cherished and expected visitors instead of what we were: the bearers of horrible news.

We stood in the parlor about five minutes then we heard the housekeeper screaming from the second floor. We all ran up the staircase, and toward the screams. I reached the doorway to the master bedroom seconds behind George and Ben.

George was trying to calm the housekeeper while Ben stood over the four poster where Cilla was lying on her back in the dress she'd had on at Morgan's funeral. Checking Cilla's carotid artery for a pulse while dialing 911 with his other hand, I heard him say quietly into the telephone, "No, there's no need to hurry."

I walked around the room. It was high ceilinged, and spacious. The front windows overlooked the Bay, and you could actually see Minaret and Plant Key from here. I knew Cilla was born in that bed, as all four of her children had been. It was there she'd slept with Hainsworth for 47 years, and I guessed that she just couldn't sleep there without him. Did she kill herself because she knew he was dead or to keep him from killing himself first? Or did they plan their joint suicide? We'd never know.

I found two envelopes and a wrapped package on Cilla's dressing table. I put the envelope addressed to Carly and the small package with my name on it in my pocket.

The other letter on Cilla's night stand had been addressed to Ben Hathaway. It was a full confession, executed and notarized by Hainsworth Waterman. If I wasn't the only one who knew the confession was false, no one else said anything about it, either. Hainsworth was a gentleman until the end.

In death, he had provided the evidence Chief Hathaway couldn't uncover. He said he'd killed Morgan because Morgan was about to cause him financial ruin with his psychoneuro immunology theory. He said he'd thrown the gun into the Gulf at the same time he'd thrown in the body. He apologized.

EPILOGUE

Chief Hathaway marked the case closed. Hainsworth's firm was up for sale, apparently over-extended on their lines of credit for breast implant litigation. His confession set out all the details. He needed the litigation to continue for another five years to cover his losses. He wanted his family to have the position in society they had always maintained and wanted to continue to maintain.

Hainsworth said he believed Morgan's findings would terminate the litigation early and eliminate the defense of all claims. He had hired ten new lawyers, added an additional floor of office space, and invested heavily in additional capital equipment to enable them to do the work. The bankruptcy of his original client left him with an uncollectible $5 million legal fee. When he picked up the defense of much smaller players in the game, he began to recoup some of his losses, but it would take several more years to break even. Morgan's discovery would cost him those years, he said.

Hainsworth's confession said he'd told his wife all of this one night while threatening to kill himself. She had persuaded him not to kill himself then, but after he was arrested, he felt he had no choice. He couldn't bear to put his family through the public humiliation of losing the business, defaulting on the loans, laying off lawyers and having office space foreclosed. I don't know if I was the only one who felt Hainsworth was leaving us a complete explanation so we'd all accept it.

Hainsworth and Pricilla had been the epitome of Tampa society for 50 years, as had their families before them. The public disgrace was more than he could bear. She killed herself because she couldn't live with it either. At least, that was the public version, and there was no reason for me to challenge it. In poker, if no one challenges your bluff, you don't show your hand.

The Waterman's joint funeral was held a few days later, and everybody there, including me and George, Kate, the Warwicks, Carly and Grover, and the rest of Tampa, was visibly saddened. Hyde Park Methodist Church was jammed. Standing room only. It seemed everyone from Waterman's firm was present, and Bill Sheffield told us his bank had been providing Waterman's financing. It appeared the firm would have to declare bankruptcy and all of the lawyers would need new jobs. The CJ sat in the family pew, sobbing like a child at the death of his only sister and his life- long friend. I wasn't sure if he'd be more antagonistic toward me, or less, because of the role I'd played in their deaths.

As far as Ben Hathaway was concerned, though, they were both dead, and Hainsworth had confessed. Case closed.

When he couldn't pin it on Grover, Ben Hathaway gave up and charged Fred Johnson with blackmail. He was disbarred, convicted and ordered to make restitution to Morgan's estate. No one's figured out what to do with the money. The legal wrangling will likely last beyond our lifetimes.

The package Cilla left for me was her diary, and the four missing pictures from Morgan's piano. The two pictures I couldn't make out on the video tape were both of Morgan and a much younger Cilla Waterman.

I never read Cilla's diary, except for two sections. I read the part about the coincidence that put both of us in Carly's apartment at the same time. She was looking for the disk, and she knocked me out so I wouldn't know she was there. She said she'd never hit anyone on the head before, and she thought she'd killed me, but she was glad she didn't. Me, too. She put the bowling ball theory to rest, though. She'd used a Steuben vase.

And I read her account of the night she killed Morgan, although I'd already guessed most of it. Once I found her name on Morgan's list of accounts receivable, and saw the nude picture of her on Morgan's piano in Robin's videotaped interviews, I'd had a pretty good idea. Saving her reputation, the rest of her money, and her husband from financial and emotional ruin was enough motive. When Hainsworth, the consummate southern gentleman, surrendered, my suspicions were confirmed. She knew Hainsworth Waterman III would never have allowed his wife to be charged with murder. She tried to save him by killing herself. But he beat her at her own game.

A few days after the funerals, I had lunch with Carly at Minaret and gave her Cilla's letter. I watched her read it, and watched her cry. She handed the letter to me, and it said what I had surmised.

Dear Carly,

I'm sorry, dear, because he was your father. He didn't deserve a fine daughter like you. You're better off without him.

He did deserve to die. When I first knew him, he was kind and caring. But he changed. Maybe it was the drugs, or the women, or the success, or the financial ruin. He became cold, greedy. The world is better off without him.

It was a long time before I knew I was only one in a long line of women for him. When I found out, I broke it off immediately, and then spent the rest of my life trying to pay him off. He asked me for money for years. He took everything but the house. Hainsworth never knew. I never wanted him to know, but it took every cent of my inheritance to keep Morgan quiet.

It was the video tapes, you see. He taped our affair, and the others. I couldn't let him show those tapes and he wouldn't give them back. I burned them all after he died.

I gave him the money he asked for, and I wasn't the only woman who did. But it wasn't enough. He wanted to destroy Hainsworth, too.

Even though you're better off without him, I'm sorry. It's a terrible way to lose your father, but I just wanted you to know that Hainsworth was a good man.

Pricilla Waterman

I tried to think of something to say to comfort Carly, but I couldn't think of anything that would matter. She cried for a while over losing her father, just after she'd found him. I think it helped that he wasn't anything worth crying over, but I'm not sure.

Carly and Kate are getting along better now that they've resolved their differences over Carly's sperm donor. Carly finally seems to understand that her childhood was a better one than she would have had if he'd been a part of it. Carly's still jealous of me. Childhood habits are hard to break. But she's trying.

Unfortunately, Carly seems quite fond of Grover, so we'll probably have him around a while. Mark's moving his family to Tampa, to become a member of the executive committee of the Tampa office of his firm. That's what he had been calling to tell me, although we never got to talk about it. Kate, the grandmother, is thrilled. And Jason, well, he called from Washington last night. He said he'd been in Romania for a couple of weeks and just wanted to catch up on the boring stuff happening at home.

A few weeks later, George and I were enjoying our sunset cocktails after the Gasparilla Pirate Fest. The evening breeze was soft, the sky was cloudless blue, and the temperature about 80. I had my feet up in his lap, and he rubbed them slowly. Harry and Bess splashed each other in the salt water.

"How much do you love me," I asked him, with my eyes closed, totally relaxed.

"More times than you can count," he said softly.

"Would you die for me?"

"You mean like Romeo and Juliet?" I could hear the smile in his voice.

"No." I said. "Like Cilla and Hainsworth."

THE END